To Leesha
I ho enjo book

ANKLE

TO THE

SOUL

Thanks so much for your support !.

Shelly McDuffie

Llumina Press

2005

ISBN: 1-932560-21-1
Printed in the United States of America by Llumina Press

Library of Congress Control Number: 2004118221

DEDICATION

This novel is dedicated to my dear husband Tony for your unconditional love, sheer compassion, and magnificent words of encouragement. Thank you for your relentless spirit and loyalty that guided me through every page.

I love you with every ounce of my being.

CHAPTER 1

The chapel was dank and dark, the way every mortuary is during a wake. Teary-eyed family members whispered softly, sitting on over stuffed velvet benches and silently inhaling foul dead person odors. A heavy, fish-eyed usherette handed me the dearly departed's death resume and pointed to the next available pew. I clutched the slick obituary program with the murky picture of the deceased on front and stepped past stout ladies with big floppy hats and gaudy jewelry. Elderly women holding embroidered handkerchiefs and paper fans with ridiculous advertising rocked and hummed eerie death chants. Scratchy organ music and old-man-mucus coughs assaulted every ear. I was terrified, but I knew my turn to view Ellis's body was coming. I imagined that his face would be lumpy with theatrical makeup grotesquely smeared over his bulging eyes and prickly skin.

As I watched, an old, hunched-over attendant in a shiny gray suit walked past each row, lifting his gloved palm to gently signal the next in line. I smelled the slightest hint of Old Spice and mothballs and heard the squeaking of his run-over alligator shoes. When he stopped at my row, I zeroed in on the fuzzy clump of spit in the right corner of his wrinkled lips. The old man's tongue darted out through his teeth and quickly traveled to the left side of his mouth and then the right. The spew disappeared as the pink fleshy forked tongue curled back into his mouth. The slurpy sound erupting from his throat turned my stomach.

The lady to my right slowly got up to pay respects to the soulless corpse. Obediently, I floated behind her. As I crept toward the steel blue casket, the woman looked back at me, staring wickedly into my eyes. With a devilish smile and a sardonic giggle, she gracefully glided past wreaths of flowers and thick flickering candles stopping at the open casket. No one dared to accompany her; the squeaky floor was clearly hers. She stood still, then abruptly cocking her head to the right and back to the left, she peered down at the empty shell wrapped in a black tux. Her disturbing jagged movements reminded me of an ostrich on crack. Ellis' hands covered his silent heart, and, just as it had in life, his black onyx ring shone on a bloated pinky finger. His fingernails were dark blue now, and his cuticles were still choppy. The woman suddenly placed her blood-red fingertips on the edge of the satin lined box, bowed her head, and fell silent.

As I stopped beside her to gaze down at Ellis' lifeless body, trying to read something from his painted expression, the woman burst into uncontrollable laughter, arching her back and head around toward the captive audience. Her green eyes rolled back into her head, and she snarled and hissed until she no longer had any wind left in her reptilian throat. Suddenly her head snapped back in the direction of the casket, shaking violently from side to side. Warm spit sprinkled my face. She leaned over the casket, her face dangerously close to the cold body. Slowly, methodically, her thick, forked tongue unrolled and landed squarely on the lips of the deceased.

As the captive audience strained forward to see, she began to lick the distorted face of Ellis Majors, cleansing his dead skin with a foamy, white substance that oozed into his nostrils and the corners of his eyes. The thick makeup blotched and creased, mixing with this acid bath, drained off into the satin pillow. The saturated puffy pillow deflated and practically disappeared from under the deceased's head. A strong steamy gust of air rose from the casket, assaulting my nostrils. The insane female snorted and inhaled the polluted fumes. I remained frozen, practically rubbing elbows with this mad woman. Then she rose up and turned slowly, peering at me, licking the thick matter off her delicate lips. A rank burp hung in the stagnant air. I quickly stepped away from the casket, stumbling over the grieving family in the front row and landing in the arms of an ice-cold elderly woman whose hands were wrinkled and scaly like the skin of a snake.

The elderly lady put her slimy hands around my throat and began squeezing the air out of me. Her remarkable strength increased with every twist. My eyes felt heavy as I fought for my next breath, straining and gurgling. I could barely see the demented woman who had licked Ellis's body clean plunge her hand into her soft leather handbag. She searched wildly and impatiently, discarding most of the purse's contents. When she located her demonic tools, the entire room gasped in horror.

She produced a steel plated lighter with tiny engraved initials and a little plastic bottle of clear liquid. She delicately doused the body and flicked the lighter. We all witnessed the fire trail its liquid until it reached Ellis's face, where there was an extra large glob of the toxic fluid.

The body exploded into a blazing inferno, blasting his head off and propelling it through one of the chapel's stained glass windows. The torso, still in the coffin, began to pop, and the steel blue casket melted and dripped onto the rickety wood floor. Within minutes, the crispy trunk of Ellis Majors tumbled to the floorboards with a nasty thud. Singed black chips floated gracefully down through the air and mixed with the melted blue substance from the casket.

The young woman laughed hysterically as she kicked the smoldering corpse out of her way. It skidded across the floor, knocking over a large funeral wreath with an "Our Beloved Son" sash draped on it. She tiptoed over the metallic fluid and dodged the bloated, airborne eyeballs of Ellis Earl Majors, which were ricocheting off the chapel walls. Stunned family members ducked and chopped away at the thick atmosphere in a desperate attempt to avoid the renegade eyeballs. The mad woman reached out, grabbed them both, and quickly swallowed them whole, then, after a ferocious burp, she waltzed down the aisle and out of the torched chapel.

The minute I realized I could fantasize such morbid thoughts, I should have known something was wrong ... with me.

☠ ☠ ☠

When I laid eyes on Ellis Earl Majors, I knew he would be trouble. A slick personality coupled with a juvenile disposition made him the most desirable man on campus. He was a spectacular physical specimen, six feet, three inches tall and 205 pounds of masculine glory. His broad shoulders and muscular arms were perfect for hugging and draining the good sense out of a female body. Ellis was definitely the type of guy who would accept a dinner invitation, not show up, not bother to call with an explanation, but expect to stop by the next night around midnight, just to see what you were doing.

It was the first day of classes at the University of St. Louis. The campus grounds were freshly manicured with blooming geraniums and sprawling elms. Someone had taken the time to delicately edge around every sidewalk. There was not a pesky weed visible. The artfully shaped hedges formed unique little balls and the freshly cut grass looked like soft velvet.

The sounds of screeching tires and loud radios blared from five-tier parking garages. Disenchanted campus policemen attempted to direct chaotic traffic with loud whistles and outrageous hand gestures.

Frightened freshmen, myself included, wandered aimlessly from building to building moving robotically, our outlook dismal. I felt foolish standing in the middle of the quad like a lost child who could not find her mother. I wanted to scream but did not dare for fear I would be carried away in an underclassmen straightjacket. I turned around to see if any one was watching me. No one was....

It was a warm, sunny morning in late August; I had just celebrated my eighteenth birthday. According to the local weatherman, the afternoon promised to be a real scorcher. Thanks to the long sleeved black shirt I had decided to wear, I was already dripping with sweat. The very least I could do, I decided, was unbutton the high collar. The fear of being too chilly in air conditioned classrooms had clouded my thoughts earlier, and now I felt both hot and foolish.

With all my schoolbooks in plastic grocery bags, I crackled as I walked. The Ballpoint pens were poking out through the thin plastic, and the heavy bags made red whelps on my thin arms. I had already snapped my new high school graduation watch while trying to maneuver the miserable bags on my weak wrists. High school was definitely much simpler. At least I had had a guidance counselor's shoulder to cry on and a locker to hide my plastic bags in.

In contrast to all of the other students with expensive designer leather backpacks bouncing off their backs and hips, I looked and felt like a homeless woman carrying all of her worldly possessions in tow. All I needed were a beat-up grocery cart and a mangy, yapping dog nipping at my feet, and I would have been all set. I made a mental note to drop-kick the grocery bags when I got home.

My first class was in Menard Hall, named after Robert P. Menard, a professor who had done tons of research in the educational field. I bit my lip and tried to open my new red spiral notebook. The wire spirals had managed to get caught in the handle of my trendy plastic gear, and the name of the grocery store was mangled and grotesquely distorted. The only good thing was that no one could make out where the bags were from. Untangling this mess made my head spin and my fingers raw. I finally got the notebook untangled, opened it, and found my campus map nicely snuggled between a freshmen orientation letter and a Wal-Mart circular. According to all the zigzag lines and squiggly arrows, it looked like my first class was on the other side of the world. I was about to enjoy a mile long walk in the hot August sun. I situated my sticky plastic bags along my sweaty forearms and followed the winding sidewalk laced with beautiful flowers and aggressive bees.

I finally made it to Menard Hall and found it swarming with anxious students and nervous teaching assistants, who tried to stand apart from the rest of the undergraduates with their large clipboards and goofy nametags. My class was on the third floor at the end of the corridor. I waded through shark-infested academic waters and located my classroom and came face to face with a standard notice of cancellation on the door. Prof. Frazier Vital was unable to attend the first day of class due to sudden illness. Class would begin a week from today. What was ailing the good professor? When I finished reading the notice, I turned around and realized this was the reason everyone was just hanging out.

I checked my student schedule to see when my next class began. Introduction to Spanish was in one hour at the opposite end of the campus. Great—another long haul back to where I had originally started. I looked around for several minutes in hopes of finding a friendly face in the group of wide-eyed freshmen huddled in knots and clumps along the corridor, but of course there were none. When I resettled my plastic bags so they'd make new creases in my arms, I heard talk of hanging out at the Student Center. I sighed and recalled reading in the freshman handbook about a candy store located there. I decided to head over and indulge in a major sugar extravaganza.

Groups of students were smoking in front of the center, someone had a radio blaring, and others were dancing erratically in the smoky atmosphere. I contemplated turning around and heading toward the library, but my sweet tooth forestalled any logical thought.

So I coughed my way into the loud, overcrowded, shabby Student Center. People were sitting on battered chairs and couches, on dusty windowsills, even on stacks of books. The noise was unbearable. Tight skirts, too small tops, and high-heeled shoes graced the bodies of practically every female in sight. Naturally, these sexpots were sprawled across the laps of popular male athletes adorned in expensive sportswear. There were more pierced lips, tongues, and belly buttons than ears. There were definitely no scholastic thoughts inside these walls. Outbursts of laughter and high fivin' came from every corner. My first thought was they were talking and laughing at me. I looked down at my first day of school attire; I was certainly a colossal glamour *don't*. Even my nail polish was boring.

My plastic bags began to crackle as if magnified by the best acoustic amplifiers in the free world. The books swayed and bumped from one side to the other while my dozen pens continued to poke out. I was a total wreck. The fact that I had lived life in a cave and gotten straight A's was obvious to anyone who glanced at me. Even my ratted hair was outdated. Either Mom or Dad would have to buck up and buy me a new wardrobe and a complete makeover, or I would have to e-mail Jenny Jones and have it done for free.

I spotted the small candy store across the room. It would be an agonizing walk past these sex-starved characters, for my bags would not allow me to travel unnoticed. I watched a young blonde sitting on the lap of an Asian Adonis flip her head back and laugh uncontrollably. Her entire body shook as if she were having a colossal orgasm. I wondered if I were the only one who could see she had no underwear on. Blondie gently fingered her beau's thick black hair and nibbled on his ears, whispering something dirty to him. The Adonis quickly ventured beneath her sweater and grabbed her left breast. I quickly cast my attention elsewhere. I promptly decided this was no place for me; besides, my bags were killing me.

There was suddenly a commotion at the far end of the Center. Although I could still hear the blonde's squeals of joy over the chaos, now I could see and hear a well-built man showing off for his friends. Ellis Majors was the most handsome man I had ever seen, a junior headed toward the five-year plan. I had heard the girls discussing him during freshman orientation. According to their descriptions, Ellis was the cream of the crop, and now I could certainly see why. He was sitting on a beat-up brown and yellow striped couch with filthy pillows and padding. The stuffing oozing out of each torn slit was abruptly airborne with his every twist and turn.

The Madonna wannabe behind me continued to be mesmerized by her Asian god. In front of me, Ellis was surrounded by a group of guys who would never be movers and shakers. All they could do was laugh at his juvenile vernacular and encourage more details of his exploits.

The sun sprinkled rays of light on the snaggle-toothed tile floor of the Center. The torn drapes were no match for the radiation. I could see tons of dust particles floating haphazardly through the air. I always wondered where these crystal floaters come from. The television perched high in the corner surrounded by cobwebs and dirty green peeling paint was turned to the local cable music video station. The current video was of a scantily clad young woman dancing on top of a yellow cab. The song, "Shake Your Money Maker," popped into my head. (My parents often played it while reminiscing about the old days.) In the video, several young men were positioned around the cab, reaching out for the singer. One pursuer grabbed her ankle, causing her to tumble to the roof of the car. She continued to sing her rap song, using every sex term imaginable. "Eat me, baby," she sang while crawling on her knees with her tongue sticking out. Now that was real talent. Singing and bumping, she managed to make it over to one of her lucky admirers, where she shook and shimmied to the beat of the thumping music. Never was a hair out of place, never was a beat missed. She arched her back like a graceful swan and flipped off the cab and into the arms of the young man closest to her, thrusting her pelvis into his. They endured each other for quite some time while the on-lookers gawked in sheer delight.

Ellis Majors was mesmerized by the gritty video. His large ebony eyes were fixed on her every move.

"Now, that's my kinda woman," he said with a leer in his eye. He was unaware that his girlfriend, Katherine Sharpe, had just entered the Student Center.

"Heads up, El," one of his cronies hissed. "Your gal just rolled up in here!" Ellis whirled around from the television and looked toward the door.

She was a stunning young woman, elegantly dressed in a dark blue silk blouse and a pleated skirt. Her designer purse and shoes smartly matched her uppity attitude. She sashayed her size six frame across the floor and sat down next to Ellis Majors. I could tell she was not accustomed to second hand furniture when she adjusted her skirt so that it would touch as little of the stained couch as possible. Katherine's nose was definitely turned up. Her soft features and long graceful legs were hard to miss. Her large green eyes were beautifully covered with soft eye shadow. The aroma of her perfume permeated the entire room, and the gold bangles on her wrists gently clicked together at her slightest move. I envied her finely manicured nails and flawless skin.

"What's up, girl?" Ellis said, showing no real interest as he kissed her on the cheek. Everyone knew Katherine was Ellis's girl. Crackin' and cussin' with his boys was more important than an intelligent conversation with his girlfriend, though, he never missed a beat while relating his creative farce. She acted as if she were accustomed to his casual behavior, as if Number Two was the one and only slot for her. How does a woman of this caliber become involved with riff-raff like Ellis Majors? Before I finished the question, I already knew the answer.

His quick wit and fancy clothes mesmerized me, too. Ellis wore a double-breasted, dark gray, pinstriped suit with Italian wing-tip shoes. His Rolex glistened in the particle sunlight while the gold chain around his other wrist accented his diamond pinky ring. The starched white shirt he wore boasted onyx cuff links with engraved initials. My mother would have said that Ellis Majors was "dapper." I bet he probably never bought off the rack. It was strictly tailor-made for this king of kings.

A long, thin cigarette dangled between his full lips. The ashes never fell; it was as if they, too, were under his spell. Standing in the middle of the Center, I listened to him spin a tale about how he'd fought off two dudes who'd tried to rob him. According to Ellis, he survived without a scratch. "Those dudes musta known my pockets was fat, but what them fools didn't know was I had my snub-nose pearl handle .38. Clicka-clicka! He made a hand gesture as if he were aiming his gun, but then he claimed the two guys were not worth shooting. He'd fought his way out.

"Ya shoulda seen me jack, I beat them boyz down! I took 'em all the way out! It was me and them and it was on." Ellis leaped off the worn couch and began shadow boxing in the middle of the floor. "I had one in a head lock like this, and the other one I just kicked to death." His dark gray suit floated around that magnificent body. Even the blonde being felt up stopped giggling and watched him. I zeroed in on Katherine and decided she was as embarrassed as I was.

I imagined Ellis as a little boy standing in his mother's kitchen tugging at her dress, begging for attention. Soon he would decide to have a temper tantrum, kicking and screaming in his scuffed up corrective shoes. His mother would continue to either talk on the phone, or watch their battered black and white Philco television. When these tactics didn't work, Ellis would devise a new plan. His mission: to break his mother's most prized possession, a flowered vase she absolutely worshipped. This would get her attention. But his plan would only lead to a vicious scolding, a painful spanking, and a night locked in a dark closet. He would continue to squeal and kick the door until his legs got numb. Ellis would then sit in complete darkness and cry himself to sleep. His mother would reluctantly let him out at noon the next day. He then would endure another merciless beating for soiling his clothes and the floor. Ellis Earl Majors would suffer from this pain the rest of his life. Even when he grew to be an old man, he would still be deathly afraid of the dark.

Now Ellis began singing a song I didn't recognize, but everyone else did. After a minute of their admiring sing-along, he switched gears and began singing off key, practically shouting. He pulled Katherine up off the tattered couch and began whirling her around the Center. Her eyes revealed sheer terror and embarrassment as students, now standing on top of the couches and chairs, clapped and whistled. When Ellis had enough of his Gregory Hines and Lola Falana routine, he pushed Katherine back down on the couch and continued to talk to his admirers, saying absolutely nothing. I looked into the eyes of what could have been a raging lunatic, but instead I saw a scared little boy pleading for acceptance. He acted like the big man on campus who had everything; however, in reality, he had nothing.

Ellis continued to move gracefully around the room, doing dance steps, snapping his fingers, and enjoying the "you be trippin'" and the "you be the man" comments. His beloved audience easily enticed him into an encore performance. After all, today was the first day of the semester and Mr. Majors had to impress. With fresh new meat to apprehend and devour, he had to lay down the ground rules.

I discreetly stole a quick glance of Katherine, the diva on high. Although she was accustomed to his childish behavior, she was humiliated. I had already heard that she was the favorite daughter of wealthy parents who did not approve of her thuggish beau. I could practically hear them screaming at her to stay clear of the dangerous Ellis Majors. Not being able to drive the Jag would be a suitable punishment if she were caught in his wicked vicinity. She would probably scream back, "So what! I'll drive the Beamer instead!"

Katherine was a very charming young lady, and Ellis was clearly out of his league. She dated him only to be accepted by the popular crowd. Now she decided to ignore his antics by burying her head in a psych textbook. She was soon deeply absorbed in the color-coded diagrams of the human brain. Perhaps she was wondering what made Ellis tick. I wondered how she could possibly concentrate on her book, which was certainly no match for either the gritty video or her boyfriend's live act. Ellis began ducking and weaving and violently punching the air with sound effects appropriate to his new story. He *swooshed*, he *pow-powed*, he *ta-da-dowed,* he was so caught up in the moment he didn't see the old man coming. I wanted to shout out a warning, but I was too low on the freshman totem pole to even speak to Ellis Majors.

The elderly janitor with his mobile cart full of mops, brooms, and cleaning solutions, was approaching the back of the dancing, chopping, swinging Ellis. Four rusty wheels squealed with every turn. Rags, ropes, keys, and trash bags bounced against the side of the cart. The janitor's dull yellow pocket protector bulged with miscellaneous pens and pencils. A tattered cap was cocked to the side and so dingy I could hardly make out the St. Louis Cardinals logo. His shirt was wrinkled and working its way out of a pair of dirty pants. There were large rings of perspiration under his arms, and the old man's belt strained beneath a protruding belly that screamed of bad diet, excessive beer drinking, and lack of exercise. He walked with his head down, as if ashamed of his vocation. He was oblivious to everyone and everything around him as he continued to walk in the direction of the vibrating Ellis Majors. When the old man sneezed, he wiped his nose with his grimy shirtsleeve, and I felt a pang in my stomach as I remembered how I used to watch our neighbor across the street do the exact same thing. When the mucus dried, it looked like a trail left by snails criss-crossing both sleeves. Our neighbor had worn his putrid shirt all summer long without washing it. I wondered if the janitor would wash his any time soon.

Then it happened. Ellis rocketed into the old man's cart without fully comprehending what was going on. Cleanser and glass cleaner went airborne, mops, brooms, and dustpans skated along the floor. The heavy-duty vacuum cleaner came crashing down and exploded into a million pieces. The old man fell to the floor, his black-rimmed glasses skidded across the tile and banged into the side of the wall. The janitor began to howl like a dog hit by a garbage truck. I would never forget his screaming.

"Sorry ole' dude," Ellis said, "I didn't see you coming." To salvage his reputation he began laughing and singing James Brown's old tune, "Sex Machine." He then proceeded to do the mashed potato all around the old man's limp body. The entire Student Center now had permission to laugh. After the dance routine was over, Ellis straightened his precious suit, checked his watch for microscopic scratches, and secured his diamond pinky ring. One hand stroke over his hair, and Ellis was back in business. Ellis's cigarette lay burning on the floor close to the old man. Its tip was a peculiar red, while the ghostly smoke rose above him with a morbid float.

The janitor was face down on the floor among the scattered toilet paper rolls and brown paper towels. His arms and legs were stretched out like Jesus on the cross. When Ellis bent down and said, "No hard feelings ole' dude," and slapped him on the back of the head, the old man began to tremble violently and his work boots made squeaky skid marks on the tiled floor. Again, the crowd burst into a thunderous roar.

"Look—a new dance!" Ellis proclaimed. He bent down again and put his mouth close to the old man's right ear. "You will now awaken and do the funky chicken!" The entertainer snapped his fingers like a magician waking someone up from a trance, bounced back to his feet, and bowed to the audience.

The old man began to squirm and make gurgling sounds. His shoes kept making scuffmarks on the tile.

"Now, old man," Ellis said, loud enough for everybody in the Center to hear, "you don't expect me to clean this mess up for you, do you?" He kicked a can of cleanser into the crowd. People ducked and cheered, and Ellis savored the moment. The old man's gurgling sounds intensified. Ellis' eyes hardened. I saw a stream of blood flowing from beneath the old man's head. Could I help him? I looked toward the diva on high. Katherine was still perched on the couch, observing with a face of stone.

Ellis must have realized that I was contemplating a daring rescue. We locked eyes like two school kids preparing for battle. The room suddenly became very quiet. He shot me one last, deadly gaze before returning to the couch and flopping down between Katherine and his empty Gucci leather briefcase. I suppose he thought this entire ordeal was over, but the old janitor was now thrashing about like a goldfish out of water. I gathered all my strength and rushed toward him. I could feel my plastic grocery bags full of books and pens thumping against my hip, and, I even lost a pen through one of the holes. Before I took another step, I dropped the bags. When I reached the helpless old man, I went down on my knees and tried to turn him over, but he was unbelievably heavy. When I finally got him on his back, everyone could see there was blood all over his face.

"Somebody call an ambulance!" I shouted, amazed at the strength in my own voice. Now I was the center of attention. Now Ellis Earl Majors had to play second string, something he was not accustomed to. Clearly, he had not given permission for the rescue to take place. Someone would definitely pay, his cold black eyes told me, and that someone would be me.

The student attendant in the candy store notified the campus police. The crowd had doubled in size. I felt like I was back in high school when there was a big fight to watch. I could see only legs and shoes surrounding me and I was hoping no one would kick or spit on me because I was in a very compromising position, sitting in the middle of the Student Center floor with the bloody head of an old man on my lap. Why I had even gotten involved, I wondered. Just a few minutes ago, I was minding my own business and trying to navigate my first day of college.

God, I silently prayed, *please don't let this man die. If you just let him live, I'll study my brains out and make all A's.* What was I doing, bargaining with God for a man I didn't even know? I remembered a movie I had seen where a man made a deal with God. The poor man could not fulfill the promise, so the devil quietly tortured his family, one by one. Would I be able to make all A's?

CHAPTER 2

Suddenly the old man's kinky hair was plastered to a wrinkled, bloody forehead, which had several deep scars scattered on both sides. It looked like he had needed stitches when these wounds were inflicted, but had never received them. The bumpy lesions had obviously healed miserably on their own.

When he opened his mouth to moan, I could see that his teeth looked as if he had hidden from the dentist for decades. The choppers across the front were rotten and his gums were black. His dark eyes had puffy circles around them. I was trying hard not to look at the open gash in his head, but it was hard to ignore. The wound was a dark red gap with torn pink flesh seeping out. A purply substance was running down his forehead and between his full lips and there was yellow mucous coming out of his nose.

Suddenly he opened his eyes and observed me looking at him. Aware of the snot, he attempted a snort to remove it, but it was stubborn. A barrage of snorts and grunts still didn't clear it out, and then I noticed a trickle of vomit coming from his mouth. I wiped it away, using my long black sleeve. The shirt that had once embarrassed me had now come in handy. It hadn't even occurred to me to grab one of the paper towels scattered in my immediate vicinity.

Now the old man began to cough and gasp. Every breath sounded more difficult than the last. His deep-set eyes were watery and dilated. My legs were beginning to get numb. I was sitting Indian-style, and longed to stretch, but when I started to move one leg, the old man must have thought I was leaving because he began to scream, "Please don't leave me here to die!" I tried to calm him down by reassuring him I wasn't going anywhere.

The room began to close in on me. I started feeling very hot; then I began to rock back and forth. This odd behavior shocked not only the crowd, but me, too. I felt like a mother trying to get her baby to sleep.

"Would someone please call again?" I shouted. "What is taking so long? Someone get us some help. NOW!" As soon as I began to bark out angry orders, I heard the wail of a siren in the distance. *They're finally here,* I thought, and then I remembered the bargain I'd made with God.

I could hear the paramedics pushing through the gawking crowd. It was just like a riveting episode of *ER.* One young policeman tripped over a broom and went sailing across the floor. By the time they reached us, I was soaked with blood. I could only imagine what it looked like.

A gray haired paramedic immediately began to work on the old man while a young red-headed female tech shouted commands.

"Everybody back. Please! Start the IV!" A young, handsome African American sergeant was obviously in charge of the campus police, tried to disperse the large crowd, but everyone was intrigued by the excitement. In all of the medical frenzy, the old man suddenly whispered to me, "Beware of Malmspada." *What in the world?* My spinning head, bone-dry throat, and pounding heart could not even react. I thought I would self-destruct at any second. I realized my face was moist, so I attempted to pat it down with my stained shirtsleeve. When I glanced up at the menacing crowd, I saw Katherine Sharpe in front, devilishly peering down at me. I could swear she knew exactly what the old man had whispered. She wrinkled her nose and hardened her eyes to send me a threatening message...

The senior paramedic, the gray-haired man, began grabbing pouches of clear liquid along with a black leather case with tubes protruding from it. I was startled by the morbid thought of death. He gently raised the old man's arm, unbuttoned the dirty cuff, and slid it up his puny elbow while tapping for a vein. When I saw the large needle, it made my skin crawl. It was so long and menacing, I was glad to see the old man's eyes were closed. When the sword-like needle jabbed into the flesh of the innocent old man, he wailed in pain and continued to cry like an injured puppy. I heard snickering and giggling from the crowd.

"You wouldn't be laughing if this were your grandfather!" I thundered. "What is wrong with you people?" I began scanning the crowd again, with the crazy thought that maybe I resembled a rambling lunatic. I felt as strong as Zena, Princess Warrior. Battle on!

My thoughts were quickly interrupted by the beeping sounds coming from a computerized piece of equipment. I have always disliked machines that calculate death. The red-head gently began to sponge the forehead of the patient, which seemed to soothe him. Nevertheless, the janitor looked up at me again, as if he had to reassure himself that I was still there. I heard the gray-haired paramedic mutter that this situation was not good.

"We'll never make it to the hospital," he whispered to the red-head. "This patient is critical. He's sure to be DOA. Call Christian Memorial!" The modem finally connected after a series of odd beeps, and the paramedic barked information into a tall black walkie-talkie type telephone. The response was so scratchy I could barely make it out.

"Christian Memorial!"

"Roger!"

"Go ahead."

"I have a white male approximately sixty-five to seventy years of age with serious trauma to the head! Please advise. BP to follow. Over."

"Roger that!"

"Clear!"

Again, the response was hardly audible. The paramedic shouted into the little black walkie-talkie, "We have to come to Christian! He won't make it to St. Joe's! I don't give a damn about what insurance he has! This man is dying! I can't hear you, Christian! I don't copy!"

How could they communicate with such inferior equipment? People's lives depended on them. I was suspended in time, angry and distraught. I remembered a special report on the news that described the crummy, outdated equipment that had cost many patients their lives. The city claimed it didn't have enough funds to buy state-of-the-art equipment. No wonder people died. The money was probably tied up in the mayor's big screen TV and fancy car.

They put a clear breathing apparatus over the old man's mouth and nose. It quickly began to fog. At least I knew he was breathing. But he was uncomfortable with this contraption on his face. He kicked and snorted, making crazy grunting sounds. I saw tears slide down both his cheeks.

"Does he have to wear this thing?" I cried as I dabbed away his warm tears. "He doesn't like it! Just look at him. Take it off! Does he have to wear this?" My demands went completely ignored.

"We're in route to Christian!" the redhead screamed.

"One, two, three—roll!" barked the lead paramedic. "Take it nice and slow." The team was putting the old man on the stretcher. He screamed out in pain.

"One, two, three—lift!" The silver-legged stretcher expanded and locked into position. The old man was finally off my numb legs. Unable to move, I remained sitting in the middle of the crowd while they rolled him toward the double doors of the student center. A student ran ahead of the entourage to make sure they would clear the doorway. *Sure*, I thought. *Now you help him.*

The crowd cleared a path so I could see them put the old man into the waiting ambulance. It reminded me of the old hearse that Herman Munster drove. I knew I would not lay eyes on the old man again. The thought chilled me ... and I did not know why.

I sat there until I couldn't hear the siren. I felt I owed him that much. It was like watching a loved one's airplane take off at the airport. It's something you felt you had to do, watch it until it was totally out of sight.

When I finally tried to stand up, I must have looked like a newborn calf on a *National Geographic Special* attempting to walk on wobbly legs. I picked up my plastic bags and slowly padded to the door. Everyone was staring at me, the plain Jane who had the guts to help an old man.

My clothes were plastered to my body by blood and sweat, and the smell was putrid. I stopped and turned around to look back at the area where I'd been sitting. There was a rust colored puddle spreading where the old man's head had lain, and no one was concerned about wiping it up. His cart still lay on its side with all of its contents scattered about the room. Students were kicking the brown rolls of paper towels toward the wall, and I heard the television cranked back up to the max. Another raunchy video was playing.

I finally made it to the double doors of the student center, pushing with all my strength to get out. I felt like a lifer walking out of the big house. The radio sitting on the sidewalk was still blasting full force, and students were still moving wildly to the beat. Under the blazing sun, I slowly crept down the path away from the Student Center. I passed a male skinhead with baggy jeans and dark glasses, and a smiling Rastafarian man with beaded dreads. A young curly headed woman with a mouth full of braces belted out a "Hiya!" but I had no energy to return an upbeat response, or any response at all. Even though it was the first day of classes, I was too grief stricken to attend the rest of my classes and decided to make a beeline for home instead. I wound my way along the university's version of the yellow brick road, and finally made it to the parking garage. People gawked and pointed the entire way. "There she is" echoed in my ears. I couldn't remember where I'd parked my yellow Ford Fairmont.

My parents had bought this embarrassing piece of steel for my graduation present. "Ta Da!" my Dad had shouted. He and my mother had put a big red ribbon on the top of the car and parked it in the middle of the driveway. It was a family event. My mother barbecued and invited my grandparents to the "Heidi-has-a-new-car" party. My grandmother made her specialty, orange Jell-O with floating fruit cocktail. "You're such a lucky girl!" drifted around me all that miserable afternoon. It didn't matter that the radio wasn't working or that the back windows did not roll down, or that it had an unremovable *Honk if you love Jesus* bumper sticker. "The point," Dad shouted, "is you have a car!"

I tried not to show the absolute horror on my face. To add to my misery, they thought it would be great to adorn the car with personalized license plates. When I saw my name sitting like a gaudy Times Square marquee, I couldn't stop the tears from falling. The car was boxy, old, and loud. Not only could you see it coming a mile away, you could also hear it. The box had as much pickup as my banana bike that lay dying in our basement. Nevertheless, it got me around and was amazingly dependable. People would honk and wave at me, either out of sheer pity or because they loved Jesus. I never knew which. I just pretended they weren't honking at me.

Chapter 3

"Heidi, are you up?" My mother's shrill voice floated upstairs, zoomed down the hall, and crashed into my ears. I was practically comatose, and could not face going back to school. I just lay there, listening to my own breathing, and feeling the cool air on my legs. It was Tuesday, my second day of school, and my first class didn't begin until late afternoon. Already wanting to skip class, I studied the ceiling. I had never noticed the large crack zigzagging under the pink paint. Things were not what they seemed.

"Heidi? Are you up?" My mother's voice had deepened. I could tell she was getting angry. I knew she was standing at the foot of the stairs, her hands on her hips and her head tilted up toward the second floor. "Heidi!"

I cringed but didn't move.

"You're gonna be late," she yelled. I listened as she stomped back toward the kitchen. She always rose at the crack of dawn to fix breakfast. The bacon smell had snaked its way through the entire house. My mother had a way of broiling it until it was practically burnt. "I'm trying to get the edges done," she always said. Next I heard my brother bump down the steps from the third floor. He was always hungry, no matter what. The house could have been on fire and he would ask, "What's to eat?" Today, I just wanted to be left alone. I wanted no part of Morgan family bonding.

I turned over on my stomach, trying hard to forget the events of my first day of college, just twenty-four hours ago. When I was younger, I always thought my bed was a safe haven; not even the monster living underneath could get me. I pulled the sheets over my head to hide from the world. Unfortunately, I couldn't escape what was rattling around in my head. I was in no condition to face another day of school.

When I arrived home from school yesterday, I hadn't told my

parents about my first day. As far as they knew it was the best day of my life. I didn't dare tell them I hadn't attended one single class. I parked the banana wagon in the back of the house and sprinted up the red wooden porch steps so no one could see the condition my clothes were in. My parents, both teachers, almost never got home before five. They were the type of instructors who tutored their students after school if they did not understand the homework. Kids often called our house late into the night.

The minute I got to my room I changed out of the blood-stained clothes. I could still smell the dirty oil from the old man's hair on my skin. I took a thorough shower, put on a pair of shorts and a T-shirt, and plopped down in front of my computer. I logged on, listening to the beeps and the grind of the modem, and took a deep breath. When the icons appeared, I typed in the word *Malmspada*. No hits. Nothing. Was I spelling it correctly? I tried several different variations of the word and came up with zilch. I even tried several foreign languages. Still nada. When I noticed my soiled clothes piled on the floor next to my bed, I grabbed them up and rushed down to the basement and threw them into the washer. I pushed the cold-water button and poured in the liquid detergent. The water came crashing into the machine, drowning the bloody clothes. I imagined the old janitor's face jumbled in the swirling water. His distorted eyes expanded and contracted, and his mouth exploded into a zillion pieces. It was as if he were trying to tell me something.

Now, almost afraid to get out of bed, I began to play the horrible scenes from yesterday in my mind. Katherine Sharpe's chilling gaze still made my blood run cold. The evil in her eyes shot out a message that could be fatal. I wondered about the condition of the old man. I realized that I would never see him again. "Beware of Malmspada," he'd whispered to me. I was afraid to say it out loud. I closed my eyes and shook my head violently in a feeble attempt to rid my head of the unwanted thoughts.

I tried to convince myself the word was merely gibberish. Something deeply planted in my torrid soul told me, however, that the words were real. Yesterday afternoon, I sat at my desk with my eyes closed until my thoughts were interrupted by a whacked-out medley floating down the stairs. I hadn't realized my younger brother was home. He was playing the dull second hand trombone my parents bought from a small hole-in-the-wall music store. I remembered him begging for the beat-up clunker when he saw it displayed in the window. The sleazy salesman guaranteed the instrument was in proper working order, but it was full of dust and could hardly do the proper trombone slide. My brother had promised our mother he would practice every day for an hour, but that never happened. He was in the high school marching band, but frankly he stank. He just liked the way the uniform looked on him, and the conversation it stirred up with the girls.

I rarely ventured up to the foreign land where my brother resided. The third floor of our house had three bedrooms, one bathroom, and a large cedar closet that I had found fascinating as a child. The cedar closet always had a peculiar smell and was very dark. It had brass-handled cabinets with drawers stacked up to the ceiling.

I remembered lying in the very last drawer pretending I was dead. I saw myself stretched out in a rose-colored casket with pink, pillowy insides of smoothest satin. I would run my fingers over the inside of the wooded cabinet, intentionally piercing my skin on the splinters until it bled. I thoroughly enjoyed the prickly sensation. Conveniently, there was a handle in the inside of this particular cabinet that made it easy to close completely. I would bump my body against the front and work it inch by inch until it was totally sealed. I used the same method in reverse to flee the box. Strangely, it was the only place my brother and sister could not find me while playing hide and seek.

Our block was fairly quiet for being plopped in the middle of the inner city. Just one block over were rows of abandoned houses with boarded windows and overgrown front yards. Stray dogs with mangy coats patrolled the area. Our private street had large turn-of-the-century homes with finely manicured lawns and neatly swept sidewalks. The entrance to the block had two mammoth stone gates that denied entry to anyone who didn't belong here. Our three-story home was the seventh on the right. It sat a good distance from the street behind a large Chinese elm that stood guard with quiet authority. The front door and first-floor windows were protected by decorative wrought-iron grills just in case an aggressive burglar decided to take his chances. Even a seasoned thief was no match for my father's security measures.

My red and pink room was on the second floor. I had two large windows across the front and one on the east side. The room had an attached bathroom, a wood burning fireplace, and an exquisite mantel and mirror. I also had a large walk-in closet that often frightened me. I had dreams that a large creature lived in the back of the closet, so I always slept with the door closed. Actually, I had a two-monster room. There was one in the closet, and the other one lived under the bed.

One night a body floated through the wooden closet door and landed at the foot of my bed. I was so terrified, I couldn't scream. The hooded carcass, draped in black cloth, carried a long, jagged knife that it violently shook at me. I tried to pull the quilt over my head, but I was frozen solid with fear. I could see the corpse moving about in the dark shadows, and then it quietly drifted back through my closet door. Even though I never saw the body again, I always knew it was there.

My room was famous for dark, unexplained phantoms on the walls in the still of the night. Shadows danced sophisticated jigs every night. I grew accustomed to the performances of jagged-edged shapes floating both gracefully and erratically. Large houses are never without their eerie sounds, and ours was no exception. The hardwood floors creaked every night, and the windows whistled supernatural tunes without the assistance of the wind. The fireplace in my room was a graveyard to unsuspecting pigeons that inevitably met their death when they were caught in the chimney. I would lie awake at night, listening to the coos of death get softer and softer ... until they finally faded away. I sometimes felt as if I were a part of the torture because I did nothing to save their timid little lives.

Our house had a large living room and dining room near the massive front door. To fill up the large dining room, Mom insisted that Dad buy a gigantic dining room table with six huge wooden chairs, a tall glass breakfront, and a nifty serving cart. A brass chandelier loomed above the table, and beneath it was a round sinister button that the hostess could push to summon the butler. I guess the people who owned the house before us had a butler, because we certainly did not. The button sat in the middle of the wooden floor, daring anyone to touch it. I tried not to sit near that dreadful mechanism, for fear it would sprout teeth and bite off my toes. It was a large, shiny, black circle surrounded by a sliver of cold steel. One toe-tap, and a morbid sound filled the air with a hideous whine that planted itself in your head forever. I always believed it triggered a trapdoor that sucked little children under who'd been naughty, or hadn't eaten their veggies. I was convinced there was a tunnel that the kids slid down that ended with a raging inferno.

I remember not eating my Brussels sprouts one cold Thanksgiving night. Mom would not let me get up from the table until everyone was finished. I held on to my seat until my knuckles were red and raw. If I was to be pulled down into a blistering fire, the chair was going with me. I was not going to hell without a fight. Eventually, Mom covered the dining room floor with light green carpet, but the hump was still visible. Once I saw the button move slightly, which verified my theory that it was still alive.

CHAPTER 4

I thought about going for an afternoon swim while the sun was high in the sky. After what I had been through at school, I certainly deserved it. Since I considered myself a sun goddess, the decision was easily made. I quickly found my red swimsuit and changed from the shorts and T-shirt I had on. I put my suit on underneath a faded black cotton cover-up, grabbed a brown bottle of suntan lotion, my sunglasses, and slipped on a pair of old flip-flops. I logged off my computer and ran down the back steps and out the back door. I just wanted to relax in the glorious sunshine and clear all the dark thoughts dancing around in my head. When the screen door slammed behind me, the pooches next door perked up from dozing in the warm sun.

We lived next door to a very old couple with five mangy dogs fenced in a filthy backyard. The husband looked like a Martian with bugged out eyes and several knots bulging out from his skull. He always wore the same shirt. His wife had gray hair, rotten teeth, and yellow fingernails. All the kids on the street thought she was a witch who could turn children to stone after severe eye contact.

Our pool had a bricked deck and a large blue pump located at the far end of the yard. The pump made an odd *ploop, ploop* sound that barely could be heard over the whirling and thrashing sounds that came from the square steel vents. The pool was ten feet deep, with a long springboard over the deep end. I was deathly afraid of the stringy, long-legged, transparent spiders that sprawled across the water floating like plankton waiting to pounce unwary swimmers. Steel ladders graced both ends of the pool, while the blue and white rope strung across the middle signaled the sharp slope to inexperienced swimmers. The pool had been a part of the back yard for almost ten years. A six-foot stockade fence with splintery edges surrounded the pool.

I recalled my father tutoring a young man whose father owned a construction company. In exchange for tutoring fees, the owner offered a cut rate for installing an in-ground pool. Dad also taught summer school to pay for the pool. It was his dream come true.

The huge yellow ditch digger had come barreling down the street early one Saturday morning, screaming and coughing up black smoke. It woke the entire neighborhood with its miserable grinding sounds. The lazy dogs next door howled and barked the entire day.

I sat on the back porch all afternoon, watching the men in yellow hard hats work. Stubborn tree roots poked through the damp dirt like large, twenty-fingered hands. I waited for skulls and bones to peer through the soil, too, but to my disappointment, they never did. When the men left, I would stand on the massive mounds of dirt pretending to be queen of the mountain. I could see into the yards two streets over. I also stood in the middle of the deep end of the enormous pit and instantly got the feeling of being buried alive. My white tennis shoes sank down until completely covered by the mud. Sometimes I could barely get up the smooth flat sides of the hole. I remember struggling and trying to claw my way to the top. My fingers sank deeper and deeper into the cool mud while it tumbled down onto my head. I could smell the dirt and watch the worms squirming and slithering through the mud as I pulled myself up the steep slope to the yard. Those were the good ole' days.

I flopped down on my favorite deck chair and stretched my legs out. The strong smell of chlorine assaulted my nose and made me blink back involuntary tears. The water was crystal clear and still, which was odd for a windy day. The pump continued to make its usual sounds as I settled in on the green canvas lounger. I put on my favorite pair of sunglasses, closed my eyes, and enjoyed the breeze. The sun's strong rays seeped into my skin, completely warming my soul.

Suddenly, I felt a surge of cool air pass over and through me. I shuddered and rose up to find chill bumps on my arms and legs. I looked around to see if anyone was watching, then folded my limbs close to my body in a feeble attempt to keep warm. It was eighty-five degrees on an August day. Why was I so chilly?

I flashed to a childhood rumor of a female ghost that lurked on our street. Whenever she was present, there was a rush of frigid air. The woman was supposedly searching for her baby. The old tale had her dressed in a low-cut, dingy white gown with a ragged hem. She roamed the street with her arms sticking straight out exposing blood red fingernails. There was talk that the ghost followed the cries of her dead baby, cries that only she could hear.

I removed my glasses, sat up, and looked around the yard. Behind me were the freshly painted red picnic table and gas barbecue grill with all the bells and whistles. The lonely gaslight stood at attention on the brick patio. Nothing out of the ordinary. I focused on the stone statue of Mary, the Virgin Mother, in the far end of the yard. The menacing cool breeze was still present. My hair began to move slightly, while the leaves on the trees were stark still. Then I heard the words, *Beware of Malmspada*, rustling in the wind. There was definitely a sinister presence surrounding me. My brother's so-called music drifted from his third-floor window. I looked up, hoping he was watching me, but the window was empty. He didn't even know I was home. The house felt dead.

A quick movement caught my eye. I could see a dark object through a slight gap in the fence, but I couldn't make out who or what it was. I did know this: *it was watching me*. I squinted to get a better look back at it. I couldn't make the shape out, and I didn't know if I even wanted to. The dogs next door were in an uncontrollable rage. They growled, gritted their teeth, barked, and rose up on their hind legs. The hair on their backs stood straight up. Who or what was on the other side of the fence? The object moved a little to the left as if to get a better view of me. I was terrified. Slowly, carefully, I swung my legs off the chair and planted my feet firmly on the ground. I looked toward the house and zeroed in on the back porch. The distance from the pool to the back porch was not that far. Could I make a run for it? Would I make it without being caught by whatever was watching me? I glimpsed another sharp movement behind the fence, but this time the motion was quick and low. Was it an animal? Or was it a person?

My entire body ached. I tried to ignore my dizzy feeling by swallowing hard and breathing deeply. The minutes ticked on and the air seemed to get colder. I then saw my father's car come up the driveway and pull into the garage. Now, just as I found the courage to look directly at the dark shadow behind the fence, the unidentified figure took off running toward the street. I ran toward the house, sprinted up the stairs to my room, and looked at myself in the mirror. I saw a frightened young woman, trembling and weak. *Beware of Malmspada.* The words were beginning to haunt me.

I remained in my room until dinner was already on the table. We had the kind of family who ate together, and virtually had no secrets from each other. I was sure my parents would want to know every detail of the first day of school. I had to remain calm.

"How was your first day of college, Heidi?" My mother asked with much enthusiasm. "Dad and I want to hear all about it!"

"I don't want to hear about it," my loving brother mumbled, filling his mouth with mashed potatoes. For once I could have kissed the little monster.

"Tell us everything!" my mother insisted as she settled down in her seat. *Beware of Malmspada* was ringing in my ears. Could my family hear it? Was someone—some*thing*—else in the room with us? I snapped my neck around to inspect the kitchen. I inspected the stove, counters, and the fronts of the cabinets, and then I slowly turned around to face my family again. My father watched me move the string beans from one side of my plate to another.

"Do you like your professors?" I heard my mother ask. "Did you do your homework? Did you hang out in the Student Center? Did you see the library? Your father and I met in the Student Center at Espy University!" She finally noticed that I wasn't answering. "Heidi, honey, are you all right?" I was sick to my stomach. I felt my face flush with heat; I could barely lift my head; I listened to my own heart beating erratically in my weak chest. I fully expected it to burst out of my body, splattering all over the surprised faces of my loving family. *Beware of Malmspada.* I felt like I was being interrogated. My loving brother came to my rescue.

"Heidi! Heidi! Heidi!" he exploded. "Doesn't anyone care about *my* day? No, of course not. Only Heidi's. Yes, I got an A on a calculus pop quiz. Yes, I'm now editor of the school newspaper. And, for your convenience, I landed a job at Murphy's Gigantic Screen Movie Theatre, where my loving family can get in totally free. How's that for a kid's day at the ranch?" My brother was a godsend.

"Ben, we didn't mean to ignore you," Mom said. "We're proud of you too, honey. I'm glad you're the editor. I know it's something you've wanted for a long time." My mother would never intentionally hurt anyone's feelings. She was the kind of woman who, if she found money in the grocery store, asked everyone in the market if they had lost it. My father sat like a bump on a log, ignoring the entire conversation. His eyes locked in on me; I could see the wheels turning. Mom was now preoccupied with Ben. One down, and one to go. I was not completely off the hook yet. I knew my father knew something was up. He had seen the way I high-tailed it up the back porch steps from the pool, but he never said a word. Probably chalked it up to my being a flighty eighteen-year-old. I could always say I was trying to answer the phone. My mother went on and on about my brother.

"Benjamin, your father and I are proud of all of our children." My mother was relentless. "We only want the best for all three of you." It was strange to hear the word three. My older sister had been away at college for so long, I almost forgot she was a part of the family. "Let's just enjoy our dinner," my mother added, winking at me and lifting her glass of iced tea.

Still watching me, my father devoured his piece of chicken. I kept my eyes away from his, concentrating on my plate. Luckily he left me alone. For once I was ahead. It was Ben's night to clear the table. I sauntered up to my room and shut the door, then lay across my bed and listened to the night bugs cry outside my window. I actually listened for the pigeons in the chimney, too, but tonight they were silent. There was death everywhere tonight. I could feel it.

I was suddenly struck by a frightening thought. I'd forgotten to take my bloody clothes out of the washer in the basement. Mom would be suspicious if she knew I was washing clothes in the middle of the day. Suppose the blood hadn't come out?

I wondered if I could get to the basement without her noticing. She would be even angrier if she knew I hadn't washed a full load. "Never waste water," she always said. "It's one of our most precious resources." We were never allowed to run the water while brushing our teeth, never permitted to take a long shower. Mom would knock on the bathroom door. "You're not that dirty!" she called through the door. "Hurry up and finish that shower or I'm coming in!"

I cracked my door so I could hear where my parents were. I heard snoring coming from their room down the hall. My father was already asleep. Ben was complaining about the dishes. My mother was puttering around in the kitchen saying no son of hers would be helpless. "You're gonna learn to be self-sufficient, Ben Morgan."

Ben wanted no part of this. I could sneak down the steps and slip through the basement door without anyone noticing.

"Aw Mom," Ben whined. "I don't want to do this. I feel like a girl. Suppose some of my friends saw me loading the dishwasher?" My brother wailed on and on. "I'm the editor of the school newspaper, for Christ's sake! Why can't Heidi do this?"

"Because it's your turn tonight. Come on, Ben. It's not that bad. You're almost finished. You're wasting more energy complaining than working." I peeked around the corner and looked into the kitchen. Ben was wiping the table. He slung the dishrag around so much that crumbs went flying to the floor. Good. Now Mom would make him sweep, too.

"But I'm tired, Mom. This is for girls."

I flipped the basement light on, and made my way down the creaky wooden stairs. The light was a single bulb with zapped gnats burning on the surface. The basement was dank and musty with rocky walls and a cool dark floor. Next to the steps, there was an old fridge with bulging ice crystals and a putrid smell. A box of lima beans lay lifeless in an eternal mound of ice nestled in the freezer. My blue banana bike rested against the wall, along with an abandoned coat rack with tarnished hooks. The overcoats and rain gear hanging on it looked like dead bodies hanging from hooks in a cold meat locker. The washer and dryer were in the far corner, next to the hot water heater.

The basement windows were small, cracked, and murky. You could see out, but never in. Beyond the main part of the basement was a paint cellar that was home to rows and rows of old crusty cans of paint, useless paint thinner, and dried up paintbrushes with missing handles. Spider webs had crisscrossed almost the entire ceiling, drooping and swaying with the slightest breeze. Near the paint cellar was a rusty commode housed in a wooden stall with a chain used for flushing. The water inside the cracked toilet was a hideous green with a dark brown ring. This bathroom was in need of an industrial strength cleaning.

I hated the basement. It looked more sinister every time I went down there, especially at night. I could hear the voices upstairs. My brother was still complaining and my mother was padding around the kitchen, dragging her right leg. She'd had an accident when she was a very young girl, and the scar on her right leg was hideous, but Mom never seemed to be bothered by it. My father teased her about it, but she always took it in stride. "I'm proud of my war wound," she said.

The scar began at her knee and extended halfway down her leg. It had never healed properly, but just seemed to sit there, daring anyone to touch it. I had always been afraid of that scar.

There were gurgling sounds coming from the hot water heater, the kind of deep warm sound that rang in your head forever. Suddenly, I was startled by a monster insect with huge floppy legs. It looked like a mix between a daddy longlegs and a grasshopper. It was greenish brown, with a cutthroat attitude. The insect hopped along in front of me, dragging its massive limbs and stopping every few steps to check my status. I tried to step on the hideous creature, but it hopped away with a sinister smirk and a bloodcurdling whine. Still nervous about the bug, I continued toward the washer and dryer. The hot water heater was lurking in the shadows with a hypnotizing glow, purring like a hungry lion waiting to leap on an unsuspecting victim.

I saw the bug creature lumbering up the wall. It crept slowly, obviously adapted to its uneven limbs. It soon crawled into the darkness, completely out of sight. I felt it was somewhere watching me, while licking each portion of its lanky, lopsided body. I clearly was not alone in the basement. I heard my family walking around above me. The sound of my mother's right leg dragging was louder than I'd ever heard it before.

CHAPTER 5

I walked slowly toward the hot water heater, whose pilot light beckoned and seduced me into an unexplainable trance. The solitary light bulb dangling from the ceiling flickered as I seemed to float past the washer and dryer. I abruptly stopped in front of the vertical aquatic-like coffin that held gallons of blistering hot water. The pilot light was in the front lower section of the hot water heater practically kissing the cement floor. It sputtered blue and yellow sparks with a violent red tinge.

I felt my body forcing itself down toward the cold floor. First the right leg, then the left bent until I was dangerously close to the hot-to-the-touch contraption that percolated year round. Why was I kneeling in front of the flame? Was this some sort of sacred fire ceremony? I couldn't stop myself from being drawn to the dancing fire. I heard whispery voices bouncing off the cold walls. Phantom shadows frolicked about, beckoning to me with jagged fingernails. What was I doing? The bug creature reappeared and hopped over to me. It too was drawn to the flame, lame limbs and all. My face came closer and closer to the brilliant blaze. The warmth frightened me. The supernatural voices were now cries for help. They clearly were not coming from upstairs. The sounds were so close, that I could feel the soft wind of each syllable in my ear, high-pitched and shaky, like the voice at the end of the old movie, *The Fly*. Instead of "Help me! Help me!" however, I was terrified to hear the words *Beware of Malmspada*. My eyes squeezed shut.

I was totally mesmerized ... until I saw it.

It was the face of the old janitor from the university dancing around in purgatory in my father's hot water heater. His features were melting, slipping away from the bone, grossly distorted. His skin was peeling back from his skull, revealing sizzling flesh and scorched bone. He had the same trauma to his head as he'd had in the student center.

My stomach was in knots, churning with acidic violence. I tried to stand, but I was locked into place on my knees before that inferno. The bug creature was also still, obviously in no condition to move. The cries for help grew to shouts. *Beware of Malmspada.* The old man's voice was laced with terror. His eyes were dissolving into their sockets. The empty holes remained gazing at me until every piece of flesh and membrane had burned away and dropped into the fire. Now there was only a floating skull, and it, too, finally dwindled away, disappearing into flaming infinity.

The spell was broken. I was released from the torment that had captured and held me against my will. Was I dreaming? Was this a nightmare? Had I really seen the old janitor's face in the pilot light? I was completely drenched, clear down to my underwear. My tennis shoes were singed. The shadows were still dancing on the walls, and when I looked for the bug creature, it was, unbelievably, still parked next to me.

I scooted a little to the left of the hot water heater, trying hard not to disturb the huge insect. I kept my eyes on it until the creature did the unthinkable. It first let out a hideous scream, then took a long flying leap, and bounced into the crackling fire. I knew now I wasn't dreaming. Inside the flames, I heard the words again. *Beware of Malmspada.* The insect crackled and burned in the flames.

I was too afraid to make any sudden moves. My stomach continued to thrash, forcing bitter, hot bile to my lips until I heaved up greenish vomit with bloody specks. My stomach ached with unbelievable pain. I wanted to crawl into a hole and die. Feeling light headed, my vision blurred, I wobbled to my feet and suddenly remembered I'd never gotten across the basement to check the washer. I walked toward it in a robotic daze and lifted the lid, fully expecting to see the old man's face in the bottom. What I saw was far worse. The blood had not come out of my clothes! It was as red and fresh as when I had tossed them in. After being covered with blood all morning at the Student Center, I was familiar with its smell. Perhaps the machine had malfunctioned, or maybe I hadn't turned it on. Possibly I had simply imagined it. I looked and saw the box of detergent on the shelf next to the powdered bleach, just where I thought I'd left them earlier. I retrieved the clothes from the washer to inspect them more closely. When I gently lifted the garments to my nose and inhaled, the tip of my nose became moist with a red glaze.

I reached for the knob on the back of the washer and pushed it in. The water came pouring into the tub for the second time. There was nothing wrong with the machine. The blood was so fresh it smeared all over my hands and dripped on the clothes I was wearing. Listening to my own breathing sickened me as I exhaled in the world of the unknown. I smashed the off button on the washer and bolted up the stairs, running directly into my mother.

"Heidi, what were you doing in the basement?" The look in her eyes suggested that I had better have a decent answer. "And what is that red dye on your clothes? You smell like fire. What's going on in the basement? You look like you've seen a ghost." Her words body slammed into me, sucking out all of my breath. Had I seen a ghost? Was the old man really dead? Was this real blood? Was I going mad? I searched for the right words. My mother would not give up until she had an answer.

"I was washing my clothes and, well, I forgot and left them in the washer. That's all. I was downstairs in the basement because I was in my room, and the clothes are still kinda dirty. I sat in on an art class today, I got red paint on … please, Mom, I hope the clothes aren't ruined. I'll get this out." The words tumbled out of my mouth. I dug my fingernails into the red material, balling it up tighter and closer to my body. Luckily, the back hall was dark, and Mom was tired from dealing with Ben.

"Mom, I gotta go study!" I ran up the stairs and closed the door, hoping my mother wouldn't follow. When I exhaled, the taste of blood was on my tongue. Spitting out red, thick clumps upset my stomach even more. I listened at the door again. Mom was not coming. Sitting cross-legged, rocking in the middle of my bed, I held on to the soiled clothing. In the darkness of my room, the clothing had a red glow that seized my pink walls. I watched as the glow floated around my room, surrounding the bottles of perfume on my dresser, choking the ballerina on my jewelry box. My prize silver-plated comb and brush were outlined with the fatal radiance. They were burning alive, branding *Beware of Malmspada* into the dresser. I lifted my fingers to my nose and smelled the aroma of fresh blood, squeezing my eyes shut. If I could only sleep without dying…

"Heidi, are you up?"

Was it the next day already? Had all of this been a bad dream? I curled up tighter into my quilt, praying for my own death. I must have slept in my clothes all night. I slowly released the quilt. The bloody clothes were still on the floor next to my bed in a morbid heap. The red, crusty stains were permanent. I knew I would have to burn them. No one would have to know.

"Did you hear your mother calling you, young lady?" Now my father was in on this. "Your brother is dressed and down at the breakfast table already. You know we always eat together. Now get up." My father was roaring through the door. "Have you forgotten that you have school today? You are no longer in high school. College is nothing to play with. Get up and get down to the breakfast table. Now!"

Why couldn't everyone leave me alone? I slowly got up and opened the door just a crack. " Dad," I said, "On Tuesdays, I only have afternoon classes. I'm gonna sleep a little longer, I'm really not feeling well. I didn't sleep very well last night. I'll get something to eat later on if that's OK."

My father sized me up through the crack in the door. I could tell he knew something was wrong, but he left me alone. I had told so many lies in the past twenty-four hours, even I couldn't keep up with them. I heard my father stomp down the stairs to report my status to my mother. "She's faking." I heard my brother reply. I closed the door and slunk back down into bed. *No, I'm not faking*, I thought. I had not slept all night. How could I sleep when I saw an old man being burned alive, and with the words, *Beware of Malmspada*, etched into my soul? Again, I shut my eyes and prayed that this was all a bad dream.

Chapter 6

Professor Frazier Vital was a short, balding, sloppy man with a peculiar walk. He padded into class and slammed down his books on an empty steel gray desk, then shuffled from one side of the room to the next, making a weird wispy sound. I never could figure out where the sound was coming from, yet it was always there. He was an odd-looking man with thinning, greasy hair parted on one dandruff-filled side and combed over to the other side of his head. His wrinkled and faded striped shirt was inching out of baggy, dingy pants that dragged on the floor. The shoes he wore were thick and scuffed with slanted heels. Rings of perspiration under his arms suggested a long walk from the faculty parking lot, and over-the-counter reading glasses slipped down to the tip of a red bumpy nose. Despite Prof. Vital's appalling appearance, he was a brilliant man. He had two Ph.D.'s and a law degree from Harvard.

Prof. Vital was harsh with his students. He never gave A's and was stingy with B's. There were rumors that he lived in an old house filled with nude mannequins. Another little nasty piece of gossip was that the good professor dressed up like a woman and frequently danced in the moonlight. He gazed down looking over his glasses and looked at each student until he or she squirmed. Awkward silence filled the room until the professor cleared his throat with a smoker's cough and began to speak.

"This is Television Broadcasting," he said. "I am Professor Frazier Vital." He handed out a thick syllabus that announced an enormous amount of reading. He revealed there would be a ten-page, single-spaced paper due every other month of the semester. There were audible moans and groans from the class. I sat up in my chair, readjusted my notebook and took a deep breath. Listening to Professor Vital was quite entertaining. He snorted a lot to clear his throat. The thick tone was disgusting. Similar to the sound an old man makes after smoking for fifty years. His raspy voice was almost a stutter, "When writing a commercial for a potential client," he said, pacing back and forth, "you must know your target audience." I wondered if he had ever been married because his eyes looked empty and his spirit lost.

As he continued to rattle on about ratings, shares, and demographics, I nonchalantly looked around the room to see if anyone was listening. My eyes fixed on a red-headed, pimply-faced weasel blowing saliva bubbles. He was scrawny and wore baggy jeans, a scruffy plaid shirt, and a baseball cap turned backwards on his head. He slumped in his seat and kept his head down toward his desk. I could not keep my eyes off his odd nose and long fingernails. He had been cutting up earlier out in the hall, mimicking different professors he'd encountered. Professor Vital had not been omitted from his repertoire. The show began with an old calculus teacher who was popular for picking her nose and eating what ever she dug out.

Then the redhead had next padded up and down the hall, his head down, impersonating the ridiculous Vital walk. He had the good professor down cold. I had even chuckled a little.

"Women eighteen to thirty-four are a totally different audience than women twenty-four to fifty-four," the professor was saying. "It is very important not to lump these two groups together—" I was just remembering how he had been viciously imitated in the hallway when he began shouting.

"Out, out of my classroom!" Why was he screaming? Professor Vital's voice was shaky, but loud. Everyone in the room turned around to see the red-headed culprit, who was already out of his seat and standing in the aisle. "Get out!" the professor repeated. "I will call the authorities. You will not disrupt my classroom. This is my classroom. Get out!" Carrot top was at it again, imitating the professor. I couldn't believe what I was seeing. How could this be happening in a college classroom? The student was dangerously out of control.

"Go, Red!" some students in the back rows shouted. The more they instigated, the more he imitated. "You da man! Go Big Red!" The redhead continued the peculiar Vital foot drag. He was definitely under a spell, a hideous spell that could not be broken without a witch or something to snap him out of it.

"Do it again, man!"

"That's what I'm talkin' about!"

"What is up with him?"

"He's got da ol' guy down cold!"

"Look at him, da ol' boy's dome is about ta explode!"

"I want somma what he's got! Red boy is whacked out!"

"I want somma that!"

People were on top of desks now, clapping and yelling for the redhead to continue.

"Stop it! Stop it!" The professor's veins were now popping out of his forehead and neck, and a deep purple hue crept over his face. Students were throwing books, chalkboard erasers, and even empty soda cans. "Stop it!" Professor Vital pounded on the desk. "I will not allow this charade in my classroom! Get out! Stop it! Stop it!" The kid didn't miss a beat. He never saw the professor coming. I watched his wrinkled, striped shirt flap in the wind, and then come to silent halt.

The confrontation had turned into complete turmoil. Professor Vital rushed the redhead, lunging forward with his arms stretched out. I was now out of my seat and near the wall. Desks were overturned. Notebooks and pens flew around everywhere.

"Go, Red! Keep going, you da man," shouted the crazed students. The other students were too stunned to move.

"I will kill you. How dare you treat me this way? I will catch you and kill you! You—you juvenile delinquent!" Professor Vital was a mad man. His eyes were spinning in their sockets. He was foaming at the mouth. "You little ... bas—I will have you expelled and thrown into jail! I am in charge of this classroom." The redhead never once acknowledged the major disruption. He completely ignored Professor Vital.

It looked like he was in his own little world. His trance continued to hold until Professor Vital reached him.

"I will kill you! You kids think you can disrespect authority! You will never disrespect me again! Ever! I have paid my dues to be in charge here! This is my classroom! I was in the war, fighting at the front. I fought for this country with blood on my hands!"

Professor Vital's nose flared and dripped. He stomped around the overturned desks, pounding on each one as he passed. "This is a learning environment. You will not disrupt the halls of learning!" He grabbed the redhead tightly around his scrawny neck. I thought I heard it snap. The professor's half-moon glasses went flying across the room, along with the redhead's baseball cap. The two of them twisted and tangled, swaying back and forth. Professor Vital exhaled as he wrung the neck of his student like a mop. His breath blew strands of the redhead's hair away from his forehead. They continued to thrash, dismantling desks and trampling students. The professor's grip was relentless. I was amazed at his strength. His nails dug into the flesh of the weakening student.

"I'll teach you to disrupt my class!"

"Ahhhaaaa." The student turned fire red as he tried to hold on to his life. Professor Vital's knuckles remained snow white. Finally the student's tongue protruded straight out. I held on to the wall, listening to the redhead's erratic breathing and praying that someone would stop this madness.

The redhead bit his tongue and screamed. His blood sprayed his attacker squarely in the face while the lifeless tongue flapped around the kid's crooked lips. "I will kill you!" cried the crazed instructor. He twisted the student's neck with more force until the kid's puckered skin stretched like silly putty. The veins in his neck snaked in different directions.

Two feet in front of me, a decorated World War II veteran was murdering a student in cold blood. I closed my eyes and covered my face with both hands. I didn't want to witness this murder. I wanted no part of it. I didn't want to have to tell the police what I saw. I tried to pretend I wasn't even in the room.

When I opened my eyes, the student's body was limp and his hair appeared to be on fire. His bird-like chest moved ever so slightly beneath his torn plaid shirt, its plastic buttons dangling from their threads. No more would this student blow saliva bubbles through his purple lips. "Ahhhhh yahhhh" his lips puckered and fluttered one last time, while choppy air escaped a twisted windpipe.

"He's killing him!" shouted an agitated female student next to me. "Someone please help him! Pleeese—someone call the police!" But no one ran for the door or reached for a cell phone. The entire room was paralyzed. I searched for the girl who'd screamed for the police. She was now lying face down on the floor.

Professor Vital released the dead body and it fell to the floor with a thud. Everyone silently watched the mad scholar release his prey and look around, as if searching for victim number two. Suddenly he sat down, Indian style, next to the crumpled corpse and began to shake the body with both two hands. "Wake up, little baby. Time to open your eyes," whispered Professor Vital. "Tickle, tickle, tickle!" He grabbed at the redhead's stomach, gripping it tightly. "I said wake your ass up! Don't you know what time it is? Do not sleep in my classroom! You will not disrespect me by not paying attention! This is an educational institution. You are here to learn something … you will listen to me!"

But this was not the voice of Professor Frazier Vital. It was deeper, raspier. His eyes hardened as he looked around the room. Everyone remained motionless. The air was thick and warm. I didn't want to make eye contact for fear he would lunge in my direction. Then the unexplainable happened. Our scholarly professor began to laugh out loud. "Houston, we have a problem. Tip-toe through the tulips, Romeo, Romeo, wherefore art thou Romeo? I'm so glad we had this time together, just to have a laugh or sing a song, seems we just get started and before you know it, it's the time we have to say so long! Do re mi fa sol la ti do! Tea for two, here's looking at you, sweetheart! Ooh e ooh ah ah, bing bang whalla whalla bing bang, ooh e ooh ah ah bing bang whalla whalla bing bang! Rope a dope! Brill cream a little dab a do yah! Chicks love the car." His head swayed back and forth, and even his massive belly was shaking. "Spin the spinner and call the shot, twister ties you up in a knot!"

Professor Vital slapped the corpse twice on the head and then thumped it with his finger like you'd thump a melon. "You sank my battleship! Ya wanna play rockum sockum robots again?" The professor changed gears again. "If you won't get out of my classroom, then I will throw you out!" He heaved himself to his knees, grabbed the dead student by the ankles, and dragged him a couple of feet. He continued to laugh as the corpse's head bumped along the floor hitting everything in its path. A lonely Butterfinger wrapper caught the edge of the deceased's belt. The student's crippled tongue fluttered from side to side between purple lips. One arm caught the leg of an overturned desk and held on.

Professor Vital could no longer drag the body. Trying to detangle the corpse from the desk, he abruptly ran out of steam and dropped the legs to the floor. Then he flopped down next to the body for the second time. "'Tis the season to be jolly, no more wires! That's it, Beav, put your foot on the lady's thumb! I'm tired as hell and I'm not gonna take it anymore! Get your bullet out, Barn! Lucy, I'm home! Danger Will Robinson! Stella!" Students were trembling and sobbing. No one wanted to be next.

The St. Louis City Police arrived with weapons drawn. "Nobody move!" a young sergeant shouted. "Everyone over to the right side." Students from the other side of the room came rushing to my side. There was barely enough room for all of us. A policewoman kept her gun pointing at Professor Vital, who seemed oblivious to the mayhem.

"Ricko, raise EMS!" barked the sergeant. "We have a 722 here. Don't let anyone in this room. Clear the hallway. No one leaves this room. Don't anyone touch that body. What the hell is going on in here? Seal this place off. Everyone be quiet!" Everyone was shock still. "Tape this place off. Maggie, talk to the old man. Silas, interview the male students, one by one. Radio Homicide! We've got a murder here. Let the murder police have this shit. Get Lt. Daniels on the radio. I don't want my ass in a sling over some bullshit like this! I'm trying to get promoted!"

The sergeant didn't seem able to stop giving orders. "I said tape this place up. Hurry the fuck up. 316 requesting an ambulance to 1369 Hardgrove, University of St. Louis! Someone call the evidence techs, someone call it in! Thomas, Elaine, help Thomas cuff that man. What the hell is going on here? All of these students are suspects. Nobody, I mean nobody, leaves this room. Do not allow these students to talk to each other. Everyone must make a statement. How old are college students? Do we need to contact parents? No one leaves this room! Someone's gonna get booked. This shit stinks. Play everything by the book. I don't want any sloppy police work. Don't let that crazy bitch from Channel 11 in here. No one makes a statement until I sort this shit out. Damn, I wanted to fucking get home early tonight!"

Professor Vital was looking around the room with x-ray eyes darting from one student to the next. No one dared to move a muscle. Then the professor closed his eyes, put his head down, and began to heave. He made gruesome, deep throat sounds while his body expanded and contracted with long smooth movements. He took two deep breaths, and then he exploded. The vomit was a putrid green with lumpy balls in it. It poured all over the front of his shirt and legs, even reaching the skin of the dead student. The vomit continued to flow like running water. He balled his two fists up and plunged them into his chest.

The police officers and the students watched in horror. His roly-poly stomach, which surrounded a large, protruding, hairy navel bounced and shook. The professor's face was ashen and blotchy, with watery, puffy eyes. Some of the vomit remained on his cracked lips. He was such a pathetic sight. The howling sounds flowing from Professor Vital hung in the deadly air. I almost forgot this pitiful man was a cold-blooded killer.

Now it was his turn to gasp for air. He rocked back and forth, making massive gurgling sounds. His head snapped back with his mouth wide open. "Ahhyahah." He was having trouble breathing through his nose, and I was close enough to hear it whistle. The professor snorted and spit, quivering all over. His dangling head sank into his chest, smearing the vomit. He choked, then coughed up a yellowish mucous. He struggled for one more breath and attempted to talk. "You … ahhh … help me, someone … ya ha."

At last, his voice was his own again, though it was barely audible. The professor was trying to muster the strength to speak his last words. His eyes rolled like brown marbles on a slick surface. His lips parted. Just barely hanging on, he managed to speak. "Be … ware—" he swallowed hard enough to wince in pain. His body made one last attempt to hang on to life. His head slowly rose, his eyes focused, and with his last breath, the professor said, *"Beware of Malmspada."*

Professor Vital's stomach stretched forward and sideways. Something was poking around trying to get out. We all watched in horror as the skin extended out in the shape of a face. I saw the eyes, the nose, the mouth just above his puffy navel. The police radios went silent.

The skin was stretched so tight over that face that the teeth were visible. *Beware of Malmspada*, growled the voice within.

The professor's stomach exploded. Flesh and blood spurted everywhere. Everyone, including every police officer, was covered with acidic human waste. The stench was unbearable. The huge hole in the middle of Prof. Vital's gut was astonishing. Veins and fleshy pink matter oozed out like running water. Heavy gurgling sounds filled the air. Silently, the professor's eyeballs popped out of his head and landed in a pool of purple gunk. The eyes stared at me.

I nearly fainted. *Beware of…? What was this?* I was dumbfounded. *Beware of Malmspada.* Had everyone heard it? Or was I the only one? Would the police know what it meant? Professor Vital had died violently with a message to me. I looked around the room to see if anyone else had heard his final words. Were they words of death? No one seemed to have heard. My heart sank. I attempted to wipe mucus and bowel from my face and listened to wailing students and screaming police officers until EMS personnel and the medical examiner arrived.

The silver haired medical examiner looked surprised to see two bodies. "I thought you only had one, Sergeant? What is this?" he asked, pointing to the pile of dead flesh.

"The older man just died, doc," the sergeant explained, "and it wasn't pretty. The fucker blew the fuck up. His gut literally exploded. Right here! Look at all the shit on the walls. On these kids! Look at me! All that slimy shit came from him, doc!" The sergeant was pointing at what was left of Professor Frazier Vital. He looked like a limp blow-up doll left over from a fraternity party.

"Aw shit," the doctor muttered. "Now I'm gonna be late getting home tonight." I listened to the physician mumble something about missing reruns of *Quincy*. Then he opened his medical bag and retrieved a pair of rubber gloves. "In forty years on the street," he whined, "I have never seen anything like this." He poked inside the carcass of professor, his gloved hands disappearing in squishy pulverized organs. The sound of the mangled flesh gushing in and out between the doctor's fingers was deafening. *Squish. Squish*

When the medical personnel draped both bodies, the cloths quickly absorbed burgundy fluids. I looked at the splattered walls and floor of the tiny classroom. The blotchy surfaces were still slimy.

Suddenly, one young female student began shouting, "He killed him! Professor Vital killed that guy!" The student had snapped under the pressure of witnessing a violent murder and a terrible death. I too was struggling with what had just happened. Until I saw her— Katherine Sharpe.

She was glaring at me with a wicked smile and hard eyes. She had not been in the room earlier, I was certain of that. I locked eyes with her and could not break away. It was as if we were the only two people in the entire classroom. I got a chilly feeling as Katherine began to breathe heavily and start toward me. She lowered her head and shook it, then stopped and pretended to be one of the students. Although her clothes were completely clean, she mingled with the rest of the students, who were attempting to frantically explain what had happened. Standing in the center of a group of coeds, Katherine whipped around to glare at me. She threw her head back and laughed.

CHAPTER 7

cademically, the semester continued to be relatively normal. My study habits were solid; and I was sure to make the dean's list. I also landed the position of assistant news director at KAEM, the campus radio station. Rumors soared about the murder of a student on campus by a prominent professor. It made both national and international news. The campus was swarming with television, radio, and newspaper reporters for weeks after the killing. The President focused on it in his State of the Union address. "I will not tolerate murders on our college campuses," he said. "It should and will be a safe academic atmosphere for our children."

Regardless of increased security measures, enrollment at the university dropped significantly as parents yanked their sons and daughters out in startling numbers. Those who did remain were frightened and unfocused. My parents insisted that I withdraw, but since I was on a partial scholarship, it was financially more feasible to remain. I did not live on campus and was ordered by my father to come straight home after class. Like everyone else, I was nervous while walking to and from classes. When would another student snap and go mad? Everyone was suspect.

The chancellor reassured the media and the parents that the campus was safe and back to normal. Campus police officers doubled and the student escort service was reinstated. A university press release stated that Professor Frazier Vital had been suffering from severe flashbacks from the war and was mentally unstable. The cause of his death, the release said, was a massive heart attack. There was no mention of his gut exploding. When the police found several nude mannequins and a dozen women's wigs in his house, the good professor's family explained that he had been conducting some sort of research.

The parents of the murdered student filed a mega-lawsuit against the university. Gossip around the campus suggested the university would fail if the suit were lost. The "death classroom" was sealed off with thick plasterboard and painted over after the police investigations ended. I didn't even like to walk past the wall where the original door-frame could still be seen. It made my skin crawl.

With all of the bad press on campus, I nearly forgot about the janitor I'd helped in the Student Center. An article about him was buried on the last page in the university newspaper. *Oliver Vaden was going to be OK, despite severe injuries to his head. Mr. Vaden had been with the university for twenty years and is married with one son.* The article continued with thanks to the quick thinking of freshman Heidi Morgan, Mr. Vaden was expected to make a speedy recovery. There was a picture next to the article of me sitting on the student center floor with Mr. Vaden's head in my lap. I didn't remember anyone snapping a picture because I'd been too busy trying to keep an old man alive.

My notoriety soared. Everyone seemed to recognize the plain girl who had rescued the old janitor. Whispering and pointing followed me wherever I went, and so I seldom went to the cafeteria and almost never visited the Student Center because college students were cruel and vicious. I heard whispers like, "You shoulda let that ol' man die," when I walked by a group of students. Because of a decrease in student enrollment, the university was forced to reduce tuition and soften strict GPA requirements. I was proud of my partial scholarship, but now it was practically worthless. Undesirable students took over the campus. It was so unbearable at times that I often sought refuge in the university library. It was the only place that appeared to be free from turmoil.

I soon began to enjoy a friendly relationship with the elderly librarian, who'd been working at the university since the foundation was poured. She guided me through rows and rows of her favorite books and periodicals, offering suggestions and chattering about the content.

Mrs. Estelle Adams was a petite woman with silvery hair and a wicked old-lady laugh. Her glasses dangled from a string that rested on her small, sagging bosom. I never once saw her wear the glasses, yet she squinted a lot. Her teeth were rotten and she reeked of mothballs. She had an assortment of tan liver spots on both hands and her fingers were covered with grotesque cheap rings that turned them green. Threadbare stockings sagged around her ankles, and her beige shoes were no longer comfortable. She walked slowly, hunched over, yet she never raised her voice. I guessed since she had been employed at the university for so long, there was no way they could get rid if her. Besides, she really knew her stuff. She padded all over the library, not once looking up a reference or file number in the computer because she knew exactly where every book was located.

No one was ever allowed in the basement of the library. Mrs. Adams told me every time I saw her, "No one is ever to go down in the dungeon. I am the only person authorized to go into the basement." She beamed with pride and smiled through rotten teeth, proudly displaying the badge that gave her permission to travel into the depths of the basement. The badge was practically worthless.

The basement steps were rickety and dangerous, and the basement itself smelled of mold and mildew. The dark cellar housed rows and rows of old tattered books and dog-eared, soiled newspapers. Everything was piled high and terribly disorganized. The light bulbs were dim, with frayed strings hanging from the sockets.

Mrs. Adams navigated the aisles like the captain of a large ship. She knew where every file, book, periodical, and microfilm was located. She shook with enthusiasm after finding her treasure. "No one knows this microfilm is here," she boasted. "Those dang computers aren't worth the money they paid for 'em. A good book is priceless."

She gave me an unsettling look and stared right through me. Feeling uncomfortable, I started toward the steps. The light bulbs flickered and swayed, their strings floating in unison. Her bony fingers grabbed my shoulder as I felt her hot breath on my neck.

"Stay with me, Heidi, I will show you something few eyes have seen." I hesitated and, against my better judgment, I followed her.

"Mrs. Adams, I don't think I should be down here if it's against the rules. Maybe we should go back upstairs." Recalling the ghastly basement incident at home, I was apprehensive about descending into the depths of hell…. Again. Death was everywhere.

She started toward the back of the basement, which was even danker than the front. I could actually taste the moist air. Spiral cobwebs full of hairy spiders were draped on the corners of metal bookcases. I listened to the sounds of massive water heaters and furnaces whirling nearby. I was near the heart of the university. I was shaken with thoughts of Mr. Vaden's distorted face dancing in the pilot light of the hot water heater at home. Thoughts of that horrible sight chilled me to the bone.

"Mrs. Adams, I really think—" She abruptly cut me off in mid plea.

"Hush, child. Just follow me." I walked with my hands and arms protecting my face from webs and renegade flying insects. When I checked my watch, I realized I would be late for my next class. I seemed to be intrigued by the basement, or I was under the spell of a wicked witch.

A fat rodent with a long striped tail scampered across the floor in front of me. I shrieked and jumped out of its way, then I remembered that no one could hear me. The walls were rock solid, and certainly scream-proof. Eventually, the ceiling turned from cracked cement to dripping, zigzagging pipes. Hot steam sizzled out of slits of rusty metal tubing, sprinkling an oily film on all who walked below. The warm sizzle lured us through an underground tunnel that extended the length of the campus. The sudden change of temperature was startling, and within minutes I felt as if I were walking on a journey to a frigid death. The tunnel narrowed and darkened. I could feel frosty air around my ankles. Mrs. Adams was nearly out of sight, but I could still hear the sound of her feet. That sound reminded me of my mother's peculiar leg drag.

Suddenly a swarm of large, flying green and red insects appeared, dive bombing my head from every direction. With the buzz ringing in my ears, I twisted and flapped, bouncing off the walls of the tunnel. Nothing helped. I screamed for Mrs. Adams, but got no response. I batted and sliced the air, but this only aggravated the pesky creatures. Finally these bugs had enough and fluttered away. Perspiration poured off of me even though it was quite chilly. Mrs. Adams had no idea that I'd been attacked, or did she? I could hear her footsteps ahead. The floor was no longer tiled; it had turned to dirt. The heels of my shoes sank into the damp soil, making it difficult to keep up. I began to feel absolutely exhausted. I wanted to plop down in the dirt and simply give up.

She finally stopped and turned around. It was a dead end. We'd been walking for what seemed like miles. Mrs. Adams had to be at least seventy, but she was not out of breath. I on the other hand was completely worn out still trying to catch what little breath I had left. She stood quietly in front of me and began to chant and whirl slowly around. It sounded like an Indian death chant from an old cowboy movie.

She put her feeble head back and took a deep breath. Her arms lifted above her head and she began to sway. The temperature became even colder than before. I tried to keep warm by wrapping my arms around my frail frame. The sound of my chattering teeth was no match for her eerie song. She continued to chant louder and louder with incredible range. *Malmspada! Malmspada! Oh, Malmspada!*

I was in a tunnel under the campus with a crazy old woman screaming *Malmspada.* This could not be a coincidence. *What was Malmspada?* I was terrified. I couldn't believe this was happening again. I flashed back to Mr. Vaden's warning, to Professor Vital's final words. And now Mrs. Adams was invoking Malmspada. What was the connection? The end of the world had to be near.

My nerves were frazzled and my mouth was too dry for me to say a word. I stood still, afraid to move a muscle. I even held vomit in my mouth while controlling my regurgitating reflexes. No one knew I was down here. I would never be able to find my way back. Something huge flew near my head. I could only imagine a rabid bat with fanged teeth. I heard the creature fly away, screeching loudly. Perhaps it knew the way out.

Mrs. Adams had worked herself up into a chanting frenzy. She began to tremble; then she lunged toward me and fell to the ground at my feet. "Mrs. Adams," I whimpered, "Are you OK? Mrs. Adams! Mrs. Adams!" I could hardly see anything; the tunnel was so black. The librarian snorted and coughed as she lay crumpled up at my feet. She began to hyperventilate. "Malmspada. Oh, God Malmspada, oh, my God … Malmspada!!"

Soon her voice was barely audible. I gently got Mrs. Adams to her feet. She was incredibly weak. How could I explain the death of an elderly woman in a hidden underground tunnel? The university authorities would surely think I killed her. I wasn't thinking clearly and my own breathing was erratic. I prayed she would not die. Again I flashed to praying for Mr. Vaden in the Student Center. I remembered my promise to God to make all A's. I knew I could not make another deal. Now the elderly librarian was beginning to weep. I propped her up against the wall of the tunnel and said, "Mrs. Adams, you've got to get us out of here. We'll die in here. Mrs. Adams, please!" I was now totally hysterical. Visions of my own death bombarded my thoughts. Her crying increased to ear-piercing levels. She'd slid down the wall and lay on the floor of the tunnel in a fetal position, whimpering like a sick puppy.

With her right ear embedded into the mud, she inched around with an erratic circular motion. Her head jerked with a nauseating tic.

Her clothes were drenched and soiled. She struggled to get to her feet, but found it nearly impossible. As I reached down to assist her again, she waved me away, covered her face with her hands, and began to scoot around on her backside like a mad dog.

I was so scared I began to scream and cry. "Silence," she said sternly. "I will hear none of that."

"But Mrs. Adams—" "Shut your filthy mouth or I will kill you." Her voice deepened, her eyes squinted. "I will twist that nasty tongue of yours and plunge needles into it. Perhaps I will cut it completely out. Then I'll gouge your foul heart out and toss it a hot skillet! You will only speak when I tell you to speak." She pointed at her bony chest. This was not the woman I had befriended! The original Mrs. Adams had disappeared.

Breathing heavily, she was determined to have my undivided attention. I gathered my thoughts and looked into the shadowy eyes of Estelle Adams. Even though the tunnel was dark, I could see the face of the witch quite clearly.

"Listen to me, Heidi." Her sweet grandmotherly voice was now back. "I want to show you something few eyes have seen." I didn't know what to expect next. There was no reasoning with this woman. She bent down and began to scratch at the earth with feeble fingers. She continued to dig with every ounce of her strength. With dirty fingernails, filthy clothes, and mud-caked hair, she continued to penetrate the earth. She was a woman possessed. Intrigued, I knelt down beside her and watched.

She resembled a dog digging up a buried treasure. Moving the earth was second nature to her, something she was very accustomed to. Her arms moved with the grace of a ballerina. The soil flew everywhere, bouncing off the sides of the tunnel. She slowed a bit when her bony fingers tapped the edge of her prize. When she lifted the object from the earth she daintily brushed it off. Holding it close to her chest, Mrs. Adams cradled her prize possession as if it were a baby. I could barely see what it was until she asked me to feel it. "Touch this, Heidi." She reached for my arm and guided my hands to the front of her body. "Please be careful," she warned. I touched the object with the tips of my fingers. It felt cold, hard, and slick. I jerked my hand back, nearly knocking Mrs. Adams off her feet. I was touching a human tibia. "It's long, thin and curved on the end. It is spectacular," she said. "Have you ever felt such a magnificent specimen?" The old woman's eyes were pierced my soul.

"Heidi," Mrs. Adams was speaking in a whisper again. Her mood was similar to a child on Christmas morning. She stroked the bone, smelled it and licked it. The tip of her nose and lips were caked with dirt. She laughed under her breath and began singing, "Swing low sweet chariot, coming forth to carry my bone." Then the lovable voice was back. The mud remained on her nose and lips while she rambled on with an absurd tongue. She reached out for me suddenly and struck me across the face, knocking me completely off balance.

I felt the blood gush out of my nose and knew Mrs. Adams had broken it. Trying to regain my composure, I jumped up and began running back up the tunnel. . I tried to block the flow of the blood with my right hand, but it trickled out anyway. I ran down miles and miles of dark passageways with no thoughts of retrieving Mrs. Adams. My entire face was on fire. Suddenly I tripped over a long, bumpy object in the middle of the path and tumbled to the ground. The object wiggled its long thick reptilian body towards me. I could see it was a mammoth snake with demonic intentions.

The serpent's forked tongue protruded with a devilish hiss, and then it started to coil its massive length around my feet. I frantically swung my arms around in the air, wiggling around in the cold earth. I batted at the serpent while trying to push it away from my weak legs. I completely forgot my nose was broken. "Get off of me!" I screamed. "Help! Somebody! Please help me! Ahhhh! God, help me, please! Oh, my God, get offa me!" My heart thundered inside my chest as I scooted around, the monster still attached to my legs, thrashing against the wall. The tunnel, still very dark and dank, seemed to close in on me. The monster's grip intensified. I could feel the life seeping right out of my body.

The serpent twisted upward, squeezing and choking off my airflow. It was now waist high. I waited for my death. I could no longer fight off a creature that was so much stronger than I was. My body wilted and gave up.

But suddenly the snake's grip lightened! It uncoiled slowly and slithered down my body. I pushed it down my weary frame. The skin was slick and hard to the touch. The scales were rough, large, and wet. It opened its mouth and hissed one last time before it slithered away. I could not believe the snake hadn't killed me. My life had been spared for reasons unknown to me. Pain shot through my body like a hot knife. I staggered and leaned against the damp wall of the tunnel. It was still quite dark. The snake had disappeared completely, gone with no evidence of its wicked presence. I heard breathing behind me and when I turned, I saw Mrs. Adams standing in the darkness.

She smiled and tried to speak, but her long forked tongue prevented any speech. She began to twist and hiss like the serpent that had almost killed me. Her eyes were neon green and her hands were webbed. I took off like a jet down a deserted runway. My heels kept sinking into the damp soil, and I quickly tired. Was Mrs. Adams the devil? I peeped over my shoulder; she was nowhere in sight. I continued to run as fast as I could, ignoring my fatigued legs and lopsided bloody nose.

Finally I came to the door leading back to the library basement, and sight of the rows of books brought tears to my eyes. I moved unsteadily toward one aisle and slowly walked down the middle. As I neared the end, I could hear a soft hum. Someone was singing. I was so happy to hear the voice of a sane human being, I ran toward it for help. I knew the person was in the next row over because I could hear them breathing. "Help me, please," I cried out. "Mrs. Adams is trying to kill me! She's a snake and I tried to get away, and …" I realized, as I got closer that the voice was familiar.

"Hello, Heidi. I've been waiting for you." She laughed wickedly. My blood ran cold. Mrs. Adams was in the library archives waiting for me. "Where have you been, my dear? I wanted to show you this set of priceless books. They're all about snakes and how they evolved." Her chuckle sounded more like a hiss than a laugh. She continued to laugh at me until her throat bulged. I turned away and spotted the rickety stairs leading out of the basement.

I headed toward the only way out and bolted up the steps to the entrance to the main level of the library, even though my heel got caught in a hole in the steps and broke off. I never liked those shoes anyway. I exploded through the door and into the library. Everything and everyone seemed to be normal. Students sat at long wooden tables with their heads bent over their books. The information desk was full of inquisitive people pushing their way to the front. I heard the voice of an angel.

Mrs. Adams was busy at her desk. There was no serpent tongue, no scaly skin, no eerie laughing. It was just plain old Mrs. Adams, university librarian.

"Heidi, my dear," she said, "where have you been? I haven't seen you for so long. I have the information you wanted for your term paper. Heidi, what's the matter, dear? You act as if you've seen the devil himself!"

Everyone turned to look at the poor girl who was as white as a ghost. I felt nauseated and chilled to the bone. "Heidi," Mrs. Adams said, "are you *OK?*" "Heidi, what is wrong with you? Are you ill? Why don't you sit down?"

I looked down at my clothes. I was soaking wet and covered by mud. I felt my nose. Nothing out of the ordinary. No broken bones, no bloody mess. I was simply dirty and smelly. How would I explain this to my parents or the people who would soon take me away if I didn't compose myself? I couldn't even explain it to myself. What had happened to me? Was I going mad? Seeing a skull in the pilot light, watching a professor kill a student, watching a thing outside my fence at home ... and now this? I glanced over my shoulder to look at the door to the basement. I began trembling when I realized that the door was gone.

The wall was covered with beige bumpy paint and assorted cheap pictures. There was a green silk tree blocking what had been the entrance to the basement to hell. I raced over to the tree, knocking it over, feeling frantically for the door to hell. I pounded on the wall like a mad woman looking for a hidden treasure. I actually felt the banging in my chest. An audience gathered to watch the insane girl. Of course everyone remembered me as the crazy girl who'd rescued the old janitor in the Student Center. I scratched and scraped and tried to peel the paint off the wall. The chipped paint pieces caught under my fingernails like devices of Chinese torture. "Mrs. Adams," I shouted, "where is the door? I was just down there. There was a door here. Just a minute ago...." I lunged toward the wall again and grabbed at thin air and slid down to the floor, where I sat in horror while everyone watched. "She's a witch!" I shouted at them. "I was just in the basement and then in a long tunnel and a snake almost killed me!" My head dropped into my stinky shirt. I felt everyone staring daggers at me. I slowly looked up into the eyes of Estelle Adams. There was a shimmer of green neon in her eyes as she put her glasses on.

The bouncing string hanging from her glasses caught my attention. I followed the string up to her ears. There was a small scaly patch beneath her left ear lobe, and her fingernails were caked with mud. And there was no door.

CHAPTER 8

I sat on the library floor, leaning against the wall for what seemed like a lifetime, trying to make sense out of what was happening to me. I could hear voices dragging out syllables that sounded like slow motion. I could not understand what anyone was saying to me. I remained sitting there because I was unable to get to my feet. At last a long arm extended out through the crowd. I looked up unsteadily, squinted, and saw a dainty silver bracelet glistening in the fluorescent lights. It was the delicate arm of Katherine Sharpe. "Are you OK?" she asked, offering her questionable assistance. I looked up at her and shook my head as if something inside my brain were loose and rolling around. I couldn't understand why she, of all people, was rushing to my aid. She was the devil, and I knew it.

I recalled Professor Vital's classroom, when she had appeared and shot me a devilish look. "Let me help you up," she said now, and I felt my body rising. She was undoubtedly very strong. "I'm OK," I managed, suddenly embarrassed by my ridiculous behavior. My legs still felt like wiggly, watery Jell-O. I wasn't exactly ready for Katherine Sharpe, be she campus diva or satanic witch, to befriend me. "Really, I'm fine," I protested. "I just need to sit down."

"Heidi, come sit at my desk," Mrs. Adams suggested. Seeing that there was no more excitement, the crowd dispersed, leaving plenty of "She's a weird psycho" and "She needs help" comments to fill my head. Gossip about me would spread over campus … again.

I walked slowly and unsteadily to the reference desk and sat down in a padded swivel chair. Perhaps I needed some psychological help. I put my head down on top of a mound of paperwork and closed my eyes. "Heidi," Mrs. Adams asked, "would you like a drink of water, dear?" I shook my head without lifting it from the desk. This ordeal had zapped all of my energy, mentally and physically. I wondered how I could get out of the library without being seen. Had I just come from a place that did not exist? The door was gone, and there was no evidence of one ever having been there. I could hear Mrs. Adams chattering with other students from a distance, but I could also feel the presence of someone or something very close. I raised my head and slowly opened my eyes. Katherine Sharpe was sitting in the chair next to me. "You dropped this," she said with a sarcastic tone. *Dropped what*, I thought without breaking my gaze. "You dropped this over by the silk tree," Katherine said. My eyes crept down to what she held in her hand.

It looked like the piece of the bone that Mrs. Adams had dug up in the basement. "It's yours," Katherine said. "I saw it come out of your pocket." She leaned toward me and whispered, "Where did you get it?" Her voice was low and sinister. I was flabbergasted. Katherine was rolling the sharp sliver of bone around in her hand, fingering every inch. It bounced off her diamond ring, making a light pinging sound. She was enjoying my total bewilderment. I followed the bone with my eyes as it ricocheted from one of her palms to the other. She never once lost her rhythm. I looked closer and spotted specks of mud on each end of the bone. Katherine kept up the sideshow until a young assistant librarian walked over to the desk. Then she slowly closed her hand and dropped the bone into her lap.

Using this distraction as a way to end this offensive maneuver, I jumped up from the desk and pushed past Katherine, but she grabbed my arm and held me in place. Her eyes were dark with a twisted stare. She was smiling the smile I saw in Professor Vital's classroom. She tossed the bone fragment into the air and caught it with her right hand. Her lips slowly evolved into something hideous. She mouthed, *Beware of Malmspada.*

Knocking the swivel chair to the floor in my fear and haste, I turned and sprinted toward the library door. I could still feel Katherine's stare on my back. Had she really said, *Beware of Malmspada*? What—or who—was Malmspada? I flashed back to the first day of school when I had searched my computer for the word *Malmspada*. I was beginning to really be afraid of the word and those who said it. Mrs. Adams had chanted the words like a death song, and Katherine Sharpe, the woman who emerges from nowhere, had now said it. These thoughts stabbed me like a knife.

I ran all the way to the parking garage before I realized I'd left my bags of books and my purse in the library. My insides instantly felt acidic, churning and practically jumping into my throat. I vomited my guts out at the foot of the garage stairs. The taste on my tongue was vile. I wiped the yellowish liquid off my lips with my sleeve and dabbed at my nose. The last thing I wanted to do was go back into the library with Katherine and that bone. I couldn't face Mrs. Adams again, either. But I didn't have a choice. I wanted to go home. I sat down on the bottom step to gather my thoughts and come up with a plan. My insides were sore, and my throat was scratchy. My head bent forward, resting on top of my folded knees. It was then when I discovered the mud on my shoes. I had been in the basement of the library. The mud was the proof.

"Hello, Heidi." Was someone speaking to me? It was a deep, rich male voice that I did not recognize. Terrified to see who might be speaking to me, I slowly lifted my head in the bright sunlight to see who it was. It was the famous Ellis Majors. How did he know my name? My thoughts jetted back to the newspaper article of the old janitor and me on the floor of the student center.

"Hello," I pathetically squeaked out, dropping my head again.

"I saw you running. Not a bad stride for a girl. Why were you running? What's up with you?" His designer sunglasses had slipped down that beautiful nose and were resting on the tip.

I was sure that I could explain that I was fleeing his girlfriend who was playing with a bone in the library that had been dug up in the basement by the elderly librarian with a serpent tongue; that made loads of sense. I was already known as the crazy girl on campus.

"I wasn't feeling well," was all I could muster. I felt like a little kid in the principal's office. He was so handsome; I wondered what I looked like. I had just thrown up my entire insides, what else could I look like? I quickly started to brush my hair back with the palm of my hand, straightened my collar, and adjusted my sweater. I dug into the corner of each eye and rubbed beneath them. I wanted to make sure there was no gook in the corners. I was sure my mascara made me look like a raccoon, a sick raccoon at that. I was positive that my cheap blush was either gone or grossly smeared. I began massaging my cheeks to alleviate the problem. It was my feeble attempt at sprucing up.

"Is there anything that I can do?" Was this the same Ellis who disrespected women and had total disregard for all human beings other than him? He bent down to my level.

"No, I was … going to my car, but my purse … the library. I don't need any … help … my books are in … the keys to my car are...." Here was my famous gibberish again.

"Why don't you let me take you home?" He flashed one of his classic smiles, and I weakened, but I wasn't buying it. I could never forget the way he'd treated poor old Mr. Vaden in the Student Center. I could still see how Ellis had slapped him on the head and danced around his limp body. He even got everyone to sing with him. It was a total disgrace. Even though I desperately needed help, I was not going to stoop to the trickery of the dangerous Ellis Majors.

"I'm fine," I said. "I can make it on my own." Slowly I got to my feet, and brushed the grass clippings and debris off my pants. Ellis also stood up.

"How did you get mud on your shoes?" He said it as if it were totally unacceptable to have your shoes caked with mud. He waited for a logical answer while I feverishly searched for one. I decided he didn't deserve one, especially since I could not come up with anything rational.

"I'm OK now," I said again. "I feel much better. I'm going to my car. Thanks, anyway." With those words I stood up, turned around, and began climbing the metal garage stairs. My one heel made a "click—thud" sound against the iron steps as I began to climb faster. The mud, now practically dried, seemed to hamper my stride.

"Heidi, wait!" I considered the fact that once I got to my car, I couldn't get into it, anyway. What was I going to do now? Remembering where my car was parked was always a problem, even though the banana boat was easily identifiable. When I arrived at the top level, I kicked both shoes off, and ran up and down rows and rows of cars. "Heidi, why are you running from me?" I could hear Ellis calling my name. Why was I running? I finally found my car hiding behind a makeshift wooden mobile home at the end of the last row. I saw that I had cracked both the driver's and passenger's windows because the days were so hot and steamy. I looked to see if Ellis had given up the chase. He had not. He was now at the top of the row, walking toward me with both hands in his front pockets. "Heidi, I only want to talk to you! I ain't trying to hurt nobody!" I glanced at my watch and guessed classes had just resumed. There was no one on the top level of the garage except me, and … Ellis.

He strolled up to the tail end of my car and smiled. I remembered my spare key under the mat of the driver's side. What good was that if you're locked out of the car? I was batting a thousand.

"Heidi, all I want to do is help you."

"I told you I don't need any help. I'm feeling much better now. Now please just leave me alone!"

He started walking toward me as I began inching up toward the hood of the banana boat. I was rapidly running out of room, and now I had no place to go. I was trapped. The only way out would be to jump over the edge of the garage. "Ellis, please! Leave me alone! I really am OK. I'm just not feeling very well." I began to lean against the side of my car. I was in a very awkward position between my car and the mammoth makeshift RV.

"Heidi, I just want to get to know you. If you need a ride home, my car is parked one level down. I'm not gonna hurt you. Trust me." Ellis's eyes were a-blaze. Trust him?

"Ellis, please just leave me alone!" He was inches from me when we both heard someone shriek, "Ellis!"

It was the voice of Katherine Sharpe. She was suddenly standing near the trunk of my car, and she had one plastic bag hanging from each arm and my cheapo purse over her left shoulder. My junk was not the style of the glamorous Katherine Sharpe. I waited for her to break out in hives.

"Ellis, what are you doing? Why are you with her?"

"She's sick and I was trying to help." Ellis replied.

Katherine shot me an unsettling look, her eyes squeezed down to two terrifying slits.

"What are *you* doing out here?" demanded Ellis. "You should be in class and not be worrying about what I'm doing. Why are you always in my business?"

It was a known fact that Katherine was only dating Ellis to be a part of the crowd. However, now it seemed that he was her weakness. A look of hopeless love covered her face. Embarrassed, she lowered her head in disappointment and began kicking at a piece of gravel in order not to make eye contact. She kicked the rock so hard that the tip of her designer shoe was scuffed. "Come on girl!" Ellis sounded tired of this juvenile charade and took over the moment. She never raised her voice to him regardless of how poorly he treated her.

"I just thought I'd bring Heidi her purse and books." Katherine held the items out so Ellis could clearly see she was telling the truth. "She left them in the library."

I didn't even remember where I had left them in the library. Why would she want to do me a favor for me? And how did she find me? Technically, I should have been in class. Ellis stamped over to Katherine and practically pulled her arms out of their sockets as he grabbed my purse and plastic bags. She gave them up without a word. He gently handed them to me as if they were laced in gold. I accepted my things and quietly said, "Thank you." I felt as if I should have bowed down to the king.

Katherine's stare burned a hole in my dignity and crippled any logical thought I might have. All I could do was stand beside the car and absorb her mental daggers. Ellis was visibly angry with his rich girlfriend. He grabbed Katherine's arm and swung her around to walk away. "Let's go!" He said, dragging her along. She was visibly shaken by Ellis and openly hostile toward me.

As the two stormed off toward the stairs, Katherine suddenly turned around and jerked her arm out of the clutches of Ellis Majors. "I'm not playing with you, Katherine. Come on!" he barked. "I ain't for all this nonsense." But she ignored Ellis's demands and marched back to me. When she got within a couple of feet of me, she hurled an object that hit me square in the face. It bounced off my cheek and hit the ground. I was stunned and too shocked to move. I couldn't believe Katherine was devious enough to throw something at me. I didn't even see it coming.

"Katherine!" shouted Ellis. Are you crazy? Stop it! Have you lost your mind, girl? What is up with you?" Ellis couldn't believe it either. Why would Katherine try to hurt me? I felt my cheek to see if the skin had broken. I didn't feel any blood. I was flushed, afraid, and embarrassed. Katherine stood and watched with piercing eyes and an unsettling smile. She felt no remorse.

"What is wrong with you, girl?" Ellis asked again. "Why are you throwing stuff? Have you lost your mind? What is that? What the hell are you throwing?" He grabbed her shoulders and violently shook her.

"It's hers!" she shouted. "I saw her with it in the library."

"With what? You saw her with what?"

"She knows what it is!" Katherine belted out nearly in tears. "She knows what it is! It belongs to Heidi!" This was the first time Katherine had ever talked back to Ellis. I was still too scared to move. I couldn't believe this was really happening. With my bags on one arm, I dug into my purse for my car keys. They weren't in my purse. Where were they?

"Are you looking for these?" Katherine held out a pair of keys with a shiny whistle attached to the ring. I knew they were mine. Why would she want my keys? Again I was too shocked to speak. Had she gone through my purse? Why would Katherine want anything of mine? I was a Ford; she was a Jag.

And Ellis was a wild man. He rushed Katherine, grabbed the keys out of her hand, and ran over to me.

"I don't know why she's trippin'," he said. I didn't know either. Ellis handed me the keys and turned toward Katherine. I began to tremble. As I put the key into the lock, I realized I hadn't seen what Katherine had thrown at me. I got the door open, threw my bags and purse on the front seat, and hopped in. I waited to start the car until Katherine and Ellis had walked the entire length of the garage. Katherine continued to glance over her shoulder as Ellis tugged and pulled her toward the stairs. Her designer purse bounced on her hip with every step. I could still hear then swearing and shouting as they ran down the metal stairs.

I waited a while longer before getting back out of the banana boat. I recalled where I'd heard the object fall. Something was lying underneath the left rear tire. I reached behind the tire and my heart was instantly in my throat. Swallowing hard and taking a deep breath, I closed my eyes and leaned on the side of the car. Breathing was nonexistent. Never in my wildest dreams would I ever imagine that Katherine would have thrown the bone fragment at me.

I inspected the bone carefully. It had been very dark in the tunnel. Was it part of the tibia Mrs. Adams had found and been so proud of? The mud had been completely washed off, and now it was smooth and slick and sharp on both ends. I was tempted to throw it away, but decided to keep it. I got back into the car and put the bone in my purse. I had no idea why I was keeping it, but keep it I did.

I started my car, backed out of the space and tore out of the garage with a chunk of human bone in my purse. While driving home I reached into my purse to look at the bone again. To my surprise, both ends were muddy again. I shuddered and slammed the bone back into my purse, and drove home. *Beware of Malmspada.* I got the sick feeling that Ellis was not finished with me, and neither was his girlfriend.

CHAPTER 9

October in St. Louis is always brisk. Leaves turn a bright yellow-orange, falling to the ground in bunches. Little kids can no longer play outside after supper for fear of getting caught in the dark. People begin wearing leather jackets and fall coats, while car dealers taunt prospective buyers with enticing end-of-the-year deals. Weekend flag football players dazzle wives and girlfriends with dynamic moves and sore muscles. Halloween costumes are all the rage, while Christmas trees sprout up in malls with lots of twinkling lights, along with little crazy donkey shaped pottery that claims to grow hair. Fall was in full swing.

I still had not completely gotten over the Katherine and Ellis ordeal. Whenever I saw either one approaching, I would run the other way. Ellis still continued his attempts to talk to me, but I honestly had no desire to date him or even be his friend. Katherine took every opportunity to shoot me full of holes with her devious eyes. I always knew when she was near, even if she was standing out of sight, because her presence was startling, even for an overactive imagination like mine. I could feel her burning in my soul.

The semester was coming to an end when I met Toni Steptoe. Toni was a full-blooded Cherokee Indian with long black hair, beautiful olive skin, and high cheekbones. She sometimes wore brown moccasins and a large colorful blanket draped over her back. The blanket was black, gold, and aqua with a hint of burgundy with images of sunburst explosions. Delicate black fringe dangled from the edges and swayed when she walked. Toni said the blanket was a gift from her grandmother, who had gotten it from her mother. The blanket was in amazing shape for an item almost a hundred years old.

Toni was a stunning young woman who had a permanent green dot in the middle of her forehead. She confided to me that the dot had never been explained to her, and she had never asked about it. Her mother's dot was black. Toni also wore a vibrant blue and gold band that was a gift from her father around her head. She wore the band practically every day, believing it kept away evil spirits and brought good luck. I watched her touch it during a difficult Spanish exam.

Toni Steptoe was a special person. She believed animals were sacred, and she worshipped the dead. "I'm not afraid of dying," she once told me, "I'm eager to travel to the other side." She claimed to have spoken to her dead grandmother many times. "I'm never afraid when she visits me. She only comes in the middle of the night in the form of a little rodent," Toni proudly explained. "She sits on the edge of my dresser and watches me all night long. I tell her everything. I watch her lick her little limbs, wiggle her long whiskers, and roll her eyes around to the back of her head. I kiss her every time she visits." She described the rodent having one blue eye and one brown eye, just like her grandmother. The rodent also had six toes on one foot and four on the other foot. Apparently her grandmother, too, had been afflicted with this defect. Toni said her grandmother had always walked like her feet hurt.

Toni was an avid swimmer. She swam in lakes and ponds riddled with deadly snakes and vicious alligators. She was an only child and never claimed to miss having a brother or sister. She was five feet seven inches tall and had a body of steel.

We met while working on the campus newspaper. Toni was assigned to cover security in the parking garages, or the lack thereof. We quickly hit it off, and I was up and running with a new friend. Toni had lived on a reservation in Oklahoma until she was sixteen. Her father, Chief Steptoe, had been killed in an uprising over land that was taken from him by the government. He had been shot while storming into city hall with a knife. "He never wanted to hurt anyone," Tony explained, "He just wanted his land back." The land had been in the Steptoe family for generations, but the city wanted it to build a strip mall with a large parking lot. Chief Steptoe couldn't scream *NO* loudly enough. The city offered the Steptoes a minute amount of money, clearly an insult. After years of quarrelling and fighting, the city decided to take the land.

When the bulldozers arrived on that dreadful day, it knocked down their small home and rolled over their crop. Luckily, no one was home at the time. Other Indians on the reservation tried to stop the white men from degrading the Steptoes' land, then the police were called, and many were arrested. It was a total disgrace. Television cameras captured the entire episode on tape so thousands of people could witness the turmoil. Indians shouted into microphones in their native tongue. After the death of Chief Steptoe, Toni and her mother had moved to St. Louis to begin a new life.

"The memories back home in Oklahoma were too painful," Toni said. "Mom and I were always reminded of Dad's death. Besides, people began pointing and saying there goes *those loco injins.*"

Toni and I became inseparable. For once, I had someone to confide in, no matter how bizarre my story seemed. I told Toni about all the mysterious supernatural occurrences that had happened to me. She listened, hanging on to every word. An ordinary person would have taken off running and screaming in the opposite direction, but not Toni. She was intrigued by a hop-along bug creature that leaped into a burning pilot light, and a floating skull that wailed, "Help me," while charring in the flames of hell. For some reason she believed me and didn't think I was a lunatic.

Toni and I began studying together at each other's houses. After telling her my story about the library and the long dark tunnel underneath it, she too refused to darken its doors again. I also showed her the bone that Katherine had thrown at me. She inspected it for a long time; it was as if she had seen it some place before. I wanted to question her about the bone, but never had the nerve. I was sure Toni knew more than she said. She, too, despised Ellis Majors and all of his shenanigans. Like me, Toni stayed clear of the Student Center and all of the nitwits who lived there. Since she hung out with me, she, too, was an outcast. Her Indian blanket didn't help the situation.

Toni and I continued to blaze through the rest of the semester. She was a good student, even though she credited the lucky headband for her grades. Her first love was swimming, but Toni also loved to run. She had run for miles on the reservation, mostly at night. "I like the cool dark breeze against my face," she told me. "The night opens the soul and cleanses the spirit. Running at night allows you to speak to the dead." When finals rolled around, Toni and I decided to spend the entire weekend studying. She packed a small bag and threw it in the back of the banana boat so we could buckle down at my house for some intense cramming. I often wondered about Toni's love life. We almost never spoke of boyfriends or the fact that neither one of us had one. I found it a little odd for two good friends not to talk about that.

I couldn't believe Toni never had a date. She was beautiful. I would always see guys looking at that spectacular body, but none of them ever asked her out. I suppose the blanket she wore and the multi-colored headband were no match for the microscopic skirts and shorts that wiggled around on campus.

My parents loved Toni and treated her like a member of the family. She was intrigued by our old house and its charm. The pool and the horse chestnut tree near the patio also fascinated her. Toni claimed the tree was a gift from God. "It is a protector of you and your family, Heidi. Look at the way it shadows the house and the backyard." Toni could make anything look interesting. Now I could almost see the limbs of the trees as long arms that could wrap around the entire house. She swore the pool was the goddess of water whose blue liquid served as holy water. "Every time your body is drenched with this water, your being gets one step closer to God, and it fills you with strength and wisdom," Toni said.

When Toni dove into the water, she always performed a water ritual. She would turn around twice, plunging face-first, with her feet exposed to the sky, and then slithering around in a circle three times. She did it so often that I began performing the ritual when I jumped into the water.

Most of all, she loved the basement. Its cool damp air reminded her of life on the reservation. She and her mother had been forced to live in the basement of a relative when Toni's father was killed. Mrs. Steptoe, a typical Indian wife and mother, was expected to stay home and care for the home of her husband and raise their daughter. Mrs. Steptoe could not drive and had never written a check. She had been completely dependent on her husband. When he was murdered, there was no way she could support herself or her daughter. She had no marketable skills and had no idea how to open a bank account. So Toni and her mother had been forced to move into the moist basement of a harsh elderly aunt who disliked children. With the financial assistance of other family members, Toni and her mother lived in one corner of the dank basement. Toni loved the basement, even though it was cold in the winter and blazing hot in the summer. Every time it rained, the basement flooded and smelled of mildew. There were spiders and guardian water bugs crawling on the blemished stone walls.

The Steptoes were only allowed to enter and exit the house through an outside basement stairwell. Their aunt rarely allowed the two in the main part of the house, which smelled of mothballs and urine and had lots of breakable knickknacks on antique tables and cracked walls. She even had a birdbath with mildewed water in the middle of the living room. The old woman's legs looked like tree trunks, which made it difficult for her to walk. She suffered from poor circulation, but Toni called it the "Mean Disease".

The Steptoes were an embarrassment to the old woman. Apparently, she was the sister of Chief Steptoe's mother, who cursed the day her nephew was born. Even though living in the basement was tough, Toni knew it was the best her mother could do. She often studied by the sunlight that shone through cloudy windows. They didn't have a shower or a phone. There was a small commode in the west corner of the basement that had green water in the bowl. Toni and her mother bathed in rainwater captured in old rusty tubs. "Water from God's eyes is good for the skin," Mrs. Steptoe used to say. There was an old stove in the east corner of the basement. The Steptoes were allowed to cook only on Sundays. It was hard to sneak and cook because the stove filled the house with gas fumes. Toni and her mother either ate fast foods or were at the mercy of relatives and friends.

Finally Mrs. Steptoe got a job cleaning the home of a wealthy woman who lived near the reservation. She saved enough money to move to St. Louis for a fresh start. Toni landed a full scholarship through an Indian outreach organization that also furnished clothes and books. They now lived in a two-bedroom apartment near campus.

Toni and I decided to tackle Spanish first. We conjugated verbs until we both were famished, and then stomped down the steps from my room and made turkey sandwiches and drank milk.

"Let's take a walk," Toni suggested, a milk mustache covering her top lip.

"But we need to study," I said. I was not up for a walk with Toni. I knew a walk would be more of a run. She never did anything slowly. "Let's walk tomorrow. Besides, it's almost dark."

"Come on, Heidi," she said, wiping her lip with her sleeve, "we won't go far." But I was in no mood for a walk, and, besides, it was starting to get cool. My parents had already gone upstairs for the night. I had no idea where my nosey brother, Ben, was. We rinsed the dishes, stacked them in the dishwasher, and headed out the back door. I didn't get a chance to grab a jacket, or put on my tennis shoes.

The night was clear and brisk. I was a little uneasy about walking at dusk, but Toni was already a couple of feet ahead of me. The dogs next door growled at her, sticking their noses through the iron gate. She ignored the canines and kept going. While Toni's moccasins flapped and scraped the ground, I crossed my arms to keep warm. She was passing an old house whose owner never allowed anyone to walk on the sidewalk in front. As a child, I was trained to walk in the street, but Toni kept on walking on the sidewalk with her long quick strides. I wanted to warn her about the old lady. Even in the dark, the wicked witch would know someone was invading her property. She must have spent her entire life sitting in the window, waiting to pounce on unsuspecting victims.

I recalled drawing a hopscotch game in bright pink chalk on her sidewalk one summer afternoon. I also managed to write the words "you stink" with an arrow pointing toward her house. The old lady charged out her front door wearing blue slippers and pink curlers in her hair and shouted for me to get off her property. She was waving a thick tree limb. She was wearing an apron with a poodle on it and looked as if she'd been baking cookies, but we all knew better. She probably had a small dog in the oven. I was queen of the neighborhood that summer. No one had ever dared to get that close to the wicked witch's house.

I was waiting for the front door to open as it always had when I was a kid. Suddenly Toni stopped in her tracks. The old lady's front door had not opened. Toni stood in the middle of the sidewalk, frozen, and I ran to catch up with her.

"What is it Toni? Why did you stop?" She was trembling. The porch light from the old lady's house was bright. I was sure it was a five-thousand watt bulb. She also had a gaslight on a pole in her front yard that was never decorated like a candy cane at Christmas time.

Toni was looking down at something furry.

"Grandma!" she screamed. "Grandma! What...?" She reached down toward a furry object with large eyes. The rodent's body never moved, just its eyes. I could see that it had one blue eye and one brown eye. The furry creature stood stark still, double-daring Toni to touch it. It was a little beast that cast a large shadow. I stood silently, too afraid to move, or breathe.

"Heidi, it's Grandma!" Then I finally remembered. Her grandmother, the rodent. The grandmother who only came to her room in the middle of the night to sit and talk with her from on top of the dresser. "What are you doing out here?" Toni asked it. "Heidi, remember that I told you that she had one blue eye and one brown eye? Well look at this adorable furry animal!" I did not want to look into the eyes of this little monster. I knew it was a killer. "My grandmother also had four toes on one foot and six on the other. All I have to do is turn it upside down to prove to you that it's really her!"

"Toni, don't touch that thing. It could be rabid!" My heart was racing. Toni was just about to scoop the creature up when it opened its mouth and hissed, causing the hair on its back to stand straight up. It had bloody fangs on both sides of its pink mouth. I could see all of this quite clearly in the light of the old witch's front porch. Toni jerked her hand back quickly, without any bloodshed. She appeared not to be fazed by her grandmother's peculiar behavior.

"Stop it, Grandma. It's me. Toni."

"Toni," I said again, "don't touch that thing. Please let's go home. You're scaring me." The beast never moved. It continued to sit in the exact same spot, glaring at Toni. It dared her to try to touch it again.

"Toni, please," I begged, "are you crazy? Leave that thing alone. I'm cold. Let's go!" Suddenly the beast turned its neck and glared at me. The stare felt like shotgun blasts. The scowl seemed like an eternity. It was me who broke the gaze.

"Say hello to my Grandma, Heidi! She's a little grouchy." Toni began to chant while turning in small counterclockwise circles. "I'll prove to Grandma that it's really me. I did this when I was a little girl."

"Toni, stop that racket," I said. "Let's go home. Leave that thing right where it is." Now I was screaming. The old witch was sure to hear us. The beast was staring at me again. I wanted to kick it into the street but was much too afraid.

Toni finally stopped the chanting and the circles and made one last attempt to pick up her dead grandmother, but the furry beast let out a hideous wail with its fanged mouth, nipping at Toni's hand and missing by mere inches. Now she let out a yelp loud enough to wake the dead. Lights began turning on in neighboring houses, including the one we were standing in front of.

The door to the wicked witch's house creaked open. I will never forget the horrible face that looked out at us. The porch light caught the evil stare of the witch's eyes. Her face was creased with age and twisted to one side. The distorted mouth was obviously the work of a horrible stroke and a life of *"Mean Disease."* The beast turned and looked toward the house and scurried up the walk to the porch steps and inside the house.

As Toni shouted one last "Grandma!" and started running up the walk to the porch, the old witch slammed the door quickly and turned out the porch light. I could not believe my eyes. Toni was stunned. She stood facing the front door. "Toni," I urged, "get off that porch. Let's get out of here!" But she was oblivious to my pleas. She continued to stand on the porch as if in a trance. She began frantically ringing the doorbell. There wasn't anything I could say or do to break the spell she was under.

I remained standing on the sidewalk by the street, watching my best friend cast a shadow in the moonlight. I knew I would have to rescue her. I stumbled toward the walk and up the cracked concrete stairs and trembled as I gently turned Toni around and guided her back down to the street. She walked like a zombie. I had never been that close to the wicked witch's house, and my heart thundered as I waited for a dagger to plunge into my back. When we both reached the sidewalk, Toni started talking in a low whisper that amounted to only gibberish. I could barely make out the word "Grandma." She was heartbroken and visibly shaken.

With the full moon as our guide, we started walking back up the street toward my house. The sky raged with an evil glow as menacing clouds floated in dead space. Toni's blank stare frightened me. I could not get the beast out of my head. Neither could Toni. Her enormous feelings of rejection had captured her and consumed her soul. Thanks to a gruesome little creature that lurked in the night, Toni Steptoe was suddenly a broken woman.

We were almost to my house when I heard a crackling sound in a neighbor's bushes. I could tell that Toni had also heard the scary sound that disrupted a still night. The police siren that wailed in the distance was no comfort. The unusual noise got louder and closer. I tried to convince myself the sound belonged to a dog hiding in the darkness. We both hastened to reach my house safely.

I saw the light on in my parents' room. The dogs next door began to bark again, but more viciously than before. We walked up our long driveway so we could sneak in the back door. I was fumbling for my door key and trying to keep a strong arm on Toni. She was still painfully quiet and appeared to be drained emotionally and physically. I finally found the key and tried to guide it into the back door lock. I'd planned to sneak up the back stairs so I would not have to explain Toni's zombie like state and why we were out in the dark.

When I finally felt the key turn in the lock, Toni fell into my back. I turned around to see what had happened. Katherine Sharpe was standing at the bottom of my back porch steps ... with the little beast in her arms. She stood in the moonlight stroking the little creature's back with her long red fingernails. Toni went completely hysterical.

"She has my grandmother!" Her shriek was deafening. "That crazy bitch has my grandmother!" Katherine looked past Toni and found my dead eyes. In the dark of night, Katherine Sharpe looked menacing and lethal. She wore a long white gown with jagged edges. It was the same dress worn by the ghost that lurked on our street. Her skin appeared transparent and gray. There were no words spoken for a couple of minutes, only intense staring from Katherine and the little beast.

Toni began sobbing and trembling like a small child. She reached out toward Katherine in an attempt to seize what she thought was her grandmother. Katherine didn't move and did not break her gaze, which was locked on me. The beast enjoyed the long strokes on its miserable back. It gently wiggled its long whiskers almost like a loveable kitten. Katherine's glare was unbearable. Now it kept Toni at bay.

"Let's go into the house, Toni." I never turned my back to Katherine Sharpe. I slowly backed through the door into the dark kitchen, where I could smell the aroma of our turkey sandwiches. Toni was still standing on the back porch, facing Katherine and the little beast. As quickly as Katherine appeared, she disappeared, floating into the night. She shot the barking dogs an infectious gaze, which instantly quieted them. As Toni watched, Katherine Sharpe floated down the driveway with what she thought was her dead grandmother. Her eyes were empty, her spirit lost.

"That's the last time I'll ever see her." She slowly walked into the safety of the dark kitchen. I ran to the front of the house to see if I could spy on the ghostly Katherine Sharp, but she had disappeared. I knew she still lurked in dark shadows, floating in the still of the night.

CHAPTER 10

My bedroom was dark, complete with dancing shadows and spooky old house sounds. Dying pigeons cooed and fluttered in the depths of my brick chimney that served as their graveyard. Toni was hysterical, repeating over and over that she would never see her grandmother again. She finally kicked off her moccasins and flopped down across my bed; she was still wearing her good-luck headband. I could hear my parents' television coming down the hall. They had no idea what had just happened, and I didn't, either. What I did know is that it was something diabolical.

Toni and I lay there in the darkness until after midnight, virtually in silence. I thought about Katherine Sharpe and her wicked spirit and ghostly appearances. Was she really the ghost who roamed our street? My mind flirted with different thoughts without any reasonable answers. I could hear Toni whimpering next to me.

"Are you OK?" I whispered.

"She'll never come back, Heidi. My grandmother will never come back. That Katherine Sharpe will put a dagger in her heart. Did you see that evil stare? Why would Grandmother try to bite me?" I remembered what Toni taught me about how some Indians believe that humans take animal forms at death. She really believed that hideous creature was her grandmother. I allowed the darkness to consume me while Toni chanted softly and spoke in tongues. I continued to listen to her broken words until she had a revelation. She remembered a story I told her when we met at the campus newspaper.

The Ouija board had belonged to my great-grandmother, Lelia Donahoo. Born in a small shack in rural Mississippi, the fifth of twelve children, she was a spunky, vibrant woman with a quick wit and a deep belief of black magic. Grandma Lee firmly believed she could raise the dead by using the Ouija board. She had negotiated the board from a gypsy woman who was traveling in a caravan through town.

One night Grandma Lee had snuck out of the house against her mother's wishes and observed the gypsies having a séance beside their wagons. All of the gypsies sat cross-legged in a tight circle holding hands with their eyes closed. They began swaying back and forth in unison, chanting a spiritual death song. The matriarch of the clan had the Ouija board directly in front of her. Grandma Lee watched mesmerized for hours, absorbing the methods and techniques of the old gypsies. They flung gold coins in the air and swung their heads around in circles. The wife of their leader placed her fingertips on the edge of the Ouija board and looked up to the moon-lit sky. They were attempting to raise the father of their leader, who had been killed by robbers in the dead of night. The Ouija board was flat and had a lot of circles and triangles painted on its wooden surface, along with the entire alphabet arranged in a semicircle. "Speak to us, dark father," the gypsies chanted. "Come to us in the black of night, from the depths of your immortal being. Speak now, give us a sign."

Although Grandma Lee never heard a sound, the gypsies acknowledged a presence. She was so absorbed in the séance that she completely lost track of time. When her mother, finding her daughter's bed empty, came looking for her, she shouted her name so loud that all of the gypsies turned around to witness a beating she would never forget. The beating did not remove the burning desire Grandma Lee had acquired for the supernatural. She later returned to the gypsy camp and traded a piece of black silk for the Ouija board.

Grandma Lee hid the board from her mother until she died, then set out to raise her from the dead. She claimed to have spoken to her mother using the Ouija board on the precise day her mother passed away. The Ouija board was never to be used again and was rarely a topic of conversation in our family. It was kept by my grandmother, who gave it to my mother, who will give it to me one day. My mother keeps it wrapped in the same red silk scarf that Grandma Lee preserved it in. I was told never to touch it until it was officially passed down to me. Until that night with Toni Steptoe, that was an ironclad rule in the Morgan family.

My mother kept the board on the third floor in the cedar closet. I was always afraid to open the closet door for fear a fork-toothed serpent would seize me by the throat and strike me dead, but Toni was relentless about the idea of raising her grandmother from the dead in human form. The idea sent chills up my spine. I knew it was a battle I was going to lose. Even the shadows on my bedroom walls enticed me to fetch the Ouija board. I tried to justify breaking a sacred vow to my mother. She would never know, I thought, or would she?

"Please, Heidi," Toni kept saying, "can we just try? It would be marvelous to speak to my grandmother just once more. Can we please try it, just once? It would mean everything to me."

"Toni, I am not supposed to touch the board. You know that. It is my family's sacred rule. I just can't do it; you have got to understand that. Now please can we just go to bed now? I'm beat!"

"No!" she shouted. "You are not an Indian, so you couldn't possibly understand. I must try to release my grandmother's soul from that dreadful creature's body. Now are you going to help me or not?" I had an uneasy feeling as I contemplated committing a cardinal sin.

We waited until my parents' television had been turned off and the house was frightfully quiet. I knew my nosey brother was sleeping on the third floor, so silence was most important. If he woke up and caught me doing as little as looking at the board, a Morgan family war would erupt. I grabbed a flashlight from my father's gray metal tool chest and headed down the hall, with Toni Steptoe right behind me.

We crept up the creaky wooden stairs, stepping over tennis shoes and T-shirts scattered along on the steps. My brother was a real slob. My mother would never let me get away with being so messy. If I heard 'because he's a boy' one more time, I would scream. My father never much complained of his pig-like habits, though. He was too busy teaching and working on his Ph.D. They both were content staying solely on my case. I could hear Ben's heavy breathing drifting out into the hallway. He always had an oily, rusty smell that consumed the air around him. Why men smelled like old nails was beyond me. Tonight was no exception; Ben's smell permeated the entire third floor.

The cedar closet was the first door on the right. The very same closet I played in as a child. I wondered if the Ouija board was there when I pretended I was dead in a coffin. I never recalled seeing it. I dared not turn on a light for fear of disturbing Ben. The door was kept closed because he said the cedar smell bothered him. How could he smell anything with the stench that floated around him like a cloud? I turned the knob and quietly opened the door. We went from dark to pitch black. I clicked on the long steel flashlight, with its dying batteries and rusty edges. I had to hit the light to make it surge to dull power. I knew exactly where the Ouija board was located: on the top shelf closest to the window. Toni was amazingly quiet. I gently took the silver handle of the cabinet and turned it to the left. The cabinet door opened as if it were expecting me. The flashlight kept flickering on and off, giving us ridiculous levels of low light. It was probably a signal to the dead.

Toni slipped into the closet beside me, ready for the unexpected. We paused at the same time, praying for some kind of miracle, as I pointed the flashlight toward the top shelf and shone the light on the Ouija board to awaken it and announce our arrival. It lay with authority, still wrapped in the antique red silk scarf that protected it for over a hundred years. The vibes I got were almost poisonous. The Ouija board was warning me it was way too early to disturb it. I fully expected to receive an electrical shock when I touched the ancient family heirloom.

Pulling it down from the shelf, I cradled the board in my arms and shone the light on it again. The red scarf was in impeccable shape for something that was over a century old. I began backing out of the cedar closet, and motioned for Toni to step out into the hallway, while I shut the main door to the hall. So far, so good. I waited to be struck dead, but, amazingly, we were both still breathing, if you called standing there in complete silence in the still of the night alive. I felt something touch my shoulder as I turned toward the stairwell and practically jumped out of my skin, juggling the board from one hand to the next. It was Toni using me as a guide to clear the railing.

"Don't do that!" I whispered

"Do what?"

"Don't touch me like that! And lower your voice. You're gonna wake Ben up. Now come on, let's get away from here!"

But Toni exhaled heavily and froze right on the spot. Trembling, I shone the dismal light on her face. She looked like she had turned to stone. Her eyes were wide and glazed over. Finally, we both started back down the stairs, hoping to make it to my room without getting caught. I could still hear the loud breathing of my sleeping brother. So far, our Ouija board theft was going according to plan. Toni and I made it to the foot of the stairs where I could hear the loud snores of my father through the closed bedroom door. From years of experience, I knew that he was in a deep, deep sleep. My mother was probably curled up on the edge of her side of the bed dreaming of a trip to Spain, sailing the Mediterranean, and eating exotic foods. They were both out for the count, at least for a while. I clicked off the practically useless flashlight and realized the loss of even that dismal light was frightening and unsettling. We were back to total blackness. We floated down the second floor hall past the girls' bathroom, as we called it. I heard a sound inside the bathroom, then remembered the toilet ran continuously. We finally made it to the safety of my room and shut the door. Again we stood in complete silence, too afraid to speak. Toni Steptoe's breathing deepened.

I gently sat the ancient board down on my frilly pink bedspread. Toni didn't move a muscle, she remained standing like a soldier guarding my bedroom door. When I turned on the small lamp on the edge of my white dresser. Toni's eyes snapped shut, then and slowly opened again. I slowly released the ancient Ouija board from the red silk that had protected it for so many years.

Grandma Lee's Ouija board was both beautiful and fiendish. It was made of wood, light tan in color, and the alphabet was printed in sharp, evenly-spaced black letters in a semi-circle. It looked exactly like I envisioned it. I was drawn to the board, inspecting it from every angle. The dark green and brown circles on the edges looked freshly painted with delicate swirls and intricate detail. To my surprise the family heirloom looked practically new. My first feeble attempt at conversation took Toni by surprise.

"What now, Toni? What do we do now? Do you know how to work this thing?"

"Lower your voice. Sit down at the foot of the bed." Toni was in charge now. I did as I was told and sat cross-legged on my bed. I remembered the story of how my great grandmother said the gypsies sat Indian style during their séances. Toni took her place at the head of the bed.

I was beginning to get tired and irritable. I was more than ready to go to sleep. "Go ahead," I said through gritted teeth. "Call your grandmother. See what she's up to this time of night."

"Keep your voice down," Toni said, "and turn out the light." I lifted my exhausted body off the bed and walked to the dresser. I listened to each click of the three-way bulb, hoping it would never get to the last level. I was now in eternal darkness, headed for a dangerous, hideous world. I returned to my designated spot in hell. We sat on the bed for a while listening to the screaming insects outside and the low cooing of dying pigeons caught in the chimney.

These sounds were even more morbid than before. One pigeon let out a coo that sounded like it would never end. Perhaps the presence of the Ouija board exaggerated the typical noises of the night. Directly across from me, Toni was breathing heavily and chanting under her breath. I couldn't understand the words, but I suspected she was trying to reach her grandmother. I supposed it was some type of Indian lingo. I could hear her fingernails racing across the board.

"Grandmother, this is your mortal granddaughter, Toni Steptoe."

"Toni," I whispered, "do you know what you're doing?"

"Shut up. Remain silent. Do not break the communication to the other side." Toni spoke in a voice that was not her own. Her features had grotesquely melted together. I could no longer make out where her nose stopped and her mouth began.

The shadows on the walls danced and watched as the party began. My digital clock read 2:06 a.m. I would be dead tired in the morning, if I weren't dead, period. The sound of Toni's words intensified. I was terribly worried that my parents would wake up and catch us. She seemed to get louder and louder ... then suddenly she began to whisper. Her voice was barely audible. Toni Steptoe became clearer. I could finally see a face I didn't want to see. There was a bright stream of light forming above her body, shooting silver crystals down from infinity. I watched in horror as Toni's face melted like a wax candle that had been burning for hours. The waxy substance dripped into her eyes burning the sockets, flowing down her nose, seeping into her lips. Her face was twisted and distorted. She didn't utter a sound. Her fingers continued to ride on the heart shaped pointer. Her lips separated, revealing bloody sores and blisters. Finally she was able to speak.

"Oh, supernatural spirit in the hellish dead of night, release my grandmother from your wicked grasp," Toni intoned in a deep voice. "Lift her body from the soiled earth and free her soul from Satan's clutches." The board shimmied under her fingers. Unable to move, I sat and watched in horror.

An invincible grip held my body captive and would not allow me to run away. I could not scream or close my eyes; not one muscle in my body performed at my mental command. *Oh, God*, I thought, *I'm dead.* I believed I had been turned to stone. I exhaled and blew my breath onto my bottom lip. I could not feel the air! All of my limbs were rock heavy.

The light brightened and the silver crystals floated in the air, covering Toni like sparkling Christmas tree ornaments The pigeons in the chimney fluttered and cooed one last time, the insects outside my window were silent, and Toni Steptoe began melting all over my bed. I could see her fingers still attached to the planchette. She was disintegrating in front of me, and the dark shadows on the walls enjoyed the show. One poltergeist did a cartwheel on the wall in front of me. The other shadows bounced and danced in the demon light. One sinister phantom did the electric slide. The air in the room was stifling. The mirror above my dresser cracked without making a sound. Bottles of perfume crashed to the hardwood floor in silence. My closet door blew open to release spirited clothing, which danced hellishly through the still air.

Everything seemed to be twirling about. Drawers opened, freeing socks, underwear, T-shirts. My small bras flapped in the demon filled air like rabid bats. I tried to scream, but I had no voice. The shadows came closer and closer; then they covered me.

Toni spoke again, this time in the high-pitched voice of an old woman. "Toni," the old woman's voice said, "it's me. Don't be afraid. I won't hurt you. I'm tired, Toni, and I am afraid. You've removed me from a warm place that is now my home. I've loved you since the first time I laid eyes on you. The day your mother brought you home from the hospital, I knew you would be special. I like my life here, Toni. I like prowling around at night, catching helpless rats in my sharp fangs. Release me. Toni. Send me back from where I came. I am no longer your grandmother. I am a fur-covered rodent who could send you to your grave. Goodbye, Toni. Never, ever disturb my spirit again, or I will rip out your heart and burn your soul in black acid water. May your body decay in the depths of hell."

The voice was now gone from Toni's melted throat. My clothes darted back into the closet and the drawers. The air became rich with breathable wind. I could see a renegade pair of underpants that refused to go back into the drawer. It frolicked about, darting to the top of my head and bouncing off the walls. Finally, a lonely sock jumped out of the second drawer and chased the panties back to their resting place. Both drawers shut in unison. I sucked in deeply, holding my breath while I watched Toni's face slowly take on its normal shape as the room brightened. I could hear her fingernails still racing over the wooden Ouija board. The silver crystals ascended back to where they came from, releasing the body and soul of Toni Steptoe.

When she removed her fingers from the board, I felt my body go limp. I, too, had been under the power of a supernatural being. Somehow I got off the bed and made my way toward the small lamp on the dresser. I clicked on the lamp. My bedroom was undisturbed, the mirror was no longer cracked, and all perfume bottles were in place. I turned around to try to speak with Toni Steptoe. She had a glazed watery look in her eyes. She had no idea that the light was on. She still sat in complete darkness. Toni Steptoe was blind.

I rushed over to Toni and cradled her in my arms. The antique Ouija board lay innocently on my pink bedspread, right where we left it. Maybe Toni was temporarily blind due to extreme shock. I swallowed hard and tried to think of something to do. I grabbed her shoulders and tried to shake her vision back. Nothing helped. I was scared. I wondered if I should call an ambulance. I could not seek the aid of my parents. I had broken a family rule that had been law for as long as I could remember. I could never explain what had just happened, especially since I didn't know myself. Why hadn't I gone blind? What would I do now? What would I tell Mrs. Steptoe?

I knew I had to get rid of the Ouija board. It was evil and deadly, capable of abducting the sight from the body of a young innocent girl. I was afraid to touch the Ouija board, but I simply had no choice. I was trembling as I reached for the family heirloom. The heart shaped planchette whipped around and aimed itself at me. It spun violently in jagged circles, and jumped off the board onto the floor. Toni heard the crash and snapped her head in the direction of the noise. The pointer landed on its tip and stopped for a second and then began to whirl and bounce dangerously in the middle of the wooden floor. Not once did it touch the area rug that could have easily silenced the performance. I was sure my parents would awaken; I silently prayed that they would. I walked toward the pointer and stood over it until it finally stopped. It seemed to be exhausted after such a turbulent night.

I realized I had made a terrible mistake. Would God strike me dead for believing in the supernatural? Did I really believe in black magic? The pointer sat still long enough for me to capture it and place it back on the wooden Ouija board. It remained still and behaved like a good little spirit, except for the nasty little burn it left in the palm of my hand. It left a scar I would have for the rest of my miserable life. I could hear the board inhaling and exhaling little bits of chopped breath. Toni continued to stare into space with an empty gaze. I wondered if the wicked board had stolen her soul and her sight. Taking extra care to avoid its lethal bite, I gently picked up the Ouija board and wrapped it back in the red silk scarf. I hid it under my bed until I could return it to its resting place.

I tenderly laid Toni down on my bed and covered her with my patchwork quilt. She stared into darkness, then pulled the quilt over her head and began to shiver. She thrashed, kicked, and twisted about for a tumultuous five minutes. Again I sat in silence, trembling, not knowing what to do. I wanted to run screaming down the hall to my parents' room, but for the second time tonight, an unknown force paralyzed me. What mysterious phantom of the night had stolen the eyesight of my best friend? I wondered if I, too, would suffer excruciating pain as punishment for my blatant disobedience. Was there a diabolical plan chosen for me? I swallowed hard and shut my eyes, wondering if this demon, or whatever it was, would eventually take my precious life. My eyes rested on the mirror over the handsomely carved mantle. It was cloudy and distant; clearly, I was looking into demonic infinity.

As quickly as the tremors started, they stopped. The patchwork quilt no longer moved. I could hear Toni breathing under the silent quilt. Soon she began to snivel and weep while the top of the quilt began to slowly pull back. I sat in horror, wishing I would be released from the force that held me captive in the chair my mother had bought from a second hand store.

Toni gasped for air. She fidgeted with the quilt, grasping and rolling it up in her clenched fists. She kept her head bowed down, hiding her face from my eyes. I could hear the commode running in the bathroom, along with the dripping faucet. My eyes were glued to my friend, who lay helpless in my bed. The patchwork quilt was moist and limp. Suddenly a mildew smell assaulted my nose. The aroma was that of damp soil, the same scent one smelled while standing in the middle of the cemetery after a torrential downpour. Toni surrendered the quilt and released it from her grip. Now I could see that Toni Steptoe's finger-nails had been removed. There was only puffy pink flesh on the tips of her fingers. My head spun as I tried to call out to my parents, but my voice had been stolen from my throat.

Toni slowly turned her head in my direction. Her long black hair was plastered across her damp face. I could barely see her once soft features. Her nail-less fingers crept up to her face and brushed her hair aside. The sensation of having no fingernails frightened her. She kept rubbing her hands together. The feeling couldn't have been a pleasant one, yet she still remained silent. Toni Steptoe's fingernails had been the first to activate the board in almost a quarter of a century, and now those nails had been taken away.

When she brushed her hair away from her face, my heart practically stopped. The turkey sandwich I had eaten several hours earlier crawled up my throat and exploded through my lips. My insides were fleeing my body at amazing speed. I began to cough up things I had never seen before. My tired eyes burned like acid. The words I tried to form were ripped from my lips. There was an invisible knife piercing my heart. Toni had lost her left eye. There was only a white, jelly-like substance where her beautiful pupil had been. There was no eyelash or brow; even her eyelid had been removed. She tried to blink but couldn't. Her remaining eye was stuck open, while the socket to the other sat like an open crater. She lifted her fleshy fingers up to the barren cavity and gently inspected the entrance that once held the window to her soul. I watched the face of Toni Steptoe as she discovered that a force un-known had viciously ransacked her left eye.

Her head snapped back as she covered her face with ten open flesh wounds. She picked and poked at the socket until it turned fire red. Purple blood oozed from the empty hole. She quickly felt the blood with fleshy fingertips and brought her hand to her nose, sniffing the rich aroma of the thick plasma. I watched her body expand and contract as she breathed heavily and erratically.

I prayed for my own death, and the death of Toni Steptoe. I could never recover from this horrendous experience. Maybe this was a bad dream. Perhaps Satan was punishing me for removing the board before its time. Toni was blind because of my greedy, foolish behavior. I prayed again for my own worthless death. I would never be worthy of a decent life. I wanted God to give my eyes to Toni Steptoe. I wanted to sacrifice my measly life for hers.

Toni seemed to glare in my direction. Her head appeared to be heavy. I imagined her skull should be lighter, since it was minus an eye and gallons of blood. She collapsed back into the bed and buried her face in a handmade pillow that read, "Put everything in His hands." The word "His" was underlined twice with thick embroidered stitches. It was a gift from Father Robert, the pastor of our church. Could God help me now? Would God help us now? Again my thoughts raced back to the floating skull in the pilot light, to Mrs. Adams turning into a serpent, and to what seemed to be a harmless rodent sprouting fangs and hissing like a snake. I was definitely going crazy. I knew the board was still under my bed. I wanted to grab it and burn it to ashes. The board was evil and dangerous, and I would burn in hell before handing it down to a daughter of mine. I closed my eyes, hoping to wake up next to my best friend after a terrible nightmare. Unfortunately, it was all reality. The hollow cavity sitting in her skull was still there.

Toni never once uttered a word. She lay face down, not moving a muscle, until dawn. I thought she was dead until I heard her exhale air from her tortured body. I vowed to take care of her for the rest of her life if indeed I lived that long. I remained in the chair next to Toni, praying that one day she would see the light of a new day, but somehow I knew Toni Steptoe would be forever in eternal darkness.

CHAPTER 11

I watched the black horsefly buzz around Toni's head as she lay strapped to a steel gurney in the disinfectant smelling psych ward. I sat next to her, lost in the many rows of beds filled with screaming females of all ages and psychiatric levels. I felt a pang in my chest every time I thought about the night of the Ouija board. I would never forget my parents walking into my room to find Toni lying in my bed with one eye and no fingernails and me next to her in a chair, sitting straight up like a vampire afraid of the sunlight. My mother's piercing scream could have raised the dead. It certainly made my blood run cold. She ran out of the room to call the police and an ambulance. I could hear her trying to pronounce our address along with the problem at hand. *I'm only your daughter Mom,* I thought. *Thanks for all the support.* In my eyes, I had only broken one little bitty rule. I hadn't meant to hurt anyone.

My mother thought Toni Steptoe was dead and that I had killed her. My father stood in silence. The room was filled with warm rays of sunlight shining on my pink bedspread. From the outside, it looked like a normal day at the Morgan home … everyone should have been blissfully happy. *Oh, happy day* as the old spiritual went.

I remembered the sun coming up after that dreadful night, but I must have fallen asleep shortly afterwards because I awoke to the squeak of my bedroom door opening and both parents calling out, "Heidi, are you up? It's almost ten o'clock. What are you girls doing in here?" And then came my mother's blood-curdling scream. Like my Mom, I thought Toni was dead. She was lying in a fetal position still minus an eye and fingernails. No, it hadn't been a nightmare; it was painfully true, every grisly detail. I tried to reason with my parents, even coming clean about the Ouija board, but neither of them would listen to me. As my story unfolded, as I began pouring my heart out, I began to understand their disbelief.

"And we took a walk down the street because Toni wanted to after eating the turkey sandwiches," I tried to explain, "and then we saw this rodent and, well, it was on the sidewalk and Toni thought it was her grandmother, and I know this sounds crazy…." I could hear the sound of my own voice sounding like a lunatic … speaking as logically as a screwball wound too tight. I heard myself trying to explain, my heart teetering and tottering on the edge of destruction. "But the old lady down the street opened her door and the thing ran inside. Then we came home, and Katherine Sharpe was standing by the back porch with the beast creature in her hands, petting it like a cat. Then, Mom, I know you're gonna be mad, but we got the Ouija board and used it to get Toni's grandmother back from the dead. Check under the bed. That's where I put it." I feebly pointed toward the floor.

My mother stood behind my father, staring in disbelief, not fully believing that I had even uttered the word *Ouija*, let alone touched the board itself. I knew it was sacred, and to be protected from little knuckleheads like me. I should not have touched the silly thing. How many times had it been beaten into my head as a child? *Never ever go near the board, never, under any circumstances.* My punishment would surely be death. I could read both of their faces as clearly as if the message had been printed on their foreheads. Well, perhaps my father would understand because it was not his family's most prized possession. He had to take pity on his daughter; after all, he had married a woman with this insane family history.

They both thought I was mad. What a tale. Stephen King couldn't have thought this one up! My father dropped to his knees and lifted the edge of the frilly bedspread. He knew the importance of the board to my mother, having heard of it since the day they met. There was no Ouija board under my bed, only dingy pink slippers, a ton of dustbunnies, strands of my hair, and mountains of lint.

The Ouija board was gone. Poof! Walked away, sprouted legs, gone. See ya. Goodbye. My father stood up with a sick look on his face; all that was right with the world had come to a screeching halt. We would never again be the nice middle-class family we once were. Now we would be labeled the family with a daughter who blinded, maimed, and tortured a smart-as-a-whip fellow college student. We could never go to the grocery store without old ladies pointing crooked fingers and damning all of us to burn in eternal hell.

The Ouija board had disappeared, leaving no parting farewells, no coherent story to stick to.

Toni, still lying on the bed but now awake, heard my insane explanation. She tried to speak, but nothing came out. I was trying to understand—and explain—why she had lost an eye, but the more I spoke the crazier I sounded. I sat with vomit all over my clothes next to my maimed best friend, listening to the siren's wail get closer and closer. When I heard it sing out and go down in pitch, I knew the authorities had arrived. Now the entire street was up, dashing to their windows, peeking out from behind trendy wooden blinds, with big question marks inside their heads. *What happened over there?* Neighbors were so nosy. They were always glad when something tragic happened to you instead of them. Now we had three police cars, EMS personnel, and the fire department pounding at our door, along with every dog in a fifty-mile radius howling.

I felt betrayed by my parents for thinking their daughter was a cold-blooded torturer. I wondered if I had been in their shoes—would I have believed such a story? Probably not. Hearing all the commotion, Toni stirred, but I still sat glued to the seat that had seized me the night before. I put my head down into a chest covered with mucous and spaghetti-like spew that covered my torso. For the second time in just a few months, I was sitting in a room as police burst in.

The sergeant took charge of the scene by shouting out orders to his men. The EMS technicians punched through the same clear plastic bags with thick liquid that they'd used on Mr. Vaden. They produced a long needle and stuck it into the veins of my best friend. She cringed and whimpered. My mother put her hands over her face and cried, and tears swelled in my eyes and dripped down my cheeks. What would I tell Mrs. Steptoe? The last time she saw her precious daughter she was whole and complete. Now she looked like a tattered jigsaw puzzle with missing pieces.

The EMS technicians darted around my bed, quickly dressing Toni's eye socket and bandaging every finger.

"Where is the eye?" Everyone was looking at me. The paramedic screamed once more, "Spread out and try to locate the eye." I could hear the police telling each other they'd never seen anything like this as they watched me out of the corners of their comfortably attached eyes. Officers searched the room thoroughly, and came up with nothing. Evidence technicians dusted for renegade fingerprints. They searched the entire house, checked the doors for forced entry, and crawled under the bushes outside. They found no evidence of foul play.

The sergeant wondered how he would communicate this one back to the commander. He began battering me with questions about what, exactly, had happened. There was no blood, no fingernails, no eyeball to be found. The sheets were not soiled, only damp from perspiration. There were no signs of a struggle; nothing was upset in the room. Even the perfume bottle that had crashed to the floor was neatly back in the circular mirror tray in the middle of my dresser. I turned to check on the mirror over the mantle, and saw that it was no longer cracked. Like I said, back to normal.

The police took me down to the station for questioning. I could hardly bear to tell the story anymore. I was put into a small room with an old splintery table with the letters "J A C K" carved in the surface. I wondered who Jack was, and how he had the tools to chisel his name in a room within the walls of the St. Louis Police Department. Perhaps Jack was the name of an old, cantankerous detective who had been drilling a prisoner in the wee hours of the morning. Maybe he carved his name in the wood to amuse himself and stay awake.

The table leaned miserably to one side. I looked down to find that one leg was shorter than the other three. I could hear screaming and shouting from the holding cells down the hall. Then Sergeant Franklin Birts walked in and asked me if I wanted a cup of coffee. I told him no thanks.

He left the little room again, leaving me to fight off the mammoth roach crawling across the splintery table. I found a tattered magazine on a turn of the century radiator and cleverly rolled it up and crashed it down on top of the roach. The bug paused, regrouped, and kept on trucking. The air in the room was stifling. I could see through the small window in the door that my parents were sitting outside in the shabby lobby. A tall bouncy prostitute propositioned my father as she was escorted to the tank in handcuffs. My mother was appalled, but remained silent. I could see Dad perk up just a little. I could tell because he ran his hand over his salt and pepper hair. Radios blared from the hips of officers, and big shots strolled through the room with nonchalant attitudes. Civilian employees pounded keyboards and answered loud telephones. The prostitute was now screaming from her cell. "Be quiet,

Terry," a policewoman yelled at the gaudy call girl. "You know the drill, and no you ain't gettin' no more calls!" The smell of stale coffee and cigarettes made my stomach turn. Sergeant Birts came back into the room and said there was no physical evidence of foul play, so I was free to go. I wondered how the police could believe there was no physical evidence. A woman was blind. She was missing an eyeball and all ten fingernails! What more evidence could they want? I guessed the police thought Toni wounds were self- inflicted. I supposed I should be happy to be free, but I was not. It took all of my energy to walk down the long corridor of the police station, and out the front door. Would what happened to Toni happen to me? After signing tons of papers in triplicate, my parents walked swiftly in front of me.

My parents barely spoke to me in the car on the way home. They were still in a state of shock. Ben would be staying at his best friend's house until they could sort things out. My father had trouble teaching class that week. It took all of his energy just to get up in the morning and get to school. My mother and I barely looked at each other. I could not sleep in my room anymore; it completely terrified me, especially at night. I only entered it when I needed something out of my closet. I slept in my sister's room. Thank goodness she was still away at college. When she came home, I would sleep in the guest bedroom. As time went by, I thought I would never be able to trust the room I grew up in. Finally, my mother locked it off from the rest of the house and ordered it off limits. Then I would stand outside the door with my right ear plastered to the wood, listening for any demonic disturbances.

It was simple. Toni wasn't sick and she didn't need wires protruding from her arms or a clear breathing device over her mouth and nose. All that was needed was the return of a supernatural being to undo the torment inflicted upon the body of an innocent young woman who desperately missed her grandmother.

I watched the fly bounce in and out of the eye socket getting covered with the slimy medicinal substance seeping out of the crater. The nasty creatures would feed on anything. Toni was lying silent and motionless in the heartless ward of the Smythe Psychiatric Hospital. The woman in the next bed began screaming and pulling her hair out. I sat quietly, not knowing exactly what to say. Toni could feel the fly, but she did nothing to distract it. Even though her arms were secured, she didn't even wiggle her nose or shake her head.

I looked around the room with its peeling green paint, dingy sheets, and worn blankets. The place was humiliating. The air reeked of urine and filth, and the windows had an oily scum two inches thick. The floor was an olive drab with speckles of blood and dirt on each tile. I could hardly believe Toni Steptoe was in a place like this. There was a rusty old sink in the corner with exposed pipes and a constant drip. The commode was hidden behind a sheet hanging from a rickety pole protruding from the ceiling. The toilet never flushed completely and was constantly overflowing. The sheet was no match for a solid door, especially since it constantly flapped back and forth. Privacy was totally out of the question. Bowel explosions were prevalent.

The food trays were grimy and covered with poisonous slop they called food. The forks arrived with dried-on food clinging to each prong. The bed gowns were old and faded with large slits and fraying edges.

I sat next to my dearest friend and swatted flies from her eye and slapped roaches from crawling up her arms. Smythe Psychiatric Hospital was the only institution the Steptoes could afford. Mrs. Steptoe didn't have insurance; therefore, she had no means to afford a reputable psychiatric hospital. Smythe was maintained by the state and had the reputation of housing the criminally insane. I screamed to anyone who would listen that Toni Steptoe was not a crackpot, but only the innocent victim of a disturbed supernatural being. Then I decided I had better not shout too loudly for fear I, too, would have to eat the lethal cuisine that was supposed to be grade A.

Women were stacked in the tiny ward with various ailments and complaints. There was one damsel in distress who thought she was a fish and made underwater gulping sounds and screamed that she was drowning. She also bugged her eyes out and made snappy head movements. In the bed next to Jaws was a woman who believed she was a sex goddess. She kept wiggling her underwear down to her ankles and propositioning the male orderlies. She made kissy sounds with her lips and pretended she was having a sexual encounter with John Wayne. "Ride me, cowboy. Let me play with your horsey. Ride my pony, Pilgrim. Saddle up, move 'em out, rawhide! Ride me, Kemosabe!"

One woman had put her child in a roasting pan because she couldn't afford a turkey at Thanksgiving. Another had stabbed her twin sons to death with an ice pick and was so hungry afterwards that she sat and ate fried chicken while dipping it into the blood of her slain children.

Toni Steptoe was not crazy; she did not belong in this deranged atmosphere.

An agitated nurse entered the ward with various medicines on a tray with written instructions. She was plump and had a witchy disposition. Her eyebrows grew together making one complete hairy line across her face, and she had cheap dollar-store glasses dangling from an old lady rope that rested on her drooping breasts. This reminded me of Mrs. Adams, psycho librarian. Her nurse shoes were a dirty white and grossly run over, and her pantyhose were torn to smithereens. Nurse Callahan's lipstick looked like a circus clown had applied it—fire red and grossly drawn out of her lip line. When she spoke, the lipstick smeared her rotten teeth. The women on the ward disliked Nurse Callahan and almost never cooperated with her. She made her rounds and soon was at the bed of my best friend.

Toni thrashed and pointed at her with her fleshy index finger. The nurse strong-armed Toni and forced a pill down her throat. She slapped some foul smelling, creamy white medicine into Toni's crater. The rough behavior turned Toni into a tiger backed into a corner. As she kicked and bit at the evil nurse, the creamy substance ran down Toni's face and into her mouth.

"Can you wipe her up, please?" I asked the nurse.

"You do it yourself. She's your blind-ass friend. I can't play fuckin' nursemaid to every crazy bitch on this ward." Nurse Callahan held Toni's head and inspected it closely. Toni had open lesions with yellow puss erupting from each one scattered on both cheeks. I figured she'd had some sort of allergic reaction or some infection not uncommon in a spook-house like this. Nurse Callahan dropped Toni's head and walked to the medicine cabinet. When she returned, there was a bottle of rubbing alcohol in her hand. She generously splashed the alcohol into the open wounds just to see Toni squirm. My blood boiled as the alcohol spread over her facial sores. I tried to feel what she was feeling ... the torment and agony. My thoughts flashed to acid, sizzling and bubbling, making hissing, steamy sounds. "Do you have to do that?" I roared. Nurse Callahan smiled at me, revealing rotten teeth and black gums. She squinted and said, "Mind your own fuckin' business." I dared not get into a squabble with this woman for fear she would later take it out on Toni. Should I tell the doctor? I made a mental note to report Nurse Callahan, and perhaps have Toni removed from her ward. I rationalized that the entire facility, every ward, floor, and cubbyhole had a mad woman playing Ms. Goody Two-Shoes shoes nursemaid. I snarled at Nurse Callahan, shooting her a silent piece of my mind. She thoroughly dismissed my "you bitch" look and kept on working.

Toni had the eye medicine smeared all over her face, including her lips. The rubbing alcohol spread over every nook and cranny, including inside her nose. The poison potion rapidly got matted into her hair, making clumpy hairballs near her temples. I swiftly retrieved a tissue from my purse to wipe her delicate skin and gently remove the poison from her hair. The movement comforted Toni and settled her down.

I began visiting her every day after my last class, reading to her and trying to keep her informed of the goings-on. I chattered about campus scuttlebutt and my struggle in Spanish class. Toni lay in silence, absorbing all my insignificant babble, gazing into a dark world where there would never be a trickle of light. I tried not to let my feelings seep through, although it was difficult to watch her day after day in an invalid condition.

She developed bedsores from lying in one position. Her doctor said that her fingernails would eventually grow back, but they never did. Soon she began to lose weight. That spectacular body was dwindling away to a skeletal frame. Her hair began coming out in patches, and the beautiful skin that once graced that stunning body was now ashen gray. Toni was suffering from a broken spirit that was perpetually lost. She no longer possessed that eternal energy that I found very hard to keep up with. I was glad that Toni could not look in the mirror and see her broken body. I did notice her touching her head sometimes and wincing at the loss of her lovely hair.

"You fuckin' bitch! I'm gonna rip your heart out. Shut up all that goddamn book reading. I'm trying to sleep here, and you makin' all dat much noise. Now shut the fuck up!" The woman next to Toni was totally pissed with me. She enticed the entire ward to kick up a loud ruckus. The screaming and shouting made Nurse Callahan come exploding into the room.

"Make her get out!" hissed Sadie, the woman who had used her twins' blood as ketchup. She was pointing a crooked finger at me. She too was tied down to her bed and trying to set herself free. She pulled and bucked until the bed shook and lifted a few inches off the floor. She tried to bump the bed over to Toni's bed. Even though she was firmly secured, I believe she would have torn my heart out if given the chance. Toni turned to listen to the commotion. I believed she wanted to speak again. She zeroed in on the rambunctious Sadie, wrinkling her forehead and shaking her head.

"I'm going to have to ask you to leave, Ms. Morgan," Nurse Callahan said. "You're upsetting the entire ward, so get the fuck out. I don't want to hear all of this loud-ass talking. It's time to get these miserable wenches quiet!" Hearing this unfair request, Toni began to get angry and started shaking her head. She clearly did not want me to leave. She enjoyed my reading to her and did not want to miss out on one word. "Get that bitch out of here!" Sadie shouted again. The others joined in and began screaming at me.

Security was called to diffuse what could have been a very volatile situation. Brutes in white shirts and pants entered the ward with sticks and mace. Sadie was the first to get sprayed directly in the eyes. As the mace drifted in my direction, I quickly closed my eyes, but it was too late. The chemical spray made me cough, wheeze, and choke. The big bullies from security dragged me from Toni's bedside through the security gate, practically throwing me out into the street. I stumbled to catch myself from falling on the sidewalk. My twisted ankle throbbed and swelled. I began rubbing it, trying to massage the pain away. It felt like the kind of pain you get when you try to stop a bike with no brakes, your feet get tangled up in the pedals, and you fall into the bar. That hurt brings tears to your eyes and sends you screaming home to Momma.

I sat down on the steps of the institution that housed my intelligent, one-eyed best friend and I reflected on my life, trying to understand the direction it had taken. I remembered all of the unexplainable situations that had occurred in the last couple of months. My parents still thought I had something to do with Toni's injuries, and Mrs. Steptoe wouldn't even speak to me. The police still cruised our street every day.

There was one thing I realized I had to do without any further hesitation, and that was to find out if the Ouija board was back on the shelf in the third-floor closet. With Toni's blindness, I'd completely forgotten about the treacherous board. I decided that would be my very next assignment. I stood up and brushed off my pants and started walking toward the banana boat. I would speak to the hospital administrator tomorrow. I was not going back in that hell hole today.

I spotted a homeless woman sitting cross-legged in a cardboard box in front of an abandoned storefront. She spooked me when I passed over her. She made a hissing sound like the rodent sitting in the middle of the sidewalk on my street. She smiled a crooked smile and pointed at me. She opened her mouth to reveal a forked tongue like Mrs. Adams at the library. She had a scaly face and red fingernails like Katherine Sharpe. She wore a dirty black overcoat with missing buttons and crusty, disgusting socks inside threadbare tennis shoes. Her salt and pepper hair had leaves and mud caked on every strand. The stench was deplorable. The box had "washer" printed on the top in bold black letters, but it was waterlogged and drooped, ready to collapse at any minute. Sitting next to her was a blue plastic Wal-Mart bag bulging with dirty clothes. A thick beige mug with crusty coffee rings around the edge was positioned between her skinny legs. This was obviously a prized possession she'd been hanging onto. A group of gnats swarmed her ears and bombarded her hairy nose.

"Come closer to me," she said in a voice that revealed years of smoking and drinking. I didn't want to believe she was talking to me. I turned around to see if there was anyone behind me. She couldn't possibly be speaking to me. I'd had enough of old women with satanic attitudes. But I was close enough to hear her next words: *Beware of Malmspada.* She laughed like a witch with a broomstick and watched me race all the way to my car. With a bad ankle, sprinting was out of the question. I looked over my shoulder to see the woman standing erect in the middle of the sidewalk. I could see her eyes had turned a neon, bulgy red. The black overcoat was blowing in the wind, which made her appearance even more sinister. The shadowy woman watched me until I got closer to my car, which was parked three blocks away. As I approached the car, I could see someone leaning on it, but I had no idea who it was. I slowed down and saw exactly who it was. Katherine Sharpe.

There was no one else on the sidewalk to rescue me from this horrible woman. She was leaning on the banana boat like an innocent young woman waiting for her good buddy. Katherine was dressed in jeans and a T-shirt, pleasantly smiling at me like we were the best of friends. I turned around to find the old woman was gone. I snapped my head back when Katherine spoke.

"How's your friend, Heidi? Has she read any good books lately or do you go and help her paint her fingernails?" She actually laughed out loud.

"Get off my car," I said through gritted teeth. "Stay away from Toni and me." I had not seen Katherine since the incident on the back porch.

"Scare me!" She said, enjoying every minute. Then she smiled and asked, "How is Toni's grandmother?" Her eyes narrowed, and she was certainly ready to pounce. If I didn't move fast, it would certainly cost me my life. I ran around to the front of my car, jumped in, and started the engine. I didn't care if Katherine fell off the back or if I revved up the engine and rolled over her skull. As I floored the gas pedal and pulled away from the curb, I looked in my rearview mirror. Katherine Sharpe was gone. But not forgotten. She left a present on the front seat of my car ... another sliver of human bone.

CHAPTER 12

As I got older, December was always a difficult month for me. Everyone was so happy, putting up Christmas lights, selecting the perfect tree, making travel plans, and buying holiday gifts. The worst part was watching young couples walk hand in hand under the moonlight with a sparkle in their eyes and love in their hearts.

I wondered what Christmas would be like this year in the Morgan household. In years past, buying a Christmas tree had been a family project. We always went to a family-owned lot directly after church on the Sunday closest to the fourteenth of December, which happened to be my sister's birthday. My father would walk around and around, being careful not to pick a tree with a crooked trunk or brittle needles. My mother picked the decorative roping for the banister and the mantel in the living room. Us kids would look around at the peculiar people who worked at the tree lot. There was always an old man with a bad back and a long beard. He could pick out the largest and most expensive tree, but he was unable to carry it. I can remember watching the *"Grizzly Adams"* types who would shove the trees in a crazy machine that whirled around with plastic spinning in the middle. The trees would come out the other end wrapped tightly in a contraption similar to what held a six-pack of soda together. I always hated cutting the tree from the plastic wrap that practically squeezed the life out of it. I can remember standing back when the tree was finally set free. The branches would spread all over our front porch like a prickly green octopus.

As the last days of the fall semester came to a close, I walked around campus with a black cloud over my head. My one and only friend lay blind in a mental institution, my parents were barely speaking to me, I could no longer sleep in my own bed, and I was to be the proud owner of a renegade Ouija board. And in the meantime, I had to duck and run every time I saw that nutso, Katherine Sharpe. How does the song go? "The mountains are high, the valleys are low, and I'm confused on which way to go."

I twirled the second bone fragment around my fingers, and the sharp edge jabbed into my skin, making red prickly points in the palm of my hand. I continued to jam my skin until it bled little red dots of blood. I made an H, not really feeling the shots of pain shooting up my arm and into my shoulder. Sometimes I felt like I was the one who belonged in a loony bin with a deranged nurse like Callahan. I dropped the bone into my coat pocket for safekeeping. Why I thought it needed to be kept safe, I didn't know.

I studied hard for finals, remembering my promise to God to make straight A's. I didn't feel that prepared, so I reread all the chapters and poured over every note I had taken in every class. But I was only going through the motions because I didn't want God on my bad side. I hoped he would understand that I am not in the habit of breaking promises, but sometimes it couldn't be helped. I made a silent vow to do the very best I could. Hopefully, God wouldn't be too disappointed in me.

The clouds were thick and puffy, lingering for hours on end, smothering the sun. I shuddered as I walked between my classes, not really feeling like the go-getter I once was. My bulky winter coat weighed me down with its deep, square pockets and huge gold buttons. I slowly made my way through the frigid wind. There were some students who seemed to enjoy this bone-chilling weather, but my nose and ears were like blocks of ice. I seriously contemplated chucking it all and going home for the day. I touched the bone in my pocket to make sure it was still there.

I passed by a notice stapled to a tree on the west side of the campus. It caught my attention by the wispy sound it made while flapping in the wind. The paper announced the opening of the university's new Olympic-sized swimming pool, available only to students, faculty, and staff.

Swimming lessons were being offered at a minimal fee. The university would soon begin holding tryouts for the swim team, but today there would be an open swim from noon to four o'clock. Typed in bold black letters was, "Refreshments Will Be Served." They really knew how to persuade poor hungry students to attend a function. Free food was the key to a healthy turnout. What would happen if free beer were offered? A university stampede, no doubt.

Thanks to lifeguard training and scuba diving in the pool that almost took my life, I was already a good swimmer. I missed our pool in the backyard. My father covered it religiously every Labor Day weekend. I always stood by the edge of the pool, while Dad pulled and tugged on the plastic tarp. I felt sorry for the pool because it looked as if the liner was choking the life right out of it.

Curious about what the new swimming pool looked like, I walked over to the new facility. The chlorine assaulted my nose from outside the freshly painted metal doors. The university pool sign stood proudly; a new plaque with gold trimming. *A virgin pool*, I thought, poking at the paint to see if it were still wet. A fly had fallen prey to the sticky paint. Its corpse was stiff as a board. Wondering if it was the same fly I had swatted away from Toni's eyes, I stood and watched the dead insect, trying to decide if I should pluck it from the paint and smash its little nasty brains out. That way, I would be sure of its death, sure that it would never aggravate Toni again. I opened the heavy door and made my way inside. There were signs everywhere, giving directions to the locker room, showers, restrooms, and offices. Everything was so fresh … so new.

I felt a pang in my heart for Toni and the misery she must be feeling. She would have enjoyed exploring new stomping grounds. There were many students casually talking and laughing in their cliques as they gobbled up the free turkey and ham sandwiches and mountains of barbecue and plain potato chips. The vegetable tray was nicely decorated, but virtually untouched. Paper plates, plastic utensils, and flyaway napkins scattered the floors and steps.

The new swim coach walked around with a large silver whistle dangling from the chain around his neck. With his thick neck and his lineman thighs, he looked more like a football coach. He had to be at least six feet nine and was as hard as nails. He carried a clipboard with a pen connected to the top of the silver clasp and wore black tight shorts with "Saint" printed on one leg and "Louis" on the other. His white short-sleeved Polo shirt sported the new university swim team logo. The matching cap completed his I-am-the-boss-of-the-pool attire. I watched him work the room, introducing himself to the movers and shakers of the university. He didn't come anywhere near me.

I stood in line to get a cup of fruit punch, and then made my way to the main attraction. The pool was the most beautiful thing I had ever seen. The deck was adorned with large aqua ceramic squares spelling

out St. Louis. The ceiling was vaulted to comfortably house a tall diving platform. I looked up the many steps to the very top and wondered
how Greg Louganis had felt when he came crashing down, hitting his
head on the edge of the platform. There were several other lower diving
boards at the other end of the pool.

Students were walking around the edges of the pool, horsing
around, pretending to push each other in. Their voices bounced off the
water and walls. A few brave swimmers were splashing around and
dunking each others' heads below the surface. The bottom of the pool
was painted with thick black racing stripes. At the deepest end, a humongous drain that could have sucked up an elephant lurked devilishly
in the corner.

I flashed back to when I learned to swim. I had been taught in another large pool with a gigantic drain. I was only five years old when I
was formally introduced to the water gods. My father wanted all of his
children to learn to swim, no questions asked, so I was practically kidnapped, taken to the downtown YWCA, and thrown into a tadpole
swim class. My mother backed him one hundred percent. At age five,
your opinion does not matter.

My mother had packed my favorite swim bag, the one shaped like
a watermelon. It was green on the outside, with black speckles for
seeds drawn on top. It had a long zipper and a long green strap. Inside
the watermelon bag was my swimsuit, my new pink brush with the soft
white bristles, and my beach towel with a longhaired beatnik holding a
sign with the words *"I love a parade"* on it. I always hated that towel,
especially since my sister's towel had a gorgeous woman on it. She always said when she grew up, she was gonna look like the lady on her
towel. She would put the towel up to the front of her body and roll the
head down and put her head on top of the towel lady's body. "See I told
ya, I'm gonna look just like her!" She teased me for years saying I
would grow up to look like the ratty guy on my towel, who clearly had
not bathed or shaved in weeks. She said it so often that I really began to
believe I was destined to be a beatnik.

I sat in the back seat of my father's green Cutlass Supreme listening to him snap his fingers to an oldies song on the radio. "I heard it
through the grapevine … something something … to be mine." My father never knew all the words to a song. He sang while I sat in
complete denial. I tried to pretend we were driving to my grandparents'
house where I would play on the swing set in their backyard. I

squirmed around, unsticking my thighs from the leather seats, praying we would run out of gas. My watermelon bag bounced next to me. While most of my friends were lying across their beds watching the Road Runner and Yosemite Sam, I was being whisked off to learn the aqua boogie.

I was put in a group with other five- and six-year-olds who were as afraid as I was. I remember my father sitting behind the clear Plexiglas wall in the section with comfortable chairs. There were other anxious parents holding their breath and praying that nothing would happen to their precious children. I stood shivering on the deck in my new pink and red one-piece suit with a daisy on the front. The pink swim cap on my head seized my brain and squeezed it. My skinny legs had gigantic chill bumps crawling all over them, and my teeth chattered so much I thought they would crumble out of my mouth. I stood on the edge watching the clear blue water gently sway back and forth. I was standing at the shallow end, afraid of the bottomless pit that lurked ahead. I kept my eyes on the pool, barely hearing the whimpers of the other children. I thought I saw smoke rising from the surface of the water, floating up to the beamed ceiling. I watched as it drifted and disappeared. The water appeared to zigzag one way and return to its original position.

I could hear instructor Dan, going over the dos and don'ts of the pool. No running or splashing … and never swim alone. The rule about not eating before swimming really bothered me. I'd had a huge breakfast just a short time ago. Dan guided the group toward the deep end of the pool. I moved slowly, being careful not to slip a single toe over the side, while the other kids hurried, following Dan like goslings following a mother goose. I looked to see if my father was still watching me. He was waving to me with a big smile on his face. I stepped in a puddle of water that startled me. I wondered if I started to drown—would my father get from behind the large glass window in time to save me? It looked like a long way away.

Instructor Dan had now dived into the deep end and was treading water while shouting out commands. The water crashed along the sides of the pool, splashing the ceramic tiles on the deck. Another instructor, Debbie, joined the party and remained on the sidelines. "Don't be afraid. I'll catch you." The words that should have comforted me only made me more afraid. The other brave little soldiers jumped into the water with belly-flop splashes. Dave quickly swam over to each child, guiding him or her over to the edge, where Debbie quickly swooped the water-logged rug-rats up and gently set every child on the deck.

It was finally my turn. No way was I going to jump into that cold, deep water. I flat out refused, shaking my head until I was dizzy, while searching for my father behind the thick bulletproof glass. He was not there. I later found out he had gone to get a Power House candy bar from the machine near the locker rooms. Debbie tried to coax me into the water. "Go ahead, Heidi. Dan will catch you. Don't be afraid. The other children have done it, so can you. Now are you ready? Heidi, are you ready? Go on, sweetie, you can do it!" I could hear Debbie talking to me, and Dan shouting to me from the middle of the pool, but I was in another dimension. Their voices sounded like a tape that was dragging in a dirty cassette player. Everything was in slow motion and time was at a stand-still. The world was no longer spinning on its axis. I bet the clock on the bank tower stopped ticking at that very moment. Debbie's face was distorted, her lips blending into her nose. The lights on the pool dimmed. I felt as if I were the only one there.

The chlorine smell got stronger and stronger. I continued to shake my head *no* until I had a headache. I could now hear the other kids encouraging me.. Children can be cruel. They quickly began calling me names like *scaredy-cat* and *cry-baby*. I was not crying yet, but it wouldn't be long. I could still feel my body shivering. I was not jumping into that pool, and that was that. No way, Jose, absolutely not. I stood frozen, looking into never-never land, trying to come up with the best plan that a five-year-old could muster up. My father had abandoned me in my time of need. I was on my own, about to be thrown to the aquatic wolves.

"Heidi, jump into the water now. Come on, sweetheart. You can do it. Let's go!" I heard Debbie clap her hands and say, "Let's go, pretty girl, hut two three four, and a one, and a two, and a three!" Suddenly I felt myself being lifted up off the deck and into the air. I was actually flying, feeling the wind against my cheeks. I was no longer on solid ground. I was taking a leap into a deep, watery grave. I could see Dan below with his hands sticking straight out. I could only hope that he would catch me. After all, he had caught the other tadpoles. Why wouldn't he catch me? There was screaming from the peanut gallery and I was sailing through the air with the greatest of ease. The water was very choppy, violently thrashing back and forth from the deep end to the shallow. As I looked down, I could see that Dan had moved. There was nothing waiting to capture me but menacing black racing stripes stretched out on the bottom of the pool. I imagined the stripes sprouting teeth… ready to gobble me up the second I hit the water.

I plunged into the deepest end of the pool, near the far right corner. The splash was like hitting a brick wall. My legs and arms stung like a million bee stings. My ears ached with tingly pressure. I plummeted to the drain with gobs of water in my mouth and nose. I tried to stroke my little undeveloped arms, but I got nowhere fast. I lay on the top of the drain still holding my breath. When I opened my eyes, I could see I was up close and personal with the other side of darkness. I knew I would never see my father again. I could barely make out the bottom of the ladder that was a few feet above my head. It looked like two big silver Slinkies crawling down the side of the pool. I could hear a dull lull coming from the scary drain.

Suddenly I could feel a pair of hands pulling me up from the bottom of the pool and pushing my little body to the surface. My father was now at the edge of the pool, shouting, and the other children were silent. I discovered that Debbie had jumped into the water, but it was Dan who was saving my life. The other parents watched in horror, smashing the palms of their hands against the glass, leaving lots of palm prints. Dan had one arm around my neck and was swimming to the side of the pool with the other. I tried to inhale, but my nose was stopped up. I could feel my body gliding along, as if I were floating. It seemed to take a long time to get to the edge. My eyes were glued shut, and my legs dangled limply. I knew Instructor Dan was a good swimmer. So why hadn't he caught me?

My father pried me out of Dan's arms and gently laid me on the cool tile deck. My eyes were still closed, and I could feel the wet suit sticking to my back. The daisy on my suit was smashed to a timid bud and cocked to the side. The skin on each of my fingertips was wrinkled and cold. I could still smell the pool water and hear the waves exploding onto the deck, along with the fierce echo of the water. There was a piece of my hair stuck in my eye, but I could not move to get it out. I felt beaten and soggy.

"Heidi, are you OK? Heidi—oh, my God, Heidi, are you OK?" My father was frantic. Dan pushed him aside and bent over me, quickly pinching my little nose and placing his lips on top of mine. I could feel his breath going into my body. I finally opened my eyes and looked into my father's face. He was smiling so brightly, it warmed the chills that had rattled my body. I could hear the other children clapping and screaming. I took a deep breath and blew the air back out. The other parents were also on the deck now, and I moved my back a little and tried to rise up. My father helped me to my feet. My knees were wobbly, my head dazed. "Should I call an ambulance?" Dan asked. "Mr. Morgan, maybe I should call an ambulance! I think she should be looked at by a doctor." My father, also quite shaken, never did answer, or if he did, I didn't hear what he said.

I could see that the area behind the Plexiglas was empty. One heavy woman kissed my forehead, leaving a cold, wet mark, and another woman grabbed me and spun me around, banging my feet on the tiled walls. All I wanted to do was go home. I never wanted to see another pool for as long as I lived. *Please, God, let me out of here*, I thought. I just wanted to go home and get the water out of my ears.

My father picked me up and carried me to the locker room where I dried off and put my clothes on. My top was on inside out, and my shorts were on backwards, but at least I was on my way home. In the car, my father tried to comfort me by allowing me to sit in the front seat with him. I can remember him saying how one little incident shouldn't stop anyone from learning something new. I couldn't believe he still wanted me to go back to the pool next weekend. I had almost drowned, and he wanted me to go and try it again.

Well, after about two months I did go back, and I learned how to swim. But I have always been afraid of pools with large drains and racing stripes. Thank God the pool at home was friendly.

Now I found myself looking into the soul of the university's pool, wondering if it wanted to rise and pull me into the depths of its being. I was frightened standing so close to the edge, even at the shallow end. I watched as other students romped around unafraid of the soul of the pool. There were underwater lights in the walls that shone brightly, penetrating the surface. The voices of the students still echoed in my ears. I began to get hot; I had not taken off my heavy winter coat. I stood sweltering, unable to move.

I continued standing and watching the water. Suddenly, I could see the same steamy smoke I had seen while standing on the edge of the YWCA pool when I was five. In a ghostly fashion, it slowly rose to the vaulted ceiling. The pool was calling me, demanding that I jump in for a formal baptism. I was mesmerized by the water, watching more smoke rise, listening to every sound of each wave. Water distorts anything if you stare long enough. I began to see the faces of Mrs. Adams, Katherine Sharpe, Oliver Vaden, and Toni Steptoe. All of the liquid faces had their mouths open, trying to articulate something to me. Mrs. Adams' face was closest to me, in the right corner of the pool. Her hair was uncombed and her eyes bulged from their sockets. I turned away to see Katherine Sharpe's face in the left corner of the pool. Inside her forehead was the little beast that Toni Steptoe thought was her deceased Grandmother. The creature had its mouth open, displaying its bloody fangs and hideous tongue. Katherine began stroking the pet on her forehead with fire-red fingernails, smiling the entire time. In the middle of the pool was Toni Steptoe's blind face. The eyeless crater was filled with water, and the other eye was closed. I could see she was trying to mouth my name. I could swear I heard my name come from the lips. Her lips came together and then started up again. It looked very much to me like she was saying, "Help." *Heidi help.* What could I do? Was she really in the water or did she need me this very second? Was Nurse Callahan strangling her, drowning her in a rusty bath tub, or pouring acid in the crater? Then the face of Toni Steptoe flowed into the large black drain and shimmied down into each metal square. I thought I heard a gulping sound.

I lingered, glaring into the water, wondering if I would make it home alive. Mrs. Adams now wanted my attention. She began sticking her forked tongue out and rolling it back into her mouth. She shook her head back and forth as if to say, "Tsk, tsk, poor Heidi." What did this mean? I closed my eyes and quickly reopened them. Now Mrs. Adams had black hairy spiders crawling all over her face.

The three of them demanded my immediate attention, all competing for equal time. Toni began to cry. Her face wrinkled up and vibrated on the surface of the water. I could not distinguish between the tears running down her face and the violent pool water.

Oliver Vaden was staring right at me from the deep end of the pool. He looked calm, yet sad. His face was the only soothing, comfortable sight. He still had the gash on his head from the fall in the

Student Center. He slowly closed his eyes and lay silently on the surface. I kept looking at the serene face that quieted my leaping heart. I could also see Katherine, gripping the beast creature by the throat, trying to get my attention. She was laughing at me. I continued to watch Oliver Vaden float in suspended animation. Had he died and I didn't know it? Again I noticed the heat escaping from my body. The black coat was becoming a sizzling inferno.

I was keeping my eyes on Mr. Vaden when he began to spin. His head spun around and around like a ceiling fan. The water rocked and crashed into the other faces. Katherine went flying into the ladder and was stuck on the top two stairs. The beast creature sank to the bottom and was trying to dog paddle to the top. Katherine's face was tangled up in the steps without the comfort of the cruddy little rodent for protection. Her face rose up and down, back and forth, with robotic movements as she tried to locate the beast creature. I saw the hop-along bug thing that was in my basement bounce on the surface of the water, its long legs making swishy sounds and little indentation patterns forming needle-tipped circles. The insect appeared to be black instead of the greenish brown it had been in my basement. It turned to look at me as if it could read my thoughts and somehow sent me a message to remind me of its morbid death by flinging itself into the flame of the water heater. It hopped on toward the deep end of the pool, bounced up the stairs of the high dive, and stood on the edge. It gracefully jumped off the edge and came bursting down into the water. There was only a small, splashy pinging sound. The hop-along bug never surfaced. It submerged and disappeared.

Oliver Vaden was now stealing the show again. He continued to spin like a horizontal Tasmanian Devil. Mrs. Adams was violently hurled against the side of the pool and plastered to the new tiles. Oliver Vaden had the entire pool to himself. He twisted and turned with his mouth wide open. His neck appeared to be getting wider and wider, as if something was crawling out. He began choking. His mouth opened wider. I quickly checked for Katherine and Mrs. Adams. They were both anchored in their corners.

Then I witnessed something I had never seen before. Mr. Vaden's thumping heart crept out of his throat and onto his lips. Expanding and contracting, it jumped out of the old man's mouth and exploded into the water. The strong pounding continued as it flopped around the surface of the water.

Mr. Vaden's face caved in and sank to the bottom of the pool. He was gone, but his heart danced on the water. This sudden burst of joy angered Katherine Sharpe's face. Angry in her helplessness, she thrashed around, sank, and resurfaced again. The heart darted around the face of Mrs. Adams, teasing it by getting close and then sailing away. Her forked tongue came out of her mouth in an attempt to catch the dancing spirit, but the muscle was too fast. It toyed with the emotions of both faces and then tired of the game.

Now I saw something out of the corner of my eye. It was only a little movement, certainly not large enough to cause alarm. It was near Katherine's face. "Plop, plop." I was startled to see the beast creature surface behind the beating heart. It floated along the surface until it was within inches of the muscle. The heart didn't hear the silent creature. It never knew what was coming. I tried to warn the heart of its impending doom, but I was afraid to shout out loud for fear the other students would think I had lost my mind. I could only assume I was the only one who had witnessed this amazing show.

The creature sat still like a lion about to pounce on a deer. It then opened its mouth twice the size of its nasty body and gobbled up the heart, swallowing it whole. Katherine Sharpe's face smiled. So did the face of Estelle Adams. They were both miraculously set free from their corners. They floated along the surface of the water, and the beast creature jumped back on the forehead of Katherine Sharpe, claiming victory. It had a large bulge in its throat. I could not believe the heart continued to beat. The beast creature tried to gulp the heart down, but it was too big. Katherine remained smiling next to Mrs. Adams. They both turned away from me and, facing each other, they sank together out of sight.

The surface of the water was again clear, free from distracting spirits. Other students still splashed around in the exact spots where all of these deadly water games had been played. I wondered if I was crazy, and needed to see a doctor. I was afraid to tell a soul, including Toni. I looked around to see if anyone was watching me. Could these people even see me?

The shrieks of the students in the pool grew louder. The water was now filled with people. I slunk away from the pool's edge and walked toward the back wall, where I slowly turned around and looked back at the water. There were no more watery faces, only real flesh and blood enjoying a brand-new pool. I padded back through the large metal-framed doors, past the locker rooms and the glassed-in executive offices. The new facility was bursting with onlookers. I was more than ready to never darken this doorstep again, but a strong, negative intuition told me otherwise.

I ventured down the steps past all of the festivities and out the door into the nippy air. The cold air distracted me. I had been in my coat for nearly an hour next to the heated pool. Now that I was outside, it felt like I didn't have a coat on at all. I decided to walk toward the parking garage to find the banana boat and go home. It would be nice and toasty after it warmed up. I had forgotten my gloves so I jammed my hands in my pockets. It dawned on me that I couldn't feel the piece of bone. It wasn't in my pocket. Where was my bone? I remembered holding it on the way to the pool. I must have dropped it along the way.

I retraced my footsteps for as far back as I remembered. No bone. I don't know why I wanted it so badly. I already had one bone at home. Why did I need another one? It occurred to me that I could have dropped it on the deck of the pool during all the face dancing, but I didn't have the strength to go back to the pool to search for a bone. I played it out in my head.

"Can I help you find what you're looking for?" someone, maybe the giant coach, would ask me.

"No, that's OK," I'd reply.

"Are you sure? What are you looking for? Maybe I've seen it."

"It's a bone. It's pointed on both ends and slick in the middle. I had it when I walked in, but then I saw some faces in the water when I was standing near the edge. One of the faces had a little rodent in its forehead and the other had its heart pop out because the rodent was hungry."

I did *not* want to play that tune. No way. I decided to go home and look for the bone when I returned to campus for Spanish Club meeting tonight. I would look for it after everyone else was gone.

Chapter 13

Spanish club meeting was such a bore. I was so sick of conjugating irregular verbs and repeating them over and over. I was sick of reading about Maria Gonzalez and her red car and Carlos Fuentes and his black dog. I needed to reevaluate whether or not I wanted to still be a part of the club. I left the meeting early and headed across campus toward the new sports facility.

The campus was quite different at night, almost spooky. There were evening classes in progress, but there was considerably less foot traffic at night. The new aqua complex stood tall in the night. I stood back, to take it all in. I almost thought I would see electrical currents cracking on the rooftop, lighting up the sky like they did in old black and white Frankenstein movies. I was afraid to go in. Standing alone like a haunted house on a hill, the building looked menacing. I was trembling as I pushed through the metal doors again for the second time that day. I could not believe they were unlocked. The halls were dark, winding around and disappearing into nowhere. I could smell the pool water from where I was standing.

Remembering the path I had taken earlier, I slowly began searching with my head down, sweeping my eyes from side to side.

"Hey, what are you doing in here? This building is closed. You shouldn't be in here!" The voice was coming from behind me. It appeared to get closer and closer with every word. I turned to see a short, fat, balding janitor with a push broom in his hand and a cigar poking out of his lips. "What are you doing here young lady? I am telling you, you kids are something else! Don't you know this here building is closed up for the evening? What do you want? I got work to do here!"

"Sir," I replied, "I lost my bracelet while touring the building earlier today. I thought maybe I dropped it in here somewhere."

Ignoring everything I said, the janitor came back with "How did you get in here anyway? I thought I locked them front doors."

"I just walked right in. The doors were unlocked."

"Well I'll be … I must be gettin' old or something; coulda sworn I locked them doors first thing when I came on tonight. Boy, I must be getting' on in years.

"Well," I repeated, "the doors were open."

"Where was you at earlier?" he asked. "Did you go upstairs or just in this area?"

"I went upstairs to see the pool. Do you mind if I take a look around?"

"No one is supposed to be near the pool after hours, young lady, and rightly so. Folks is always found drount at the bottom of these waterin' holes. Have no business in or around these pools There ain't no life guard on duty now, and I can't swim a plum lick. Can you swim at all?"

"Yes, sir, I swim very well."

"I was just up there sweeping and I didn't see hide nor hair of no bracelet."

"Oh please sir, my grandmother gave me the bracelet, I would simply die if I lost it!" *I'll probably die anyway.* I caught myself pleading for a bone. I could hardly believe it. "I did find a tennis shoe, girl's size seven," he offered. "You didn't by any chance lose a tennis shoe, now, did ya?"

"No sir, only a bracelet."

"Well, if you says you can swim, I reckon I can let you in for a minute or two. I shouldn't. I could lose my job, but you looks like a nice young lady. Have at it, but I can't turn all the lights on fer ya. The campus police would wonder what in the sam hill was going on around here! I shoulda been cleant up and finished this whole dagblame floor by now. These peoples think I'm some kinda youngsta, but I ain't. Look what happened to poor ol' Ollie Vaden. Blame job like to kilt em. I'm not lettin' that happen ta me, no sirree Bob, no way. I'm just gonna takes my time and be done when I'm done. I'm pert near sixty years old. I'm too old for this mess now. Told Mista Bob that I wanted to stay in the library, but, no, he wants me over here. I can't clean this whole dag-gum place alone, mah self! I needs me some help. Yessir, I do. You chillen don't know how lucky y'all are. I wishes I had another chance ta go ta school again. People always breathin' down my back, tellin' me what ta do...."

He walked away, babbling on and on, shaking his head. I was deathly afraid of dark, still water and wanted to follow the old janitor and ask him to accompany me to the deck of the pool. I could not ask him to turn on the lights, or protect me from the faces that lurked on the water's surface.

"Thank you, sir," I shouted to his back. He raised his right hand to acknowledge my gratitude, but continued walking in the opposite direction. I could hear the keys bouncing on his hip as he pushed the mop back and forth. The pine cleaner he was using was rancid. It   smelled ten times worse then the stuff used at Toni's hospital.

I crept up the stairs, while the sound of jingling keys got softer and softer. I could now hear the massive pumps that kept this large pool alive. I had not noticed the sounds earlier because there were so many people around. The gurgling sounds were much louder than our pool at home. As I got closer to the pool, my heart played leapfrog in my chest. The air was steamy and thick. The whirl of the pumps frightened me. I wondered where they were. Sometimes the pumps were below the pool. The thought that I might be standing on top of the large pumps nearly sent me into cardiac arrest. I was now right outside the doors that led to the deck of the pool. I had completely forgotten to look for the bone as I came up the stairs, but, hopefully it was somewhere near the edge of the pool. The gigantic doors had two glass windowpanes in each panel. I stood on my tippy toes and peered inside. The water lay dormant in almost complete darkness, totally still and sinister. It looked like a colossal empty grave that had been filled with rainwater. The racing stripes were engrossed in murky darkness. Fearing I'd risk my sanity, I refused to even think about the drain. .

There was a small dim spotlight shining on the exact same spot where I had stood earlier today. The pumps hummed like a gigantic gas burner on a kitchen stove. That *wooosh* got me every time, and this one was on a much larger scale. My palms dripped with sweat, not from the heat, but from sheer terror.

As I opened the door, the new hinges squeaked painfully. I guess I'd disturbed its beauty sleep. I was so afraid of a dark, still pool that I crept across the deck with my eyes practically closed. I tried not to think about where I was, but blocking out a dark Olympic-size swimming pool was not easy. The pumps played a death song with every step I took.

I remembered my purpose for this dark journey. I had to open my eyes to find the bone. When I did, I realized I was not alone. I felt someone's presence on the deck with me. I was hoping it was the janitor trying to hurry me along, but I knew that was impossible because the presence was in front of me, not behind me. I was almost certain there was only one way into the pool area. Suddenly I felt a chill, and the water in the deep end began to swirl. Half the pool was moving, the other half, deathly still. The high dive stood in the shadows, standing guard over its aquatic master. I had never been so afraid, but there was no way I could scream. I took baby steps, carefully walking on the glowing blue-green squares only, until I made it to the spot I'd occupied this afternoon. The spotlight there was no match for the huge florescent lights that poured from the ceiling in the daylight. I could hardly see my hand in front of my face. I dropped down on my knees, feeling around on the deck, tile by tile. For some reason, I had to find that bone. As my eyes adjusted to the dim light, I kept crawling around in total terror. I would rather have met the boogey-man himself than be on my hands and knees on the deck of a dark pool. The water at the deep end churned and rose above the pool's edge, spilling out onto the deck. I wanted to blast out of there!

I had just about decided to forget the bone and stood up to look at the water one more time when I saw a figure at the far end. "Mr. Janitor, sir, is that you?" I called. Silence. "Hello, down there!" I called again. I thought I could bluff my way out of an early death. The figure at the other end of the pool stood still. "Hello," I tried again. "What do you want? Who are you?" I tried to make my way to the door. No bone is worth this much agony. Still not a peep from the far end of the pool. Then the pump symphony kicked in again, this time with a vengeance. The figure came toward me, walking on the water, and with it came the ripple effect. It had just passed the half-way mark of the pool when I saw who it was.

"Hello, Heidi." Katherine Sharpe was coming closer. "Looking for this?" she asked. She had my bone in her hand. I could see there would be a problem. Her face was rabid. The water rolled with her non-stop. I bolted for the door, but supernatural strength and speed were no match for a mere mortal. Almost before I could move, she blocked the exit doors and snapped the locks shut.

CHAPTER 14

My heart stopped. Total fear riddled my entire body. A diabolical presence was walking across the pool. A neon green light flashed across the vaulted ceiling. It lit up the entire pool for a split second. The water was no longer a clear blue. It was now a dangerous black.

The locks on the doors vibrated and clanged, and I could hear locker doors banging off their hinges in the distance. The neon electrical light flashed again, this time with a deadly red flame. I could see a figure across the pool, standing very still on the deck. The red light didn't last long enough for me to identify who or what it was, but it didn't look like Katherine Sharpe.

I lunged toward the doors and grabbed at the handles, jerking the knobs in a feeble attempt to break off what I knew was pure steel. I banged on the unbreakable windows. Now I knew how Toni Steptoe felt existing in eternal darkness. "Help," I cried out. "Someone help me, please! I'm locked in the pool! Help me, someone—anyone, please! Mister Janitor, please help me!" I began to hyperventilate. Perspiration poured off my forehead into my eyes. My eyes began to sting, seriously blurring my vision. "Help … me … someone, please!!" I cried out again. Where was the janitor? Couldn't he hear me? Had he forgotten I was in the building? He was probably puttering around the halls mumbling some nonsense about how bad college kids can be.

A sudden wind around the pool blew so hard I was lifted off my feet. I tried desperately to fight this mad force, but there was nothing to swing at, nothing to bite into, only a wind that was pushing toward the edge of the water. I was still in complete darkness I could hear bubbling and sizzling sounds and, I was locked in this place.

My hair blew back in the wind, which warned me that the danger was coming from the center of the pool. The locks continued to bang even louder than before. The centrifugal force of the wind was unbearable. I could hardly keep from falling into the bubbly water, which was thrashing from one end of the pool. It splashed on my feet, and I screamed out in pain. The water had turned to acid. It scorched my shoes down to mere scraps of material, ate away my flesh, burned down to the bone.

"You came here looking for a bone, Heidi. Well, now you've got a new one … your own." I couldn't for the life of me recognize the voice. It was deep and raspy, like it belonged to a twenty-year three-pack-a day smoker. I heard a laugh echoing off the squeaky clean walls. It went on for what seemed like an eternity. Whoever was laughing was enjoying my misery.

I was in excruciating pain. My feet were on fire. The scent of my own flesh burning was making me sick. Standing at the edge of the acidic water, I screamed and screamed. "Oh, God, somebody help me! Please—anybody help me. Please!" I stood crying and twitching in agonizing pain, watching sparks dancing off the tops of my feet. The pain crawled up my legs and spread like wild fire, consuming my weak frame. I felt like a limp scarecrow in the middle of a field that had been intentionally scorched.

I finally had no voice left to scream with, no more energy to fight for my life. The water in the pool popped and gurgled and sizzled. I was totally helpless. Giant waves hurled toward the high ceilings. The faint light coming through the windows in the doors enabled me to witness an indoor title wave. I prayed to God for a quick death. I could feel the small bones in my feet poking out of my singed flesh. The feet I once had were charred black blocks. I was standing on two nubs. This had to be Hell.

Suddenly, both of my arms stretched out from my sides. My fingers were extended and stiff. I had no control over my limbs. Then I felt a strong pain in the middle of each palm. The pain became greater and greater, and I could feel the blood running down from the middle of my hands. Everything was suddenly terribly quiet, and I could hear my precious blood dripping on the deck, drop by drop. I was being nailed to an invisible cross. The nails went deeper and deeper into my hands. "Help me someone please, help me," I whimpered.

Now I began to hallucinate that I was being burned at the stake. I could feel the blaze rising from my feet and slowly making its way up my already scalded body. Black ashes drifted from my body and floated into the air. The blaze reached my neck, piercing my throat and blistering my lips. My cheeks roasted and sank in. I tried to see through slitted eyes that would soon become smoldering green marbles. Flesh hung off of my brittle frame, slipping little by little off my bones.

I shook myself and came to grips with the fact that I was still standing on the edge of the pool, stretched out like Jesus on the cross.

Then I heard the locks unlatch, one by one. The two large metal doors opened wide, the light from the hall shining through was extremely dim. The locker doors banged and banged, and above their noise I could hear someone walking with chains shackled around their ankles. *Drag, thump, clink, drag, thump, clink.* Mobility sounded like a chore, as if the walker were tired or hurt. I could hear soft crying, whimpering, and an occasional sniffle.

I was barely hanging on when I saw the source of these horrible sounds: a figure with a bag over its head, hands tied behind its back. I heard the faint jingle of keys. I recognized the beige work pants and shirt. It was the elderly janitor who allowed me to look for the bone. His head hung low as he trembled with every step. *Drag, thump, clink.* The sobbing got louder. "Help me, mister," I mumbled so low even I could barely hear it, but his sobbing only got louder. Behind the elderly janitor was the dark robed figure mentally pushing him toward the edge of the pool. It was the same robed figure that had appeared earlier at the far end of the pool. It lifted its arms to the ceiling, triggering an intense lightning bolt that raced across the pool and struck the acidic water, turning it into a boiling frenzy.

The splashing of the water tortured my burned feet, but I was too weak to scream. The sinister figure approached the janitor and pulled the bag from his head, revealing a burned, disfigured face. The helpless janitor had been beaten and tortured. He had one eye missing from its socket … just like Toni Steptoe, and the empty socket was dripping blood, which trickled down one side of his bloated face. His other eye was glassed over with a thin black film and was barely open. His nose was broken and was a squashed mass in the middle of his face. The teeth in his mouth hung by threads from his weak gums. The janitor could hear the water whirling and coughing up black acid. He stood stark still right next to my extended arm, shaking his head back and forth like a blind man. He whimpered again, pleading for his life with slurred words. "Please, sah, I done nothin' wrong. Don't keel me, sah, you done already blinet me. Leave me be, I'm beggin' ya, paleeze! I done everything ya tole me ta do. I let this lady in heah. I sends huh up to you, jest like ya wanted me to. Please, suh, don't keel me, paleeze!"

The dark robed figure lifted its arms toward the ceiling once more and lightning blazed again. It traveled down the walls to the tiled deck, sending electrical currents sizzling and buzzing throughout the entire surface. The old janitor began trembling again.

Then the unspeakable happened.

The dark robed figure lowered its arms, moved closer to the sobbing janitor, and pushed him into the scalding water. As soon as he hit the surface, the old man let out a blood-curdling scream. Steam rose from the surface, and the smell of human flesh burning violated my nose and made a rancid taste inside my mouth.

The water consumed the janitor's battered body and he sank completely out of sight. The ripples made bubbly, steamy sounds that never seemed to fizzle out. The dark figure and I watched in silence. I was too weary to scream. All I could do was watch an old man die an agonizing death. At last the water was calm again.

The ceiling suddenly lit up, and I heard a morbid gulping sound in the middle of the pool. It got louder and louder … and then I heard a terrifying heaving sound that I recognized as someone about to regurgitate their food. The water spun like a top, round and round, until it expelled the bones of the elderly janitor. They floated on the top of the black water and I heard the ghastly chuckle of the dark robed figure.

"You came here looking for a bone," it said. "Now you've got plenty of bones. Your own or his—it's your choice!"

I closed my burned eyes and wept. "Why are you doing this to me?" I asked. The dark figure could hear my weak words. "What have I done to you?" I asked. "Why don't you just kill me too?" I gasped in the dark thick air.

The dark figure began to laugh so loudly its laughter shook the building. It pointed at the bones as they drifted haphazardly on the water. The janitor's skull finally popped to the surface and floated along until it was directly in front of my charred feet. The skull's mouth moved into a twisted smile, like a snaggle-toothed jack-o'-lantern. It spoke to me in a booming voice. *Beware of Malmspada.* The skull floated away and joined the rest of the remains bouncing around in the middle of the dangerous pool. *Beware of Malmspada.* The death words.

I stood still, spiraling into darkness, and the dark figure stood and watched the bones float in the menacing water. Somehow knowing I would be thrown into the water next, I began a silent prayer. I prepared for death. I wondered what time it was. Was it past midnight? How long had I been here? The dark figure glided down toward the deep end of the pool. I was sure it was my turn to die. I braced myself. I was determined to die with a clear conscience. I lost track of the figure, which had faded into the black air.

Then I felt the release of my body from the invisible cross. First my left arm dropped to the side, then my right. There were no nail holes in the middles of my palms. I looked down at my feet. They were no longer charred nubs. I was standing at the edge of the pool, watching the old man's bones banging into each other. With careful steps, I backed away from the pool. Every step was painful. My entire body ached. Rabid thoughts were tumbling around inside my head and I could no longer think rationally. I just wanted to get out of the building and never ever come back. Again I had witnessed unspeakable horror.

I made my way slowly through the doors outside the locker rooms. The lockers no longer banged unmercifully off their hinges. The hallway looked and felt normal. I was so afraid to turn around that I just kept walking down the long corridor toward the stairs. I finally made it to the outside doors.

The night air was magical. I had finally attained my freedom. I ran down the long path leading away from the building. When I checked my watch, I saw that it had stopped at midnight. How ironic. I kept running until I reached the end of the path, where I felt a sudden urge to stop and turn around and look back at the eerie structure. The moon was shining above the building, casting a virulent shadow. From where I was standing, I could see something moving on the roof. It was the dark robed figure. It floated to the middle of the roof, where it stopped and raised its head and arms to the dark sky. A turbulent crack of lightning traveled across the sky, illuminating the heavens above. The figure stood in place for a couple of seconds and then let out a sinister bellow.

Beware of Malmspada. The words rang through the campus, shaking the trees and rattling the buildings.

It was directed toward me, but I was tired of the turmoil and no longer wanted to play their death games. I threw up a mental white flag, caving into the evil that was following me. I was physically and mentally beaten. I thought of Toni Steptoe, helpless and innocent, and, no longer wanting to believe what had just happened, or even think about it, I turned and began my journey home.

I started navigating the path to the parking garage, trying to figure out what I would tell my frantic parents when I got home. I should have been back hours ago, sleeping safely within the walls of my family's domicile. The cool wind caused me to hasten my steps. I wanted to check and see if the dark figure was watching me, but I just didn't care. I was totally wiped out. For the first time, I remembered exactly where the banana boat was located.

I was just about to trudge up the metal stairs of the garage when I heard the explosion. It rocketed across the sky, illuminating the entire campus. The flames engulfed the new pool building, shattering glass windows and crumbling the brick walls. I could hear the fire engines racing toward the scene. Campus policemen sped up the grassy hill from all directions, with lights and sirens blaring. Fire trucks soon roared up the path, mowing down finely manicured hedges, disrupting natural order. As I watched from afar, policemen and fire officials shouted out orders and scrambled to contain the fire.

I hoped the robed figure had perished in the fire, leaving me free from any more turbulent occurrences. Fire was so final, almost a perfect end to malicious maneuvering and manipulation. Transgressions seemed to come face to face with some type of judicial system, then disappear into thin air. I flashed back to the old janitor, the one I could not save. I suppose I broke even.

CHAPTER 15

I did what every red-blooded American college student would have done … I went straight home and snuck in the house. Once again the campus was in total chaos. Three deaths in a semester were more publicity than a university could handle in a lifetime. Students walked the grounds like zombies searching for their graves. The media bombarded the campus with flashing light bulbs and endless amounts of videotape. The charred debris of the new facility lay in a miserable heap smoldering for days after the fire. ATF agents, along with bomb and arson squads, combed the area for weeks and weeks. The old janitor's remains were found, complete with his jingly set of keys. Authorities assumed the old man had been killed in the explosion.

Only I—and the horrendous dark robed figure—knew the truth. I could still hear the old man's scream as he hit the acid, and the sight of the acid eating him alive would haunt me for the rest of my life. Did he have a wife and family? The campus newspaper quickly answered my question. He had a wife and one adult son. "He will be missed," the article said. Local television stations ran sound bites of his widow crying uncontrollably. She was totally distraught about losing her husband of nearly forty years. "How could this happen?" she sobbed. "He was my life, my entire world. Now he's gone. My life is over!" The camera captured a full shot of her standing in the living room of their home. The clothes she had on were old and worn, and so was the furniture. She's right, I thought; her life was over.

I was the accomplice to that murder. If I only hadn't wanted that stupid piece of bone. I had no business at all begging the old man to let me onto the deck of the pool. If I hadn't been so selfish, he would still be alive. Would the authorities find out? Had I dropped anything that would put me there that night? I thought long and hard, but could not come up with a single clue. Would my parents realize that was the night I had been out so late? My mind flashed to Toni Steptoe ... helpless. Damn that Katherine Sharpe. I felt like killing her.

Was I capable of murder? Was I capable of draining the life out of another human being? I shuddered at the way my mind was racing. What about Toni? I was reduced to thinking on Katherine's level. I would have to play her game to stay alive, or simply give up. If given the chance to fight Katherine, I wasn't sure I could defend myself. I decided it was time to make a major change in my life.

Mom and Dad were furious with me when I told them I was taking the next semester off. All we did these days was argue. We never just talked. Ever since the night Toni had been blinded, our relationship had gone sour. I wondered if we would ever regain what we had. In the back of my mind, I already knew the troubling answer. They would rather see me attending a school where there'd been three grisly murders than no school at all.

"Are you crazy, young lady?" my father asked me. "This puts your scholarship in jeopardy. You're throwing all of this away because you want to find yourself?" my mother asked. They were double teaming me. It was the most we'd spoken to each other since that dreaded night. My father was usually the calm one, but this took the cake. My mother, as usual, was borderline hysterical. She would soon have to take two aspirins and lie down. I could see my brother standing in the corner of the kitchen with the face of a sibling who would never make a mistake like mine. *That's right, Ben*, I thought. *Take it all in. Watch your older sister make a mess of her life.*

I can't concentrate anymore. I have no direction, no purpose. I remembered this line from a movie, except the actress who delivered it sounded more dramatic than I did. "Look," I said to both of my parents, "with everything that's happened, I just can't take another day on that campus." They realized I did have a point. The campus was in complete turmoil. "I would feel a little better," I continued, "if I could take a break."

"Finding myself" was the only excuse I could think of on such short notice. I'd heard other kids use that excuse, but somehow it just didn't seem to work for me. I always knew exactly who I was. What I couldn't tell my parents was that if I didn't get away, a crazed student might kill me.

"What will you do?" my father asked. "Will you get a job or were you planning to lie around all winter and watch soap operas and eat cheese puffs?" That wasn't fair. He knew I hated the soaps and almost never ate cheese puffs. He was in rare form tonight, complete with flaring nostrils and bulging neck veins. This was a losing battle, but I had to win. "I'm waiting, young lady! What do you intend to do?"

This had gone way too far. I hadn't thought about what I would do. "Maybe I could nurse Toni back to health," I finally said. "She really needs someone to watch over her in that hell-hole." Good answer. Poor Toni Steptoe. Just the mention of her name made my parents soften a little. My father glared at me, then at Ben.

"Go to your room, Ben. This is not for you to hear." Ben stomped all the way to the third floor, but if I knew that little sneak, he'd creep back down to listen from the stairs. There was nothing I could do about that. I could hear him calling me "dumb-bell" and snickering under his breath. Even my little brother knew I was off my rocker.

"Now," my father said, "I understand your wanting to help Toni, but you can still attend to her needs while going to school. We'll hear no more about it. You're not quitting school, and that's final."

I tried to tell my father that I was afraid of the campus, and that no one liked me, but the words would not come out. Besides, it would have sounded so juvenile, and right now I needed to be as mature as possible. I tried to poke my chest out and look a little more responsible. My mother had not made the aspirin announcement yet.

"I have already notified the admissions office of my plans." I told them. "They're reviewing the status of my scholarship. I'll be notified by mail of their decision." I thought my father would explode. It was the first real decision I'd made for myself. I felt it was the right thing to do, but my heart ached. It would only be a matter of time before Katherine Sharpe would come after my family. She'd kill them for sure. I had to do something. She was evil, and I knew it. But the horrible part was that she knew I knew what she was capable of doing. The only thing I didn't know was *why*.

We sat in silence so long my legs began to fall asleep. I tried to shift my weight from one hip to the other to keep from falling out of the chair. My father stared into space with an "I'm disappointed in you" look in his eyes. His head shook with deep sadness. This was the kind of thing that had to simmer for a while. I tried not to make eye contact with him. It would only make matters worse. I was eighteen, old enough to make my own decisions and mistakes. There was not much my parents could do.

I realized I would get the cold treatment now more than ever before. Our home was in turmoil and I was the cause. I knew I had to say something intelligent. I grasped for just the right words, because this would be my only chance. I cleared my throat and went for the gusto.

"I was thinking … if I could find a paid internship that could also be counted as college credit for a semester, I'd still be learning and getting a small paycheck. I'd get some work experience. I could put it on my resume." This sounded good to me. I waited for a response from my father because my mother was too distraught to speak. Again, complete silence. "I'll check with the placement office tomorrow," I said. My father got up from the kitchen table and walked calmly up the back stairs practically knocking Ben over as he went up. When he got like this, it meant he had washed his hands of the entire situation. I let out a sigh of relief and remained in the chair. My mother stared at the floor, shaking her head. I couldn't bear to meet her eyes. She looked beaten, almost helpless. I didn't like the unsettling feeling of hurting my parents, but in the long run, it would be the right thing to do. In my world, things that go bump in the night were capable of despicable murder.

"Mom? Can I have a bowl of ice cream?" Ben was marvelous at breaking up a cool moment. My mother's spell was broken as she switched gears and was back into her mother role. I supposed I was on my way to a semester off. My family had no idea I was saving their lives. The thought of any one of them in the acid pool sickened me. Their frail bones would float on the top of the deadly black water? No way. Katherine Sharpe was a maniac.

I visited the student placement office the very next day. The smell of charred remains from the exploded building hovered above the entire campus. Notices of part-time jobs and internships covered the bulletin board outside the office. There were plenty of students looking in catalogs, punching on keyboards, peering into computer screens. The place was buzzing with job frenzy. I felt a rush of excitement. Maybe I would get my own apartment! But I quickly shook myself loose of that thought. It was just a little too far over the top. My father had not spoken to me this morning. The silent treatment would go on for some time. Ben would wallow around in it, soaking up all the attention. I signed in at the front desk and sat down next to an old fashioned coffee table to wait until my name was called.

"Heidi Morgan!"

I heard the advisor call my name. She led me down a hallway past glassed-in offices with students seated in front of desks. Liz Galloway's office was at the very end on the left-hand side. She was quite young and spoke with a harsh lisp. Her clothes were outdated, even more than mine, and her hair shouted for a new cut. She was definitely in her own world and didn't care what others thought. I liked her instantly.

"What can I do for you?" she asked. While I explained my dilemma, she smoked like a fierce chimney. The "This is a non-smoking environment" sign in the lobby didn't intimidate her in the least. She listened as my story tumbled out and landed squarely on the table. Most advisors would have told me to grow up and sent me back to the classroom, but not Liz. She seemed to understand. She sympathized with the part about Toni. When I told her of the problems with "a female student," she squinted her eyes and wrinkled her forehead. For some unknown reason, I only revealed the parts about Katherine Sharpe's stalking me. I told Liz I hadn't done anything to provoke this student. I didn't dare mention Katherine Sharpe's name, and Liz didn't ask. By the look she gave me, I guess she chalked it up to an adolescent squabble that she herself wasn't long past experiencing. I explained that this was affecting my family life, my grades, and my sanity. I shifted in my seat a little and looked down to my feet.

There was a noticeable lull in the conversation. I looked up and focused on Liz Galloway. She was waiting for me to continue. She sat patiently as I tried to find the correct words. "I'm afraid of this student," I finally said. "I think she's trying to kill me and I don't exactly know why. I've never told anyone besides my best friend Toni. My parents don't even know." I paused to gain my composure. Still nothing from Liz. I could hear other students complaining about poor grades and typical college disenchantment. I guessed I was not alone. "I was wondering if I could look for an internship and get credit for it," I said. "It would be a wonderful experience for me, working in a real professional environment." I was searching for the correct words. "My parents have agreed to let me try, and I was hoping I wouldn't lose my partial scholarship. Lots of students do it. It's a great opportunity. This would really give me a chance to figure out what I really want to do." I paused again to let Liz take all of this in.

"Do you think I'll be able to keep my scholarship?" Now I was squirming big time. This was not going well. I wanted to run out of the office. Liz must have been thinking I was a real idiot.

I guessed she was pondering my dilemma. I was sure she would try to talk me out of this. I sat quietly with my eyes on the floor and took a deep breath. "Do you think I'm making a mistake?" I asked. Just then, the telephone rang out so loudly I jumped. Liz slowly picked up the receiver without taking her eyes off of me. She took a long drag off her cigarette. The hanging ashes captured my attention. I waited for her to recommend that I see a psychiatrist. It was the counselor thing to do. It was her obligation to tell me I was completely out of my mind. She waited a beat before speaking.

"Student placement," she said into the phone while taking another long puff off her cigarette. She held her breath and then exhaled. "This is Liz." Her face lit up like a Christmas tree. "How are you Kay? Fine, fine, they're fine. Thanksgiving was great!" She tapped the ashes into a white ceramic ashtray full of butts. I don't know what was worse, inhaling the smoke or the fumes from the ashtray. Smoking was a nasty habit. "Yes, yes, OK," Liz was saying. "I like living there. It's much larger than my other place." Here I was, pouring my heart out to this woman, and she was discussing her living arrangements with a friend. "Yes, the car is fine," Liz continued into the phone, "but I really need a new one. I've had it for five years!" I continued to study the floor and fidget with the buttons on my coat. "No, no one special," Liz said. "I can only wish! How's Ellis?"

Liz finally looked up to give me the one-more-minute sign with her index finger. *Ellis?* I thought. *She couldn't be talking about Ellis Majors. No—that would be too much of a coincidence.* I tried to settle my nerves and focus on the problems at hand. "OK," Liz said, "don't forget to call me about Saturday. See ya, Kay." She dropped the phone into the cradle and said, "I'm sorry, where were we? That was my cousin, Kay. Her real name is Katherine. She's a student here, maybe you know her. She's a beautiful young woman with an A average. She drives a Jag. I suppose I'm a little biased. Her boyfriend's name is Ellis Majors. Do you know him?"

I froze. *Liz and Kay are cousins?* Did Katherine Sharpe know I was here? Liz began chattering on about their two families and how much she loved Kay. "She's like a little sister to me," she said. "Maybe you two could get together some time and talk about your problem. She's a marvelous listener. Perhaps she could speak to this student who's bothering you. Tell you what—I'm gonna call her back right now so you two can meet! You won't have to go away at all; Katherine could be like your big sister. She'll straighten this entire thing out for you."

Liz was shaking with every word. The cigarette smoke danced eerily around her face. For a minute I thought I saw an image of a snake reflected in her eyes. The room was suddenly very cool. "No that's OK," I managed. My throat had suddenly closed up and my voice was so faint I could barely hear myself speak.

Liz spun around in her chair and focused her attention on her computer screen and began banging on the keyboard. "Let's see what we have here." She scratched her head and continued her search. I knew what she was looking for: the name of the crazy college student doctor. "Good," she said a minute later. "It's still available. I do have an internship that would be perfect for you. There's one hitch, though. It's in beautiful downtown Joplin, Missouri. It's at KAEM Joplin 31. If you decide you'd like to check it out, I can set up an interview for you with the General Manager. Let me see, yes, it's a paid internship. Maybe you do need to get away for a semester. I can speak with the dean about your scholarship. Perhaps we could work this out."

My heart raced and my stomach took an upward turn, though I didn't want to seem too excited. I could blow the whole deal. I somehow squeaked out, "Thank you for helping me," before I left Liz's office. I could hear her picking up the phone and dialing. *Who was she calling? I asked myself—Katherine or the General Manager? Why would she call her?*

I could just imagine what Liz would say to her cousin. "Kay, I saw this young woman a few minutes ago in my office. She's deeply troubled, seems she believes that someone is trying to kill her. Her name is Heidi Morgan. I know this should be completely confidential, but you're family and I know you won't say anything. Isn't that the craziest thing you've ever heard? Imagine actually believing someone wants to kill you!" Katherine would listen closely. She would listen with compassion while Liz repeated my entire story. She would ask pertinent questions, absorbing every detail. Katherine would definitely lock in on the part about traveling to Joplin.

I took a deep breath as I walked through the door and into the hall. My skin was clammy and dry at the same time. I believed with every ounce of my soul that Katherine Sharpe already knew of my plans.

CHAPTER 16

Winter break was the perfect time to pack and organize for my temporary new life in bustling Joplin, Missouri. My parents took the news a little better than I anticipated. My father whined about how I would be alone in a small town without any supervision, but I argued that if I had chosen to attend college in another city, I still would have been completely alone and making my own decisions. I think my parents knew this was a good opportunity, but they both had to complain a little. After all, they were parents.

I felt this was the right move to make. The university was going to allow me to keep my partial scholarship. The dean of student affairs thought it was a marvelous idea. "Most students never get such a wonderful opportunity," she said. "You'll get work experience and learn to manage your money. Don't disappoint me. Heidi. You won't get another chance if this doesn't work out." The dean continued to rattle off a list of do's and don'ts. She must think I'm going to Chicago or L.A. What trouble could I get into in Joplin? Trust me. There would be nothing to do.

Alexander George, the General Manager of KAEM Joplin 31, immediately agreed to an interview. The southern twang flowing from the other end of the phone was refreshingly innocent. I faxed him transcripts and a resume, and we agreed to meet the following Monday. I bought a dark gray business suit with black patent leather pumps and a new leather handbag to match. I also treated myself to a special pair of black sheer pantyhose and a thin silver necklace. I was not accustomed to such extravagance, but now I needed a business-like appearance. Now that I was set in the clothes department, however, I only had one more problem. How would I get to Joplin? The banana boat would probably make it, but I would die of embarrassment driving around in that contraption. Joplin or not, I needed a nice compact car, rented at my parents' expense.

I decided on the right course of action and went in for the kill. My argument went from making a good impression to breaking down on the highway. I wanted to go alone. "I'm eighteen," I argued, "and I need to experience life on my own." This all boils down, of course, to the fact that you need a major credit card to rent a car, so my parents caved in and bucked up. Thank goodness they both needed their cars for work, or I would have been hitting the road in a large bulky sedan.

Ben was beside himself. "Heidi, Heidi, Heidi. The whole world revolves around Heidi." I silenced him before my parents could change their minds. My father and I rented a new red Pontiac Sunfire with a CD player. The chrome was so bright I could see my reflection in it. I drove the car home and parked it next to the banana boat. I think my car lost its soul after that. It was never the same.

I could hardly wait until Sunday. The plan was to leave on Sunday morning, stopping only at largely populated gas stations for rest breaks. I promised to call every couple of hours to announce my progress. With a "Trip Tik" from AAA on the front seat and a change of clothes in an overnight bag in the back, I was finally ready to go. Dressed in blue jeans, a T-shirt, and my favorite tennis shoes, I jumped into the fabulous rental and started up the powerful engine. My parents had made reservations for me at the Holiday Inn for Sunday night. The hotel was right off the main highway, and about fifteen minutes from the television station. If I got the internship, I would look for a small apartment because this was a five-month commitment. *Joplin, Missouri, here I come!*

I waved goodbye to my parents and Ben. My mother looked as if she would cry at any second. It was a big step for all of us. Although I would certainly miss them and was a little nervous, I would never let on. I backed down the driveway and drove into the brisk, sunny December air. I cranked up the CD player and headed toward the highway with a full tank of gas and a bag of roast beef sandwiches packed by my mother. The Sunfire had a burst of energy and was ready for the drive. I flirted with a carload of guys at a red light … I was on top of the world.

Suddenly I thought of Toni Steptoe, still blind and bedridden, confined to a horrible institution and at the mercy of deplorable nurses. I was experiencing the thrill of a lifetime (for a college student), while she was a total invalid. I had stopped by the hospital yesterday to tell her all about the trip. She'd listened, quietly staring into a dark unknown world, and when I was finished, she smiled to acknowledge how happy she was for me and hummed an Indian prayer for my safety. It was the first time I'd heard Toni make a sound since that dreadful night. I was excited to hear her weak voice. Perhaps she was getting better. Then the girl in the next bed shouted at Toni for disturbing her quiet time, as if there were such a thing in that miserable place. After Toni finished the prayer, she performed an extraordinary act. Her frail arms lifted up toward her head and pulled her good luck headband from around her dirty hair. "I want you to have this," she whispered. "It will protect you and guide you into the light. There is darkness ahead, Heidi. I can feel it. Look to the band for guidance. Never be without it." Her eye and the crater where her other eye used to be filled up with water, but the tears never fell. Toni had finally spoken! She was no longer on the dark side.

I felt a chill. Toni Steptoe was warning me about something, but I didn't know what. She'd always had an unbelievable knack for seeing directly into the future. I remembered her telling me how she'd felt her father would be murdered on the morning he was killed. I was hesitant in taking the special band, but then I remembered that Indians are offended when their gifts are not accepted. It was seen as an insult. So I reached for the band and took it from her thin fingers. It was dirty and worn, but now it was my most prized possession. I knew how much it meant to her. She would never have parted with it unless she felt I really needed it. Before I left the hospital, I gently brushed Toni's hair and lined up her tattered moccasins at the foot of her bed. I kissed her on the forehead and walked out. All the way down the hall, I could hear the woman in the next bed shouting at Toni.

The headband was now safely in my purse. I felt foolish about bringing it, but somehow I just had to. As I drove south, I reached into my bag and got it out. The vibrant blue and gold were now faded, and her dark, thick hair was still wrapped around the edges. I didn't dare wash it for fear of damaging it or washing away its magical powers. I plopped it down on the seat next to the brown bag of sandwiches. I also had my bone in the side pocket of my purse. I never could figure out why I still carried it. The surge of guilt chilled me. I vowed to spend more time with Toni after I got back from Joplin. She certainly deserved that.

I was about an hour south of St. Louis, and had just passed the popular restaurant that throws rolls at the customers. It was nationally known and had been the subject of countless news magazine stories. The parking lot was full of Sunday breakfast patrons. I suddenly missed my family.

I mentally went over what I would say to Mr. George, the General Manager at the radio station. I would work very hard and make everyone proud. Looking at the bag of sandwiches, I began to get hungry. I wasn't interested in roast beef. I craved a candy bar and a soda, something that wasn't good for me. I was on my own now. I could make crazy decisions. My mother would have been appalled. I noticed a bright gas station with a Quik Trip just off the highway. The words "highly populated" rang in my ears. My parents sure knew how to get a point across. There were several vans and four-wheel drive vehicles parked on the lot. This place was certainly well traveled by weary drivers. I saw a little boy running into the store behind his mother. Surely this place would fit the safety bill.

I parked the Sunfire right in front of the door and turned off the ignition. I grabbed my purse off the front seat and skipped into the store. I chose a can of diet lemon-lime, a candy bar, and—remembering my father's snide comment—a bag of cheese puffs. I paid for my feast and headed toward the door. I walked to my car and froze. There was a small rodent on the hood of my car, licking its fur and staring at me. I dropped the can of soda and watched it bounce on the cement, squirting everywhere. The candy bar and cheese puffs followed it. When my eyes left the sidewalk, I looked in horror as the rodent with one blue eye and one brown glared at me. Then it sat up, exposing four toes on one foot and six on the other. It was clearly the beast creature. How could I have thought it drowned in the pool at school? It was very much alive. I stood and watched as it innocently stroked its body with the pink forked tongue that I so vividly remembered.

"Mommy, look at the bunny rabbit!" A little boy with chocolate on his face was pointing at my car. "Can I pet your bunny rabbit, lady?" I was numb, petrified, still standing in a puddle of fizzing soda. "I'm sorry, ma'am," the boy's mother said. "He thinks every little fur ball is a rabbit. Don't touch that thing," she said to her son. "It could be rabid!" She turned him around and led him toward a fancy green van parked two spots from my car. I watched her as she strapped her son into his car seat and handed him a bag of popcorn, then pulled out of the parking space. When I turned back around to look at the beast, again, it was gone.

My knees shook as I got into the car and picked up the headband of my blind friend. I felt my body tremble as I looked at the spot where the beast had been sitting. Katherine Sharpe was sending me a message, one that I could not ignore. I sat for what seemed like a long time, just waiting for the beast to return. I never moved a muscle. I just sat stark still waiting for more communication from the other side.

I finally snapped out of the trance that captured me for almost an hour. I could feel the eyes of other customers watching me. I bet they were wondering if I was on drugs, or maybe a juvenile runaway. I continued to sit and gather my thoughts quietly behind the wheel of a shiny new rented Sunfire. Checking my watch, I realized I was behind schedule for the check-in call to my parents. Still hanging onto the headband, I searched for the cell phone in the glove compartment. I saw the dreaded low battery message that often haunted me. What good was a cell phone if you couldn't use it? I recalled my mother also providing me with a calling card in case of emergency, or if the stupid phone didn't work. Now I realized I hadn't memorized the PIN. What a technological fiasco. I would have to call home *collect.* .

I took a deep breath, almost afraid to get out of the car again. I had to regulate my breathing so my parents wouldn't suspect I had a problem. I walked toward the pay phone at the end of the parking lot and dialed the operator. She quickly connected me with my home number, asking me for a name to relay to my parents. I could hear by my father's tone that he was not only worried, but a little angry.

"Yes, operator, I will accept the charges," he said. Then, "Heidi, why are you calling collect? Where's the cell phone? Where are you? Where are you calling from? I knew I shouldn't have let you drive alone. I never should have let you go in the first place!"

"I'm fine," I said. "I got caught in traffic, some sort of accident on the highway. It was backed up for miles." I felt awful, but I had to lie. I could hear my mother pick up on the extension.

"Heidi, are you OK?"

"Yes Mom, I'm OK, but I need to get back on the road. What's the PIN to the calling card? The cell phone's dead."

"Heidi, I don't have a good feeling for this trip," my father said. "How far are you? Maybe I could catch up to you and drive—"

"I'm fine," I said, cutting him off. "I really I am. I just hit a little backup on the highway. I'm only an hour behind schedule, but it's still early. I'll make it to Joplin way before dark. I'll check in and rest the entire evening. Really I'm fine." I fingered the telephone cord, hoping the conversation would be over soon. I watched several cars speed past me. My parents rattled on about being responsible. After I promised to call again in precisely one hour, I was back in the car and on the road.

I went over the beast episode in my head. After deciding to toss it out of my mind and to only concentrate on the interview, I felt a little bit better. Highway signs told me that I still had several hours to drive. Suddenly the aroma of the roast beef sandwiches filled the air. I devoured a sandwich while driving toward what I knew would be an unforgettable experience.

CHAPTER 17

The Shetony Motel in Joplin was in the middle of nowhere, USA. It was located at the edge of town, and its parking lot was full of dirt, Stag beer cans, broken glass, and fast food wrappers. There was also a rusty brown pickup truck sitting high on bricks. I was afraid to go in alone, but I had no other choice. I was dead tired and needed a place to rest. I couldn't call home and complain about these conditions, so I decided to hit this problem head-on, and walk right into this dismal, broken-down motel like I wasn't afraid. Just in case I needed a quick getaway, I parked the car right in front of the door. I got out and looked around for any undesirable scary characters. There was an old man sitting on the sagging porch of a small wood frame house with a busted roof nearby. He tipped his crumpled hat at me and smiled a gummy smile as he watched my every move. His ratty pot hound barked a welcome to me and wiggled a dirty, thick tail. I was sure this old man could have told me a thing or two about the goings on of this house of horror. If Mom and Dad knew what kind of hotel this was they would blow their stacks. I hoped I had not made a mistake.

I walked to the front door of the motel and could barely open it. It was swollen, rusty, and had a spider web crack in the glass. Once inside, I found the air musty and thick. I did not see any other guests in the lobby, nor any potted plants. All I saw was a creepy desk clerk with a pierced tongue, rotten teeth, and a bad case of body odor. She wore black fingernail polish and had a zillion earrings in her ears. She spoke with a southern accent and was not very hospitable.

"What do you want?" she said.

"My name is Heidi Morgan. I have a reservation." I tried to use my best big girl voice. She continued to read a tattered *Road and Track* magazine that looked like it was a hundred years old. Each finger on her hand had a lettered tattoo on it. I couldn't quite make out what it spelled, though, because the letters were smeared and crooked. The nails on these graffiti fingers were short and raw. I could swear she had saliva on each nail because every one looked wet. She finally looked at me. I could tell she thought I was a city slicker and a troublemaker.

"Can I have my room, please?" I said with as much authority as I could muster. She slammed the magazine shut, stood up, and kicked her chair over, glaring at me with the look of a python and taking a deep breath.

I'm sure my heart stopped. My eyes never left her face.

"Sign the book." Her scratchy voice assaulted me. She turned the dirty registration book around towards me and slammed a mangy pen down. I slowly picked up the tooth-marked black pen and scribbled my name. I hoped I wouldn't get a dreadful disease from using that pen. She glared at me and said, "Room 13 is on the first floor. Sweet dreams." She threw the room key at me and smiled a curious smile as I backed out of the shabby lobby. I bumped into the door and pushed it open with my backside. As I walked back to the car, I seriously considered calling my parents to come and get me. I was scared. I opened the car door, grabbed my bag and marched right back through the front door.

Room 13 was absolutely deplorable. The shower had mildew growing in the corners and the lamps had black blobs on the shades where the bulbs had burned through. Everything was nailed down, including the loudly humming digital clock. There was neither a bible nor a phone book in the drawer of the nightstand. The sheets on the bed were thin and worn, and the gray curtains were limp and torn. The loud heater only blew out cold air. The lock on the door was cheap and flimsy, and there wasn't even a chain on the door or a little safety sticker that announced the fire exit. The only sign on the door indicated what time to check out and half of it was torn off. I shivered from the cold air and looked for an extra blanket. There was one at the top of the bent rack inside the closet, but it was filthy. The smell in room 13 was a mixture of mothballs and garbage. It felt like there had been a murder in this room.

I was so tired that I lay down across the lumpy mattress anyway and quickly went to sleep. I dreamed of fiery demons living in a dimly lit basement … poised at the foot of the stairs waiting to pounce on the next victim with their burning, ripped flesh.

I awoke with a start, popping up from the damp blanket. For a minute, I didn't remember where I was. Then I realized I had slept all night in my clothes. My back and neck hurt from sleeping on a paper-thin mattress. I rubbed the back of my neck with both hands and arched my back to unkink a deep-rooted pain that consumed my entire body. My throat was sore and scratchy, and I was tired and cranky, certainly not in the mood for an interview. I checked the clock on the nightstand. It was 5:30 a.m. My interview was at 8 a.m. I padded into the bathroom and gawked at the dark circles under my eyes. I looked as terrible as I felt. I wished I had a continental breakfast of bagels and juice to eat. No, what I longed for was one of Mom's big pancake breakfasts with sausage and eggs. I thought about what my family was doing at this very moment. Ben was probably begging Mom to get up and cook. Dad was probably still asleep taking up most of the room on the bed. The television in the kitchen was almost certainly blaring while my brother rummaged through the cabinets for his Captain Crunch cereal. I had never missed them so much.

Thinking of my family raised my spirits. I had to get ready for the interview with Mr. George. I jumped into the grungy shower, washing my hair and watching the mildew in the corners float away with the trickle of tepid water. The clumpy globs of gunk broke in tiny pieces and circled a while before falling victim to the stopped up, hairy drain. It made me sick to think of the germs I was standing in.

I brushed my teeth with what seemed to be clear water and blow-dried my hair. I carefully dressed and applied my make-up from the free J.C. Penney cologne pack Mom had given me. I was careful not to get the war paint on too thick. I looked in the mirror and admired what I saw. The suit and shoes were perfect. I looked at my hose, sheer, shiny, and glamorous. I was glad Mom had made me bring two pairs, even if I only needed one. I dabbed on my new perfume and was a new woman, fully energized. I watched the weather on the rickety old TV perched on the scarred dresser. The perky weather girl was forecasting rain. There were large graphic raindrops dancing across the screen. She was from the station I hoped to be working for. "Happy Monday morning!" she screamed like an exaggerated Pac-Man. Her mouth had the same choppy motion as the old video game. I hoped this was not a bad omen.

Now the clock read 7:05 a.m. Wondered if it was correct, I decided to strike out and find the station. I would be a little early, but I'd planned to people watch from the lobby. I grabbed my bag, made sure the directions were in the zippered pocket, and headed toward the front desk. Katherine Sharpe was a million miles away and nothing was going to ruin my day.

The same clerk was at the desk clerk and she failed to bid me a good morning. She even had on the exact same attire she'd worn the day before. She gave me the evil eye as I passed the reception desk. I wondered if she had been up all night, as vampires often are. I was almost afraid to turn my back on this miserable wretch. When she uttered a deep throaty grunt, hiccupped, and raised her black-nailed hand, I shivered and ran the rest of the way to the cracked door. I could hear her laughing and hissing.

I stood in the doorway looking up at the sky. Dark clouds were threatening a torrential downpour. I hoped I would make it to the television station before the rain did. I was walking to my car, planning what I'd say in my interview, when a mammoth grasshopper sitting in my path suddenly startled me. It was green and dark brown and downright ugly. Was it was the same one I'd seen in our basement just a few months ago? Yes, it was the exact bug I saw jump into the pilot light of our hot water heater. Now it was sitting in the middle of the walk in front of a motel in Joplin. I could see the details on the top of its ugly head, along with the red glow of its eyes. The insect's skin had obviously been badly burned. I was more than certain it was my friend from the basement.

I slowed my pace, instantly afraid of what this thing was capable of doing to me. I was a hundred times its size, yet it dictated my every move. The creature's eyes never left my face. It dared me to pass. I foolishly looked behind me for help. Yeah, I could just hear myself saying, "Could you help me? This grasshopper mixed with King Kong won't let me pass." I decided to move slowly to the left of the walk. It was a feeble attempt to get around this incredible freak of nature.

Its eyes burned a hole in my soul. I could feel the flesh of my beating heart tearing away from the muscle. I expected to collapse any minute. How could I be afraid of a grasshopper that should still be dead? I took a deep breath and decided I was being silly. I was a human being, and a sane human being at that. This was a grasshopper the size of a small brick. I gave the bug creature plenty of room. If someone was watching me from his or her motel window, I probably looked like a lunatic.

The heavens opened up and it began to pour. Finally, an excuse to make a mad dash for the car. I made it to the car, and while I fumbled for my keys looked up toward the Holiday Inn. The desk clerk was watching me from the door and laughing. She had her head back, revealing a snake like throat. Was anyone normal anymore? While the rain soaked my freshly blow-dried hair and my new suit, I found my keys and thrust them into the lock. I jumped into the car and looked toward the walk where the bug creature had set up shop. I was not surprised to see that the thing had disappeared.

As I turned around to put my keys into the ignition, I could see that something was sitting on the windshield of the car. Although the windows were steamed and cloudy, I knew exactly what it was. The bug creature was parked on my windshield! I frantically started the car, reaching for the lever to start the windshield wipers. I turned on the bright lights, cruise control, and air-conditioning. After pushing every button on the dash, the wipers finally whipped across the glass and flung the monster bug off to the side. I cringed at the hideous wail. I took off like a jet and headed toward the station. I could only hope I had run over the bug creature.

Getting caught by the red light at the corner rattled me, but it also gave me a chance to catch my breath. I checked my watch. Now it was 7:30 a.m. This ordeal had taken almost a half hour? I was due at the station in exactly thirty minutes. I groped for my directions, which should have been in the zippered pocket of my purse. They weren't there.

The light turned green and I was off again, trying to remember the way to the television station. The rain tortured my rental car while I drove blindly down the wrong road. Somehow I'd gotten turned around and was no longer in Joplin. I didn't recognize any of the signs I saw. I was the only one on the road. Wasn't it Monday morning? Didn't people go to work in this miserable town?

I couldn't see in front or behind. It was just miles of dense rain and fog. A sense of panic took over my intelligence. A million times, I wished my parents were here. Why hadn't I listened to them? It was still thundering and lightning so hard that I wondered if I should pull over. The road got muddy and bumpy, and the skies were covered by black clouds. I was having a difficult time maintaining control of the car. Where was I? Where were all the people? There were no traffic signals. Bursts of lightning lit up the entire sky. In the instant flash, I could see a farmhouse. I drove the car toward the house to try to get directions. I was so excited at the thought of getting help that I didn't notice the pool of water just ahead. The car hit the crater and stalled, sputtered, and died. It would never move again. I was helpless, and the cell phone was dead and there was no one in sight.

Remembering the house I'd spotted a few minutes ago, I searched the back seat of the rental, hoping for a courtesy umbrella. But people were not as thoughtful as they used to be. I was stranded. Time check: 7:47 a.m. Thirteen minutes to the interview of a lifetime, and I was stuck in a ditch in the middle of nowhere, USA.

Tears streamed down my face in buckets. I was in no position to get hysterical, but that's exactly what I did. The rain was really coming down. I had to get out of this car, or risk being flooded out. But the doors seemed to close in on me. The air inside the car got thicker and thicker. I wiped at the steamed-up window to find that I was closer to the house than I thought. I also found saw it was no farmhouse. It was clearly a large, elegant, older home with a tall iron gate surrounding the property. The house had a long curved drive, which made me wonder what it was doing in this hick town. Maybe it was the mayor's house, or perhaps the police chief's house. I felt a surge of relief. In any case, it was the home of someone who had a phone and could help me. I grabbed my purse and opened the door. Forgetting about the hole that caused the trouble in the first place, I stepped out of the car, fell into the hole, and practically lost my shoe. I was now soaked from head to toe. I had to make a run for it.

CHAPTER 18

My mind flashed to Toni Steptoe as I ran toward the mansion. She would have been full of energy, sprinting with the grace of a cheetah. I wondered if she was still lying in the nastiest nuthouse on the planet. I made a mental note to call home and check on her condition. As I stumbled to the iron gate, I broke the heel on one of my brand-new working-girl shoes and plunged down to the wet soil. The lawn was soft and cool, like a satiny pillow. I lay still for a few seconds, absorbing the raindrops on my cheeks and lips. My new suit was now a muddy brown, but I had held on to my purse.

I struggled to my feet and continued. I hadn't realized how high the heels of my new shoes were until I felt the up and down motion of walking with one broken heel. The shoes were completely ruined. The squishy sounds reminded me of walking in oversized galoshes when I was a kid.

The house was surrounded by a seven-foot iron gate with sharp points on top. I was convinced the magnificent gates would be locked, or maybe there would be ferocious guard dogs waiting to sink their teeth into my soggy flesh. As I neared the fence, what I saw were two monstrous stone lions, one on each side of the gate. I looked up at the beasts, faithfully guarding the life and blood of their sacred masters. They were perched on cement pillars that were easily six feet tall. The eyes of the statues were black sockets that cast fatal shadows. Their stone mouths stood open in cold growls. I noticed that the yard beneath the lions was mostly dirt, with only a few strands of grass. The ground was grossly uneven. It looked like a graveyard kept by intoxicated gravediggers who buried coffins lopsided in the earth. I noticed there were large black birds circling above the house. I quickly searched for a dead horse or cow.

What kind of people live with intimidating lions adorning the front of their home? I wondered. Maybe the owners didn't like visitors, especially those in need of help. I could only hope this was not the case. I would graciously offer to pay for the phone call and leave as soon as possible.

Luckily, the gate was unlocked. Glaring up at the lion over my shoulder, I pushed the squeaky metal monstrosity open. The lion reminded me of a picture of the Virgin Mary in my grandparents' house. No matter where you moved in the room, she was always watching you. I had always been afraid of that picture.

The long walk to the front door seemed like an eternity. *Up, down, up, down.* I should have thrown my tennis shoes in the car. The rain had finally subsided to a drizzle. Something was going my way. I wondered what I would say to the person who opened the door. "Hello," I would say, "my name is Heidi Morgan. I am a stranger in town and I need to get to a job interview. My car is practically submerged in a humongous puddle about a quarter of a mile down the road, but I need to get to the most important interview of my young and dumb life. Can I use your phone?" Suppose no one was home? Would I sit on the front porch and wait or would I up-and-down it back to town? Should I offer these people money? Should I have them call me a cab? I figured I would feel out the situation once someone opened up the door. As I got closer to the house I began to have an eerie feeling. The home was massive, three stories and a huge porch that wrapped around the entire first floor. The numerous windows had huge wooden frames. There was no sign of human life. It was a dark, cloudy morning. If someone were home, wouldn't they need to have a light on? Perhaps everyone was still asleep.

I noticed thick green ivy covering one side of the house. I always wondered why anyone would want this growing on their home. I finally made it to the foot of the wooden stairs to the porch. I took it one step at a time, reminding myself that I was definitely trespassing on private property. It took six steps to reach the porch. There were large windows on both sides of the huge front door. I noticed something very unusual about the walls of the house: they were completely dry. I turned to see if the rain had stopped, but it was still drizzling. The walls of the house should have been totally drenched, but they were bone dry.

I was searching for the doorbell when I heard sniffling sounds, as if someone were crying. My head snapped around. Someone or something must be directly behind me, but no one was there. Still searching for the source of the crying, I walked around the side of the porch and leaned over the edge. There were only bushes, small trees, and decorative rocks. When I walked back around to the front door, I found the cause of the faint whimpering. It was the windows. There were enormous streaks of water falling down the windows closest to the door. I could not believe it, but the windows were crying! The tears soaked the thick panes and plopped to the floor of the wooden porch. I reached up and touched the liquid with the tip of my index finger. It was a light clear substance. I rolled the liquid around using my thumb and second finger. It felt almost gooey. The windows appeared to be prisoners of the house.. I checked on both sides of the door. They all had the same moisture. Were these windows trying to tell me something?

Suddenly, I felt sure I was not alone. Standing dangerously close behind me, lurking with the strength of the Jolly Green Giant, Godzilla, and Mighty Joe Young was one of the stone lions. It was standing at the bottom of the porch in all of its strength and glory. I watched the immortal creature watching me with eyes set in black sockets. I let out a blood-curdling scream. I felt nauseated and weak and my stomach turned flip-flops, producing acidic liquid that I fought to keep down. I was trapped on the porch with nowhere to go but into the mysterious dark house.

As I backed toward the front door, I noticed the other lion was still on its perch. Maybe only one of these animals had a real soul. For a fleeting moment, I turned my back to the brute that was just below the porch, found the doorbell, and pushed it as hard as I could. It had a curious sound and feel. When I looked back at the lion; it was gone. I turned back around and found that the doorbell was in fact an eyeball. It was squishy and wet. My fingertip practically disappeared inside the pupil. As I got closer to the bell again, it blinked. It had delicate lashes surrounding the top lid. The eyeball followed my every move silently pleading for me to pluck it out of the deadly wall. I checked for the lion again. It was now up on the porch, standing beside me. I began to tremble and cry. Not again. I checked my watch: 8:30 a.m. I felt my future sink before my eyes. I would never be able explain my tardiness to the general manager. I had no energy to scream or run away. I prayed that someone would open the door and be civil and gentle.

I needed help. I wanted to push the doorbell again, but didn't for fear I would hurt the unprotected eye. Whose eye was this? Were they alive or dead? The wind began to howl and the windows continued to cry. The lion remained on the porch with me.

I noticed a large doorknocker in the middle of the door. I grabbed the handle and pounded. It was a lot louder than the doorbell. Finally, the massive door creaked open. I stood there, waiting for something to grab at me or perhaps suck me into some deep dark hole, never to be seen or heard from again. The door slowly opened. There was no one behind it.

I walked in without any hesitation, knowing I was doing the wrong thing. Somehow I knew that screaming would not help. There was no other house as far as I could see. This place was my only chance. It was quite dark inside. My shoes touched a slick hardwood floor, and I nearly fell down in the front hall.

"Hello?" I called. "Is anyone here? Is anyone home? My name is Heidi Morgan. My car stalled and…." I believed I was speaking only to the chilly, thick air. There was a massive chandelier with crystal attachments dangling from the golden prongs hanging in the middle of the ceiling of the entranceway. I had never seen such a spectacular fixture. I could also see a staircase disappearing up into darkness. Was the house empty?

"Hello," I called again. "Is anyone here? Please, I need help!" There was a room to the right of the front door that seemed to be a sitting room with a large, burgundy couch, matching chair, and love seat. In the middle of the room sat a coffee table with an exquisite silver tea set on top. The lamps on the side tables had thick gold fringe hanging from around the edges. It was the kind of room your grandmother forbade you to enter.

I walked a few steps further into the house when the chandelier started to rock. It swayed back and forth while the front door slammed shut. I felt the front of the house shake itself and then quietly settle. I was definitely trapped. Now individual crystals on the chandelier began to tumble and crash to the floor. I thought my heart would jump out of my chest. In a minute, the chandelier looked like a tree without its leaves. The swirly golden prongs were barren, almost scary to look at. I turned around and tried the brass doorknob on the front door. The knob was gone! There was no way out.

"Somebody help me, please!" I shouted. "Somebody, please. Is anyone home? Can I use your phone?" My shrill voice could have awakened the dead. The crystals on the floor started scratching and bumping into each other. Most of them stood upright and danced along the wooden floor to the cracked wall. The crystals moved about in unison scraping the floor with a peculiar swish. The crystals actually gnawed into the wood as if they had sprouted sharp teeth. Wood chips flew around everywhere, including up into my eyes. I had never felt this kind of pain. I could hear what sounded like a sawmill. Rubbing and digging into my eyes was no comfort. Then the chips began to burn. I just knew I had been blinded.

When I finally came to my senses and could barely open my eyes, there was no sign of the crystals. I squinted and looked down toward the baseboard. Even in the darkness, I could see what looked like letters carved there. I bent down to get a closer look. *Y-O-U A-R-E D-E-A-D. You are dead?* I collapsed onto the floor in a heap and lay there for what seemed like hours. I was vulnerable, at the mercy of some unknown force. No one knew where I was. I had not called my parents before I left for the interview. I would surely die in this mausoleum. I had not learned my lesson. My outlook was bleak.

I felt a rush of cool wind and shook myself and tried to get to my feet. My ankle hurt from trying to support a body without a heel. I was wet and miserable—all for an internship in a hick town. What was I thinking? Were things that bad at home? I shuffled toward the stairs and noticed another room on the left. I peeked in. It was a vast dining room with a massive table in the middle of the floor. This room, too, had a chandelier with hanging crystals. I counted six large cherry wood chairs covered with dark red velvet. The tall breakfront matched the table. Inside the cabinet was radiant china arranged on every shelf. The wine glasses were surrounded by plates that stood up on their edges with no assistance. An old-fashioned skeleton key protruded from the lock of the breakfront. The key wiggled to free itself from the hole it was housed in.

Standing in the center of the dining room table was a black iron candleholder similar to the candelabra Jewish people lit for Hanukah. It was the oddest thing I had ever seen. It had eight long slender holders but no candles. Eight flames flickered above the empty holders.

"Hello," I called out for the third time. "Is anyone here?" My voice was desperate. "Someone, please, stop playing games. I need some help. Can I please use the phone?" I know I sounded crazy, even to myself. There was probably no phone in this hellhole. I bobbed up and down into the room, where I decided to kick my shoes off. I would certainly be more mobile if I needed to run. Hanging onto my purse, I inspected the candleless flames. I slowly put my index finger into the flame closest to me. It was indeed hot. I felt myself going mad. My body temperature was rising rapidly. I thought I heard faint voices around me, squeaky, high-pitched voices, something like cries for help. Now I heard multiple pitches, high and low, as if I were in a room with a dozen people. "Where are you?" I cried. "Show yourself to me. Come and get me if you want, but at least show yourself. Only cowards hide in corners!" I must have been out of my mind, talking like that to an invisible phantom waiting to kill me. I paused for a second, waiting to be crucified.

The voices got louder and louder. The flames swayed. The voices were now hollow, as if they were coming from a deep cave. The ear-splitting echo was unbearable. I covered my ears with my hands. Suddenly, all was quiet. No more voices. *Help me*. I heard the words so close to me it could have been coming from my knees. I looked under the table. There was only a thin layer of dust. I felt around the edge of the table, afraid my fingers would be snapped off. Nothing. Everything was so dark.

Please, over here.

"Where are you? Show yourself to me. Tell me where you are!"

The voice seemed to be right under my nose. I looked at the chair at the head of the table. It was massive, the only one with a high back and armrests. For some reason I kept watching it, drawn to something beneath it. I slowly knelt down beside the chair and inspected the deep, rich, velvet covering.

The voice was practically in my lap now. *Help me. Touch me. Release me, please!*

I looked beneath the chair. Even though it was very dim, the sight was unbearable. Skulls. Four of them, bound together by a thin, brown leather strap. Pleading for help. Speaking to me. I heard them again: *Please help us!* My eyes stung in their sockets as I froze and watched one bony mouth form intelligible words. *...prisoners in this hell-hole for years and years.* The other three skulls simply whimpered, tears flowing from their empty sockets down cheekbones. The tears dropped to the hardwood floor in blotches, forming little pools of water. The voice I was hearing was that of a middle-aged man. Although he was frightened and agitated, he was clearly the chairman of the skulls. *We were innocent victims of these horrible people. I died in 1967, the father of teenage twin sons. My wife, was left alone with no job and the task of raising my boys alone. I was on my way home from work. It was the middle of July...* The chief skull cringed. I don't know how I knew that it was flinching. The skull had no flesh to indicate a wince, but I knew that's what it was doing. Another large tear dropped to the floor. The other skulls remained silent, not a whimper, not a gasp. They listened intently, as if they had never heard this story before.

The chief skull continued its miserable story. *It was my sons' sixteenth birthday. We had plans to go out to dinner. I had never been so happy. A dirty old lady, walking ... bent over like old ladies do ... she came out of nowhere! She was in the middle of the street! I panicked and slammed on the breaks to avoid hitting her. I could not stop in time ... my car ...* He hesitated and coughed. A skull under a dining room chair was speaking to me. I could tell he was speaking directly to me by the sound of his now pitiful voice. He had no eyes to watch me. I flashed to the eyeball doorbell—was it his? *My car,* he continued, *it crashed into the frail body of the old woman. I was mortified that I had hit someone. It was 4:30 in the afternoon. Her twisted body was thrown to the sidewalk. The sound was absolutely deadly. I jumped out of my car and ran to the old woman's side. Her broken body lay half on the grass, half in the street. The contents of her bag were scattered around her twisted body. "Ma'am," I cried, "I am so sorry. Are you OK?" Of course she wasn't OK. I kneeled and tried to lift her. She shouted out in pain, and took one last breath. I started to call for help. I was sure the old woman was dead.*

Before anyone got to us, she came back to life. She cursed me, looking me straight in the eye. She was no longer hurt. Her bloodshot eyes pierced mine with sharp daggers. I was instantly blinded, tumbling off my knees to the cold ground. I started to rub my blistering eyes as if they were on fire. I knew ... then ... I would never see again. But what I didn't know was that it would be my last breath. She seized my heart right then, cutting off my airflow. The pain was so excruciating, I completely forgot about the punishment in my eyes. The old woman plunged razor-sharp knives into my heart. I could actually feel my spirit slipping away, out of my feeble body. I watched my soul burst out of my chest and plunge into the depths of hell. There was not a drop of blood on me. I longed for a quick death as I lay helpless on the sidewalk. It was the middle of rush hour and no one saw a thing.

The last thing I heard before death, the skull concluded, *were the words, Beware of Malmspada.*

The skull was silenced by the sound of its own words. It was so quiet I thought it was dead. Again. Then words hit me like a lightning bolt: *Beware of Malmspada.*

Now the skull spoke again. *Before the police arrived, the old woman got up and walked away. No one knew I'd even hit her. No one knew how I died My death certificate read Death by Cardiac Arrest.*

My funeral was quite depressing, the skull continued. *The old woman took me to the service in her ratty cloth bag. My soul banged around in the bag as she intentionally slung me around. I listened as the priest spoke about my life. My wife was hysterical and there wasn't a thing I could do to help her. My two sons screamed for their dad as they stormed the casket. I couldn't console my family. I will never be able to touch my wife again. It was unbearable. One night after the burial, I heard erratic digging sounds. The old woman unearthed my corpse from its final resting place and sentenced my soulless carcass to burn in eternal hell.* The skull had now become breathless. The other skulls were still silent. .

His story was finished. I remained on my knees, my own head under the chair. The other three skulls sort of rattled as if to get as comfortable as possible. Their leader was silent, and then so were they. The horrible words had wounded them all.

"How in the world did you get tied to this chair in the middle of nowhere?" I finally asked.

You will soon see the journey we have all taken. This, our eternal resting place, will be made clear to you.

The mouth no longer moved. The skulls were just skulls. I slowly rose to my feet and walked toward the chair to the left of the head chair and bent down to look underneath. More skulls tied with a thin brown leather strap. They were quiet. To my surprise, one skull was smaller than the others, obviously the result of the death of a young child. The skull make sucking sounds like infants often do. Next to the infant skull was a skull with a nurse's hat on it. Her bony, empty stare mesmerized me. I was chilled to the bone. I could not bear to check the other two remaining chairs.

The dining room was suddenly freezing cold. The flames without candles still flickered. I stood near the grand dining room table wailing like a baby. The tears flowed out of my stinging eyes like a faucet. I realized again that no one knew where I was. The blue tinged flame turned to a wicked yellow. There was diabolical trouble ahead.

CHAPTER 19

The skulls danced in my head for quite some time. They also triggered thoughts of the swimming pool on campus, and that horrible night. That thrashing black acidic water with the skull of an innocent janitor floating on top had been no nightmare. I remembered the smell of his innocent flesh burning … the burning flesh of a grandfather who gave out shiny nickels at Christmas time.

The chair skulls were still quiet. I wanted so much to cut the thin leather strings and release them all, but an inaudible voice inside me, along with a deep-rooted feeling, forced me to leave the dining room exactly as I had found it. I feared the skulls would try to coax me back, but they didn't. Relieved, I ventured toward a large butler's pantry with its large glass cabinets extending to the ceiling. The cabinets were full of antique glassware that was worth a fortune. Mom would have gone bonkers over the gold-rimmed glasses and teacups. I was amazed that I could think positive thoughts. I was still admiring the plates and saucers when I felt that someone, or something, was standing behind me. I whipped around, fearing that my life would be taken at any minute.

There was no one there. I peeked into the large dining room to check for the lead skull. He appeared to be sleeping, although the other three watched me through their bony eye sockets. The wind outside became blustery. I could hear tree branches screaming against the side of the house, scratching and begging to get in. I no longer heard the rain.

I continued my journey past the pantry. "Hello?" I called again. "Is anyone here? My car broke down. My name is Heidi Morgan. Is anyone home?" When I reached the large kitchen, I could hear the skulls rattling and whispering. The kitchen was large, with high ceilings and beautiful woodwork. The wallpaper was orange and green striped, with a hint of gold. The tiled floor was puffy in places and soiled in others. It cracked and squished under my feet. The double stainless steel sink was spotless. It sat in the corner beneath brown wooden cabinets with dull handles. The spray water gun, as I called it, had rust crusted around the bottom. I'm positive it would send water flying out from every nook and cranny when turned on. The old avocado refrigerator hissed and coughed itself into a dying frenzy. It probably had ice buildup in the freezer, the kind I got my tongue stuck to when I was little. I didn't dare open it to find out. I was sure I'd find a frozen head nestled in the thick ice in the freezer. The green marble table in the middle of the room, surrounded by five swivel chairs with puffy green padding, commanded my attention. The table had no centerpiece. I do not know why I expected to see salt and pepper shakers; that would only apply to normal people. The marble table had been wiped clean, but crumbs were still lingering in wet swirls. *Someone or something had been lurking about.* A wicker lampshade dangling from a tarnished chain hung limply above the table. The light was so old, I imagined it displayed in a '60s decorating magazine with a lady who looked like June Cleaver sitting under it.

The air in the kitchen was very hot and thick. There was a renegade house fly buzzing around on the coils of the scratched stove. I watched it as it landed and walked around the edge of the stove. My mind flashed to Toni Steptoe. I hoped there were no flies annoying her. The stove looked cool to the touch. I could hear water boiling but there was nothing on the stove. The sound was close, as if it were right in the kitchen with me. The water gurgled and thrashed with the energy of a large pot. The kitchen smelled of beef cooking; but the empty coils were covered with caked-on food. The aroma of beef became stronger.

I stood in the middle of the kitchen trying to locate the smell, which seemed to be coming from everywhere and nowhere. When the fridge kicked on, its hum was familiar and comforting. I was still hoping I could find a phone. "Hello," I screamed at the top of my lungs. "Is anyone here?" Someone had to be here. I noticed the wooden back door with its frilly beige curtains covering thick glass. I tiptoed across the room, moved the curtains just an inch, and peeked outside. The red wooden porch seemed to be freshly painted. The paint was blood red. The mailbox looked practically brand new. I wanted to know whose name was on the mail if there was any. The cooking-beef smell intensified. "Who are you?" I asked again. "Show yourself! Help me please!" There was definitely a presence near me.

In the dining room, the skulls began to rattle again, and I could hear the lead skull barking out commands. He was quite agitated. Even the dishes in the pantry were chattering and clanging together now. The beautiful gold rimmed glasses pinged the loudest.

"Stop it please!" I implored the invisible presence. The main skull was now shouting. *Leave us be! Leave her alone!* I was almost too terrified to run back into the dining room, but I knew I had to. I raced through the pantry and into the room where the feasts fit for a king had been served. The skulls were screaming so much I almost didn't see her.

She was an old woman with thinning gray hair and wrinkled skin. She had a pair of reading glasses hanging from an old chain that bobbled on sagging breasts. Her watery blue eyes were surrounded by dark, baggy circles. A red and white striped apron hung off her sagging, bony body, and her fingernails were long, yellow, and curled up at the edges. The shoes she wore were old and worn, and her big toe protruded through the left shoe.

She stood in the door that led to the hallway. The skulls were clearly upset by her presence. I was so stunned I could hardly speak.

"Ma'am," I finally said, "my name is Heidi Morgan, my car ... my car broke down, and ... I am so sorry to be in your home. I needed help, and, well, the door was open, and I walked in. There was a lion on the front porch." I knew I sounded like an idiot. The old woman stared at me with cold and empty eyes. She appeared to be very upset that I was trespassing in her home.

I tried again. "Can I use your phone? I'm a college student from out of town. I'm from St. Louis and I need help. It was raining and my car stalled." I was babbling again. She stood still, watching me like a hawk on its perch. She had not uttered a sound.

Now the chief skull began to speak. *Please Ma'am, don't hurt her, spare her. She didn't know. She had no idea. Please my lady, do not hurt her. Spare her, please! My lady, please take pity, she is young and innocent. Please choose another. Take me again—my life is over! Do not take this child!*

The second skull now began speaking. Its voice sounded vaguely familiar, but I couldn't place it. Who were these bones that were trying to save my life?

Tiptoe through the tulips, the lord is my shepherd, tea for two, skip to my Lou, my darling; Romeo, Romeo wherefore art thou Romeo,

Houston, we've got a problem. It was Professor Frazier Vital! I was shaken. Professor Vital. My professor, whose life had been snatched away when his gut exploded. His skull, sentenced to a dark eternity, was one of those strapped beneath a dining room table. I bent down to see the soul of the good professor. It was him, all right. *Women eighteen through thirty-four are a totally different audience than women twenty-four through fifty-four.* Now he was reciting his television broadcasting class lecture. It was what he had been teaching when he snapped.

Suddenly Professor Frazier Vital's skull began sniveling and choking. As I turned around to see where I could run to, the skulls went back to their rattling. The old lady was still watching me. She knew I was trapped. I knew it too.

The beef scent was very strong, and I also heard the strong rush of the boiling water. I thought about rushing toward the old lady and knocking her down. I felt bad about it, but it was the only way. The lead skull was still whispering faint pleas of mercy. He was praying for my soul. The others joined in. I decided to make a run for it. I was just about to slam into the old woman, but she was no longer there. I stopped in my tracks. I thought my heart would stop. The skulls were going crazy again. I was definitely in big trouble. The house was suddenly dark. I heard the chandelier crystals jingling in the front hall. The beef smell was in my lungs.

"Welcome, Heidi. I'm glad you stopped by." Katherine Sharpe came into the room. She was wearing an off-white double-breasted suit with pearl buttons. Fingering a fine gold chain around her neck, she smiled at me, showing her beautiful white teeth. The bangles on her thin wrists clanked gently together. She looked like an angel, but I knew she was the devil.

"Katherine," I burst out, "what are you doing here? What is this place? What do you want with me? Why can't you leave me alone? Why are you here? Did you follow me? What the hell do you want? What in God's name do you want with me?" I was more mad than scared. "Why can't you leave me alone? Where's that old woman? Can she help me? Let me out of here!" I turned around to see if the old lady was behind me. Katherine's eyes deepened. Her head went down and then came up again. Her lips twisted with a voice that reminded me of the possessed girl in *The Exorcist*.

"Doesn't that smell grand?" Katherine took a deep breath and exhaled. "I love the smell of beef in the morning. There's nothing like it!" She looked deeply at me. Suddenly I could see that she wasn't alone. The fierce lion sat obediently behind her. The grasshopper creature landed on her shoulder, and the furry rodent creature hopped up into her hands.

"Meet my friends, Heidi. Oh, that's right. You've already met."

"Let me out of here, Katherine!"

She laughed. The grasshopper nearly fell off her shoulder.

The lion began to roar loud enough to rattle the windowpanes. I ran to the pantry through the kitchen. The old lady was standing in front of the sink with her back to me. Katherine and her pets followed.

"Grandma," she said, "I want you to meet my friend, Heidi Morgan. We go to school together. She's one of them."

The old lady slowly turned around to face me, revealing an apron soaked in blood. She smiled at me, showing blistered gums and fanged teeth.

"Hello, Heidi. Welcome to our home. I am Martha Vaden, Katherine's grandmother. We've been expecting you."

CHAPTER 20

"I brought some of your good friends to visit you," Katherine said. The bug creature, still singed from the fiery pilot light, rose on its hind legs to greet me like the stallion did in the show *Fury*. It was still perched on Katherine's shoulder. The furry beast creature with four toes on one foot and six on the other smiled at me, showing off its bloody fangs. "I wanted you to feel right at home," Katherine said.

"What is this place?" I asked again. "Why am I here? Why did you lure me here?"

"It's because you're special," Katherine snarled. "Liz is my cousin, you dumb little girl! How could you be so stupid? Poor, pitiful Heidi. Don't we all feel sorry for her! I see you've already been talking to Professor Vital. He's been so lonely without you, Heidi. Although he looks a wee bit different than he used to, he's just as nutty as he was before his unfortunate accident."

The lion roared again, practically knocking me off balance. Katherine and her grandmother laughed. There was a secret between them ... a deadly one. The house got darker. I began to tremble and feel sick to my stomach. The nauseating beef smell permeated the entire room. I could still hear the boiling water. I tried to hold my head up, but I couldn't.

"Lemme outta here!" I began spinning around, tearing into Katherine. I knocked her off her feet, and she hit the floor with a hideous thud. I staggered into the front hall.

"I'm gonna kill you!" As Katherine let out a hideous shriek, the bug creature hopped on top of my head and began clawing at my scalp. It clung until my head bled.

Katherine was now back on her feet and charging. "You will pay for this, little girl! I am in charge here! You and all the others will pay for what you've done!"

Still dazed, I tried to get the killer insect off my head. The blood ran down my face and onto my new suit. I wailed in pain.

Suddenly the main skull shouted out a warning. *Run, Heidi, run while you have a chance! Run!* Professor Vital began humming the "Star Spangled Banner." The other skulls screamed at me while I tried to understand what was happening. The chandelier began to swing, its crystals rocking and banging into each other. *Death to Heidi!* they chanted, *Death to Heidi!* The lights grew dimmer. The lamps in the living room blinked on and off. My head throbbing, I tried desperately to stay on my feet. My entire body ached. I knew this was Hell.

Katherine's eyes were ablaze. "Go to work, my children. Make her pay for what she has done to me! Make her sorry for causing me much sadness!"

Obediently, the furry beast creature jumped off my head and began clawing and mauling my skin. Its nails ripped my cheeks and arms, slicing and dicing. The bug creature pecked my hair, tugging viciously at my scalp. The pain was excruciating. Pieces of my raw, bloody scalp were caked in the claws of this nasty beast. I turned around and around in my weak efforts to escape its sadistic attack. I fell to the floor, scratching and squirming on the rough, hard wood. I crawled under the massive head chair and managed to look up. The lead skull shouted survival commands as the claws of a savage beast tore into the meaty part of my head. *Pull it off of you, Heidi! Get up and throw it against the wall! Your head is bleeding. Heidi! Look out—the big bug is coming your way! Don't give up, Heidi! You don't want to live as we do. Fight back, Heidi. Don't give up!*

And Bingo was his name-o! Professor Vital was awake and singing.

"You little bitch!" Katherine snarled at me. "Heidi, Heidi, Heidi! Poor sweet little Heidi. Look at those clothes bought right off the rack! Your dumb parents aren't even members of the country club! And that awful yellow shitbox you drive! What a fuckin' disgrace! I never used curse words before! I have stooped to your level. Look at me! This is a five hundred dollar suit. But you, you little tramp, you get all the attention, even from that prick, Ellis! Admit it—you're in love with him, aren't you? Admit it, you little bitch. You've wanted him from the very beginning. Poor little Heidi Morgan … saving souls and breaking hearts."

What was she saying? Me in love with Ellis Majors? I was still trying to free myself from a virulent insect and the rabid fuzzball with razor sharp fangs.

"Stop it!" Katherine Sharpe bellowed. Automatically, her two lunatic soldiers stopped and took their place beside her. Katherine's grandmother stood sneering at me with the look of a rattlesnake.

"I didn't even like him!" I shouted. "He came on to me!" The minute I said it I knew it was a mistake. Katherine was livid.

"He did not come on to you, you little slut!" she shrieked. "I saw you two sitting on the stairs by the garage! I saw the way you looked at him! It was you, not him! I saw the way you strutted around Ellis. And those stupid grocery bags that you carried. You looked like a homeless old tramp. I ought to kill you right now! I should have killed you months ago! You and your good little girl act, you make me sick!" The veins in her neck and head popped out. She looked like a lunatic. "How dare you to be in love with my boyfriend! You're not even pretty. I am beautiful and smart!"

I could not believe my ears. Me? In love with Ellis Majors? Coming on to him? How could she … how could anyone possibly think that? "He kicked the old janitor," I said to defend myself, "and never tried to help him. I've hated Ellis Majors ever since that horrible day in the student center."

"Oh, you loved it didn't you?" Katherine said, "having all the attention. The girl who saved the poor old janitor's life!"

My head was spinning. Katherine's threats were terrifying me. *She should have killed me?* What?

"By the way, Ms. Goody Two-Shoes," she snarled again, "how's your friend, Toni Steptoe? How'd you like the way I took care of her? How's she seeing these days?"

"What does Toni have to do with this?" I dared to ask. The lion roared again and Katherine's grandmother glared until her neck bulged. It looked like she had swallowed a huge rat. I flashed to Estelle Adams at the university library. As I watched, a forked tongue came tumbling out of grandmother's mouth. Her eyes were bloodshot.

"You're wondering about Estelle Adams," the old lady hissed in a scratchy voice. "She's my sister."

Again, I was stunned. Estelle Adams, the sweet old librarian who had turned into a scaly snake—the sister of this deranged maniac?

"She's a wonderful ol' gal, ain't she?" Grandmother asked. "I hope you enjoyed your journey with her, you know, the voyage to the bottom of the library? She told me all about it! You stupid little slut. You looked like an idiot banging on the library wall looking for the secret entrance. How stupid can you be?" The old woman was so excited she began to cough up putrid green phlegm. She grasped her neck, straining to breathe. Katherine didn't move.

"If she dies," Katherine murmured, "you die … sooner."

The old lady stifled her cough and plopped down in the middle of the dining room floor. I was alone in a house with two insane women. I wished I'd never come to this horrible town. Perhaps if I closed my eyes and quickly opened them, I would be back at home, waking up from a terrible nightmare. My head throbbed from the vicious assault inflicted by the ferocious animal army.

"How are you gonna get yourself outta this one, Heidi?" Katherine was now dangerously close to me. I could smell the mint on her breath. "Tell me, Heidi, did you think you would get away with this? Did you think for a minute, for one lousy, stinking minute, that I would let you take Ellis away from me?"

"It's my turn," she said. "Heidi, you are no longer in control of your own destiny. I'm gonna bring you down, and believe me you're gonna fall long, hard, and painful. I've been waiting for this. You might as well know that I stopped my Aunt Estelle from killing you in the library tunnel. She was very displeased with me. You ought to be thanking me. I actually saved your life!" Katherine leaned into me and fell silent. I could still hear the water boiling and the heavy breathing of her grandmother. The bug creature scratched the top of its burnt head with a hind leg. "You owe me … big time. Now, let's play a game, shall we?" Katherine was smiling, and my colossal headache was incredible. The blood on my head began to dry, but the aching continued.

"Let's play the game, *Remember When*," Katherine said. I'm sure you played it when you were a kid. I'm gonna make you remember the good times of your life. Remember the night at the university swimming pool, Heidi? You put that poor janitor's life in jeopardy. Because of you—yes, you, Miss Wonderful—he died an agonizing death. Grandmother wanted me to kill you that night, too, but I saved your miserable life! Again. I could have stabbed you right through the heart, or I could have tossed you into that pool of acid. Instead, I spared you and allowed you to witness the gruesome death of the lovable janitor who carelessly let you in after hours. You put his life in jeopardy! I had to kill him! I would not have been accepted if I hadn't! Yes, I nailed you to the cross that night. That was me who burned your feet and healed them in the same breath. How did it feel, Heidi? How does it feel to know that because of you a nice old man lost his life? Live with that, why don't you, for the rest of your short miserable life." Katherine was steaming. "I trust you've already met him in his tormented afterlife. Yes, he's one of the low-lifes under the dining room chairs. I've taken good care of him. He's been waiting for you!" Tears fell down my cheeks. Katherine remained in my face. I was frozen.

"That's it, little girl," she sneered. "Cry. Cry for Professor Vital. Cry for the janitor. Know that because of you these men lost their lives! And, by the way, remember the red headed kid from Vital's class? The one who seemed to be in a trance? The one Vital killed with his bare hands? Go into the dining room! Now!" She snapped her head away from mine and pushed me back into the dining room.

Katherine's grandmother slowly followed us. "Go over to that chair," Katherine said as she marched me over to the chair closest to the windows. "Bend down, you stupid bitch."

I was trembling; I didn't want to see what I knew I would see under that chair. As I slowly got down on my knees, I could hear sniffling and whimpering. A red glow coming from beneath the chair nearly blinded me. When I could see, I saw a skull with a baseball cap turned backwards. The skull faced me, gazing through empty sockets, straining to keep its composure.

"Oh no!" I was breaking down. "Why, why did you kill all of these people? Why? My God, why?"

"You're not as big and bad as you thought you were," Katherine snarled, "are you? I wish you were a worthy opponent. I'm really tired of winning every battle, though I must admit it has been entertaining. Take a good look, Heidi. Take a good, long look at what you are solely responsible for."

"I've seen enough! Let me up!"

"Stay down there!" Katherine forced my neck down to the floor, locking it into place. "You haven't met everyone yet. Let me introduce you to the redhead's chair mate. Heidi, meet Ms Simmons. Remember her? She's the lady who lived down the street from you. You remember that night you and Toni Steptoe took a nice after-dinner walk? She never allowed you or any other children to play in front of her yard. I don't know why I killed her. She hated you as much as I do. I iced her just for fun." The introduction was not needed. I could hear the voice of the witchy woman clearly.

Stay out of my yard! Get off my grass! The old witch was always screaming at us kids. The skull was still screaming.

"No," Katherine reflected, "I really don't know why I killed her. She was such a nice, gentle lady."

The witchy skull was greatly agitated at the mere sight of me. There was a yellow frilly poodle on the top of the skull, the same poodle that was sewn on her apron. I hated her, but I'd never wanted her dead.

I looked toward the other corner of the chair. The nurse's skull moved in a graceful way. Suddenly, the skull screamed, *Blood! We need more blood over here! Doctor, we must save this child, and fast. We're losing her! Oh my God, she's flat lined!* The nurse skull bounced around nearly strangling herself on the leather strap. I couldn't take my eyes off of her. I didn't even see it coming.

Katherine's hand came crashing down on top of my back. She hit me so hard that the bug creature and the furry animal went tumbling to the floor and the grasshopper made a whining sound as it hopped around on the slick floor. Its nails made scratches in the grain.

"Are you enjoying this?" Katherine asked. "Are you?" I lay on the hardwood, virtually lifeless, willing to give into Katherine Sharpe. And then I looked up at the next chair and saw … my friend. Toni Steptoe's skull was also under one of those cursed chairs.

Heidi, Toni's skull whispered, *Beware of Malmspada. I was blind, but now I see. I see clearly in death. Beware of Malmspada.*

CHAPTER 21

"Surprise, Heidi dearest! Hey, you look kind of pale. You want to use some of my make-up?

I'll loan you my eye shadow! Perhaps you can help your precious Toni apply it on her one eyeball! I'll help you pluck it from the doorbell! Katherine was singing and laughing at the same time, tickled by her dark humor.

I closed my eyes and wept. Toni Steptoe was dead and it was my fault. I looked up again to see Toni's skull under the chair. It had her lucky headband around it. She'd given it to me. I cringed while trying to figure out how she got it back. Her eye sockets were dark. Toni's skull stirred a little, trying to get comfortable. She banged against another skull and woke it up. She knew I was watching.

It's not your fault, she said. *I was dying, anyway. I wanted to be free of that lousy loony bin, anyway.*

"Oh Toni, I'm so sorry," I wailed. "What have I done?"

Heidi, don't worry about me, I'm already dead, Toni's skull whispered. *You're my friend, kemosabe. Just try to get out of this horrid place. These people are evil. They will destroy you if you let them. A word of warning: Beware of Malmspada. Go to the old man. He will protect you.*

"Silence!" screamed Katherine, her green eyes ablaze with evil and hate. "I've got a secret to tell you, Miss Heidi. We're still playing *Remember When*! Remember when you rang the doorbell just a while ago? Remember the eyeball doorbell? Did it seem squishy? Did it look familiar? Can you figure out whose precious eye I stole? Did the eye seem like it was crying? You're a smart girl, Heidi, but you're a dumb bunny, too. Well I'm here to help you out. It belongs to your friend there. It's Toni's. Go ahead—ask Ms. Moccasin how it felt when I gouged her eyeball out of its socket." Katherine paused to take a deep breath. "You see, Heidi, she was your closest confidant. I had to make her death really special. She was such an easy target, lying there so helpless in the crazy house. I told the attendant she was a dear friend of mine. I smiled so sweetly. They actually left me alone with her. I even made friends with that nice woman, Sadie." Katherine gracefully positioned her hands as if she were praying.

"Shut up!" I shouted.

"Temper, temper, Miss Goody-Goody. I haven't finished my story. Remember 2:06 a.m., Heidi? Does that time ring a bell in that sweet little head of yours? Do you recall that wonderful, dreadful night in your dinky little bedroom? Remember the voice you heard through Toni's lips? That was me! Can you recall how Toni was blinded? How about the melty gunk that burned into the windows of her weak soul? That was my masterpiece! I enjoyed the pain I caused her. Of course you realize that it was all your fault, you selfish little cunt! Oh, dear me. I never used to swear before."

I thought back to that night. I closed my eyes to recall the agonizing details. Toni had been determined to raise her dead grandmother. I knew we should not have disturbed the Ouija board. Mom had forbidden me to even touch it.

Katherine shrieked with laughter. "I even made you throw up that turkey sandwich. But there is one particular piece of information I would like for you to recall, and that's the removal of the fingernails. Do you recall Toni losing those precious little unmanicured nails? I haven't seen such messy looking hands in my life. Don't Indians get manicures? I suppose you're pretending like you don't remember. Well, I've got something that will help you remember." Katherine walked into the sitting room next to the front door, reached down behind the couch. She pulled out an antique picture frame. "I've been saving this for just the right moment. Ta-da! For you!" Katherine bowed down as if I were the Queen of England and extended the picture to me. "Take it," she shouted. Trembling, I reached out for the frame, not knowing what to expect. Katherine laughed again. "Merry Christmas, Heidi."

The room was extremely dark. Katherine was anxious. "Look at it!" she screamed. "Look at it real good. What do you see?"

Slowly my eyes left Katherine's face and crept down to what I held in my shaking hands. I fully expected a snake or a lizard to jump out of the glass. When I focused, I saw it was not a picture at all. It was a display of fingernails, neatly lined up from thumb to pinky. A neat metal plaque attached to the frame read, "Toni's Fingernails." I dropped if and the glass shattered on the floor. All ten fingernails were dislodged from the cardboard. They scattered on the cold, hardwood floor. Katherine and her Grandmother laughed out loud.

Leave me alone! The crystals on the chandelier began to chant, *leave me alone! Leave me alone*! They were laughing at me. I sank to my knees and wept. Katherine was truly enjoying the walk down memory lane.

"Oh no," she said gaily, "this party isn't over yet. We've got a long way to go. I hope you had your Wheaties this morning!" Katherine was tickled at her joke. "Ellis used to make jokes just like that. I suppose you already know that. I'm gonna really miss him, but that fun starts later. I just hope I can decide what to wear."

Katherine's grandmother was beginning to tire. "Kay," she said, "I need to sleep. I'm old and tired. This kinda work takes all my energy. We can continue these festivities tomorrow." Old Grandma smiled a crooked black-gummed smile at me. "Wake me up early. I don't want to miss any of the fun." She padded up the dark stairs and disappeared.

Katherine turned back to me. "You better be glad my grandmother is tired," she said, her voice full of menace. "Now clean this mess up!" She stood over me like a drill sergeant and made me pick up every particle of glass with my bare hands. Her delicate gold bracelets gently clanged together while she folded her arms and tapped her feet. My mauled skull pounded like a jackhammer. I was sure there were open wounds that needed stitches. I had to take every morsel of glass to the kitchen trash can.

"You wouldn't be in this mess if you would have just left Ellis alone!" she said.

Here we were again, back to Ellis Majors.

"Katherine." I was putting my life on the line with this, but I thought she would appreciate the truth. "I must admit, I did find Ellis Majors very attractive at first, as did every other girl on campus." He seemed to be charming and fun to be around. I found his beautiful clothes and that Rolex watch almost irresistible."

"I bought that damn Rolex watch," she screamed at me, "and those black onyx cufflinks, too. I *made* that piece of shit, Ellis Majors! Every stitch of clothing he owns, I picked out and bought! He doesn't have any money! He lives with his mangy old aunt in a shack on Hamilton Avenue that's practically falling down. I pay for the old bitch's medicine. I used my inheritance money and my college fund to buy him anything he wanted! I even bought that Gucci briefcase he carries. He's a poor ignorant stupid fool I fell in love with! I had to clean him up for show! My parents are rich. I drive a new Jaguar—why would I even pay attention to a parasite like Ellis Majors? I just wanted to fit in. I was tired of being the weird little rich girl. He made me feel alive! He ignited something inside me that I'd never felt before … with anyone. I hate the fact that I can't get him out of my system. Why do I love him so much? Why? Well, I'll tell you. I hate him, I … hate … Ellis Majors."

Suddenly Katherine was a real person again. Her face was covered with genuine human pain. I wanted to put my arms around the girl who was very obviously hurting inside.

She shook the tears from her eyes and went on. "That nitwit had no business with a girl like me!" She pointed to herself. "I could have gone to Princeton or Duke or even Yale! Yes, I was accepted to Yale University, but I settled. I settled for a state university in my own home town! My parents are ashamed of me because of him! That goddamned Ellis Majors has practically ruined my life!"

Now Katherine Sharpe was the one who was trembling. Her nose was running, and the tears flowing down her cheeks were smearing flawless expensive makeup. "After all I did for that ignorant moron, and he likes you! Someone whose parents are school teachers! You'll never amount to anything! I was an idiot to even think he was anything but an imbecile!"

I could smell Katherine's perfume heating up the room. The animals were absolutely silent. The lion sat on its hind legs poised behind Katherine just in case she gave the order to kill me. For a minute I felt sorry for her. She was a sick, lonely girl with all the money in the world to buy whatever or whomever she pleased, and even that didn't make her happy.

I had to take the chance and defend myself. "I didn't once approach Ellis, Katherine, not once! After the accident in the Student

Center, I couldn't stand the sight of him! You saw how he kicked and disrespected the old janitor. He never apologized for something that was completely his own fault! All he could think about was making sure that he still looked good. You were there. You saw his childish behavior! I had to save the old man's life! Everyone else thought it was funny! Honestly, Katherine, you have got to believe me. I never had any thoughts of taking Ellis from you! I wouldn't do that. I *couldn't* do that, even if I wanted to. I am in no way a match for you. Every guy on campus would die to even take you out. You're the most popular girl on campus! There's no way I could compete with you! Like you said, I drive a shitbox, you drive a Jaguar! You have got to believe me, Katherine. I didn't try to hurt you, and now I can see that you clearly have been hurting for a while."

I could see that my words stung Katherine Sharpe. She had her eyes toward the floor. The room was now silent. "Please, Katherine," I repeated, "you've got to believe me, please!"

But Katherine looked at me with those dazzling green eyes of hers and said, "I don't believe you. You did try to take my Ellis from me, and now you're gonna pay ... with your life." She was as cold as ice. Mascara had run down her cheeks, and now she looked like the monster I knew she was.

"When are you going to let me go?" I asked her.

The lion roared.

"Never." Katherine snarled. "Never."

CHAPTER 22

"**I** want to tell you about the bone."

I was awakened by Katherine standing over me in a long black silk nightgown and robe. I had been taken to a small room with no bed, windows, or lights. There was only a thin torn blanket on the floor. The door had been locked all night. I had had nothing to eat or drink, though I was taken to a small bathroom that reeked of urine and feces. The sink was rusty and grimy, the toilet, deplorable.

I had been thrown in that dark, cold room long after midnight when Katherine had decided she had had enough of me for one evening. Even after all of my begging and pleading she wouldn't let me call home to let my parents know I was at least still alive. They must have been out of their minds with worry. I was in Joplin, Missouri, with two maniacs who enjoyed the art of murder.

Even at the crack of dawn, Katherine looked beautiful. I had no idea exactly what time it was because she had taken my watch the night before. My entire body ached and I was trembling from cold and fear. My head desperately needed medical attention. I struggled to my feet and tried to stand up straight. My new suit was crumpled and torn.

"Good morning, Heidi. I trust you slept well." Katherine waited for my weak response.

Where I got the gumption, I'll never know. "I slept well, thank you." I slowly faced her as she glared at me, practically foaming at the mouth.

"Well," she said, "we'll see how funny you get when you find out what's in store for you today." Katherine slammed the door to the small room. I heard her lock it from the outside. I slid down the wall, not even imagining what I could look forward to today. I sat quietly so I could hear what was happening on the other side of the door. Katherine was talking to her Grandmother. The lion was roaring ferociously from the back yard.

Finally the door opened again and Katherine appeared, spruced up ready to go. She blindfolded me and led me down a set of old steps, where I was locked in another cold room. I could hear footsteps above me. It sounded like the old woman was in the kitchen because pots and pans were banging together and I could hear water running. The old witch was cooking breakfast. I wanted to bang on the door, but I had no energy to do so. I convinced myself I would need all of the strength I possessed to stay alive.

I guess I was locked in this room for at least four hours before the door slowly opened. I had removed the blindfold and could see that Katherine was now dressed in a double-breasted black pantsuit with patent leather pumps. She had a tray in her hands, but I could not see what was on it. Katherine stooped down near me and left the tray on the floor.

"Enjoy … I'll be back."

"Can I please go to the bathroom?"

"No way. Go in your pants." She walked out of the room again and shut the door. The room was dark with the door shut. There were no windows. I had no idea what was on the tray. I pulled it closer and felt around on it. I was so hungry I didn't care what it was; I was going to eat it. So far, I felt nothing but the surface of the tray. I had covered three corners and was slowly approaching the fourth. My fingers crept anxiously toward my breakfast. I felt a smooth bowl and a plastic spoon. I picked up the spoon and began to stir. The substance was thick and lumpy. I stuck my finger in the bowl and scooped up a fingerful of the thick mess and brought it to my nose. It felt and smelled like oatmeal. I used the tip of my tongue to reach out and taste it. It was sweet like cinnamon, but it was also very cold and chunky. Trying to avoid the lumps, I gulped down what I thought was oatmeal until there was nothing left but the little lumpy balls. I pushed the unidentified floating objects around the bowl. I was still so hungry I considered eating them without even knowing exactly what they were. I rolled the hard little nuggets around in the palm of my left hand.

"Did you enjoy your breakfast, Heidi?" Katherine was back. She stood tall, filling the doorway. "But I see you didn't get to the best part." With the help of the light coming through the door, I could plainly see what the hard balls were. They were eyeballs. Not the squishy kind, but very hard, dead eyes in different colors.

Katherine laughed. "I thought you would like to see what real eyeballs look like. Out of the socket, of course! The only way I knew was to make you eat the breakfast of champions!" She laughed out loud, practically choking on her own spit. There was another surprise in the bottom of the bowl. It was the dead bug creature, covered in cinnamon oatmeal. Its singed body lay helpless, its neck twisted and broken. "It was always a nuisance," Katherine said, "so I decided to break its neck. Oh, but I didn't want it to go to waste. I just knew you would enjoy it. *Heidi.*" Katherine had a way of saying my name. There was always much emphasis. The entire contents of my stomach exploded through my lips. I continued to vomit until I was too weak to move. Again Katherine stood over me, sinking those green eyes of hers into my soul. "Get up," she snapped. I barely heard her. My suit was covered with green vomit and rejected oatmeal. I lay against the wall trying not to breathe my own vomit.

"I said get up!" I could tell that Katherine was in no mood to be kept waiting. I managed to get to my feet. "Clean all of this nasty shit up", she ordered. "You will not make a mess in my grandmother's house." She handed me a filthy kitchen towel and forced me back down on my hands and knees. "Now scrub it all up," she barked. "I want to see a squeaky clean floor. Right now! I want to be able to see my beautiful face in it!" But the room was too dark to see a reflection. I could only hope she was rational enough to realize that.

After I finished cleaning the floor, I was escorted to the filthy bathroom. There were dirty towels hanging from the racks next to a cracked cloudy mirror. I looked at my reflection in the cracked mirror and saw a scared, dirty little girl with open sores in her head. Using the filthy towels, I made a feeble attempt at washing my face and wiping my clothes, but there was no hot water or soap.

"Hurry up," cried Katherine outside the door, "We've got a lot of catching up to do." Her words made my blood run cold. I sat in the corner of the bathroom trying to think of something, anything to do.

"That's it!" Katherine burst through the rickety door and flew into me with the rage of a caged alley cat. "I've had it waiting on you, Heidi." The cracked mirror crashed to the floor and exploded into a million jagged pieces. I had no choice but to walk right on top of them.

The sharp pieces of glass pierced the bottom of my shoeless feet like little prickly knives.

"How'd that feel?" Katherine asked. "Didn't I tell you to hurry? Listen to me when I tell you to hurry. I mean HURRY. We've got work to do!" Her nostrils flared. "You are not in charge here. I am! You will do as I say, is that clear? Is … that … clear … Heidi?" Katherine was gritting her teeth. I stared at her, afraid to utter a sound. She was clearly expecting an answer, so I finally managed a measly, "Yes."

She grabbed me and pulled my weak body down a dimly lit hallway. I stumbled, nearly falling to my knees a couple of times. "Keep this up, you stupid little bitch, and you will be sorry," snarled a disgusted Katherine. She was in no mood to drag me along to keep up with her own rapid pace. I was barely hanging on.

The hall was long, dark, and cold. The walls were a dingy green and decorated with pictures of old people dressed in turn-of-the-century clothing. The picture frames were large and dusty. There were rows and rows of these eyesores, complete with those little metal plates at the bottom with long names of old painters. There were also multiple doors along the hall of different sizes and colors. Each door had a crystal doorknob above the keyhole. There were probably dead bodies in those rooms, dead bodies suspended from a spider web-covered ceiling with garden snakes tangled in a maze on the floor.

Suddenly I could smell the beefy scent again and hear the sound of water boiling. Katherine stopped in front of a green door with rusty hinges. The beef smell was now unbearable. There was heat coming from underneath the door. The warm air covered my feet.

"Allow me to introduce you to an old friend," Katherine beamed. She took a skeleton key from her pocket and carefully inserted it into the keyhole. The sound of the lock turning was squeaky, high-pitched, almost like a scream. Katherine was actually licking her lips with excitement. I began to tremble, not wanting to see what was behind the door. The lock sang out once more and finally clicked, and the hinges caterwauled as the door slowly opened.

I stood in the doorway, frozen, as Katherine whizzed past me, nearly knocking me over. I couldn't believe my eyes. The room was large with vaulted ceilings, the walls were gray and slick, and there were no windows. Florescent lights loomed across the slanted walls. It looked like a mad scientist's laboratory. The beefy smell was now all over, creeping into my lungs.

The room was blazing with large water tanks filled with boiling hot water. The liquid thrashed against the sides of the steel walls of the tanks, gushing over the top and splashing onto the floor. Two of the tanks had blue flames dancing below them. One tank had a ladder next to it. Katherine climbed up the ladder and peered into the tank. She inhaled the fumes, closed her eyes and then exhaled. The steam oozed deeply into her pores. "Ahhhh!" she said. "I love the smell of beef in the morning."

I thought about turning and running, but the stone lion I suddenly noticed standing guard behind me foiled my plan.

"Heidi, come here." Katherine extended her arm to me. *Not a hair out of place,* I thought. *She really thinks this is normal behavior.* I couldn't move a single muscle. "Get over here!" Her loud voice startled me into movement, and I slowly made my way toward Katherine and the watery steel coffins. Crawling back down the ladder, Katherine invited me to climb up and look into the tank. The smell of the beef and the scent of my own vomit made my stomach turn.

"Take a look, Heidi. Take a good look. Get up that ladder." I made a queasy climb up the ladder while Katherine stepped aside with a Vanna White move. I closed my eyes on the way up feeling the moist, hot air on my face. "Look into the tank, Heidi," Katherine demanded again. I shook my head no and started to climb down the ladder. "I said look down in the damn tank!"

"I can't!" I screamed. The breeze from the tank blew my hair back onto the open sores on my head. "I don't want to! Please, I want to come down!"

"Look into the tank or you'll be sorry! Look into it! Look into it or I will kill you now!" Katherine was now screaming at me.

Slowly I opened my eyes and looked and saw what I would never forget the rest of my life.

CHAPTER 23

Katherine's eyes were ablaze with fire and evil energy. I crawled down the ladder, step-by-step, sick to my stomach. I swallowed hard to keep the acid in my stomach from seeping through my lips. The tank was filled with boiling water and floating diced vegetables. There were green peppers, onions, cloves of garlic, grains of corn, and clumps of broccoli.

"Oh," Katherine said, scooting across the floor to a cart full of ingredients in little bottles arranged neatly in a row. "I forgot to add salt and pepper. Let's see, now. Parsley, red pepper, cloves, cinnamon … aha! Here they are! Salt and pepper." She was bubbling with joy. "Now, Heidi, this will only take a minute."

I collapsed to the floor and lay in a helpless heap. I watched Katherine climb up the stepladder with a salt shaker in one hand and a pepper mill in the other. The water continued to splash and tumble to the floor. Katherine moved her body to avoid the fiery drops of water while delicately sprinkling the salt and pepper. She smiled and hummed like she was preparing Thanksgiving dinner.

I had lost track of the time. I didn't even know what day it was anymore.

Katherine carefully stepped down the ladder, then jumped from the last rung to the floor. "See, I can be a gourmet cook, too! Now that I'm finished with that, I simply must tell you about the bone! Get up, you puny little bitch. Just look at that gash in your head. You really need to see a doctor." She chuckled evilly, while the lion stood guard as I stumbled to my feet. I felt dizzy and nauseous. I rubbed my eyes and massaged my face. I knew I was going to be tossed in the tank with the veggies and the salt and pepper.

"Please," I begged, "may I call my parents? They must be sick with worry. I was supposed to call them as soon as I got back from the interview at the television station." I was feeling groggy. "What day is it, Katherine? What time is it? May I go to the bathroom? I think I'm going to be sick."

"If you soil this floor with your foul mouth, you clean this floor up with your tongue!"

"Haven't I suffered enough? Have I not been the target of gruesome disturbances for months? You blinded and murdered my best friend, sent me through excruciating terror, and now I must endure more pain from you! And what about the other people you killed: Professor Vital, the redheaded kid from school, the innocent janitor, and that poor father of twin boys? What about them, Katherine? Are they destined to suffer in this purgatory forever? When will this ever end, Katherine? When am I dead? Why don't you just kill me now and get it over with? Just kill me now!" I was totally hysterical, surprised at the words that were spilling out of my mouth.

"Shut up!" she shrieked. "You will do as I say! And, no, I am not quite finished with you yet, missy. You will pay for what you have done to me! I don't even know why I care. You're nothing! Nothing! Such a plain, ordinary girl. You got in my way first, with your stupid grocery bags and your stupid looking clothes! Oh, yes, you will pay, Heidi, and Ellis will get his too!"

The lion roared as if it understood exactly what she was saying. I could barely stand on my wounded feet.

"Please, Katherine, why are you torturing me?"

"You still haven't figured it out, have you?"

"I told you. I was not, and am not, interested in Ellis Majors. What more can I say?" I was practically shouting at her.

"You liar! You are still in love with that low-down, miserable excuse for a man. You two make me sick!" Katherine was quiet for a minute, searching her mind for just the right words. She looked at me, gritted her teeth, and cocked her head to the side. Squinting, she straightened her head and pointed at me with her index finger. "There's one other thing you did. You had no business sticking your nose into it, but you just had to play Miss Good Samaritan and lend a helping hand. The almighty Heidi Morgan, here to serve and protect! Why couldn't you just mind your own business?" Katherine was wild with anger. She checked her watch and waved her arms in the air. "Yes, it's a Rolex, in case you were wondering."

The boiling water pounded the walls of the tanks and the lion roared. The moisture in the room made my filthy clothes cling to my dirty body.

Katherine glared at me, with her sinister green eyes and said, "I'm tired of this kiddy play bullshit. I've got something to show you." The furry creature came from out of nowhere and landed on Katherine's shoulder. She was clearly annoyed by the interruption and tried to hit at the animal, but it was too fast. It made a gruesome sound and jumped to the floor. I was still standing near the tank when I heard the sound of someone screaming and pounding on a door. The furry creature scurried across the floor toward a closed door and stopped. The water in both tanks was suddenly quiet. The pounding intensified. There was someone on the other side of the door, trying to get out.

"Do you recognize that voice, Heidi?"

"Let me out of here!" the voice cried. "I'm afraid of the dark! Katherine, please, let me out of here!" The man's voice was panic-stricken. "Katherine, are you out there? Katherine! Katherine! I've got to have something to eat! Please let me out of here! There are mice in here! I think one has bitten me. Please, it's so dark! You know I'm afraid of the dark!" It was the voice of Ellis Majors! Ellis Majors was locked behind that door.

"Ellis? Ellis, are you OK?" I shouted. "It's me! Heidi!"

"Heidi, is that you? Get me the fuck out of here! Is that crazy bitch out there? Is that old hag Grandmomma out there? Heidi, get me out of here! Is she out there? Heidi, Katherine's gone crazy! Heidi, please! Get me out of here! She's gonna kill me! She's gonna kill us all!"

Listening to Ellis plead for his life, Katherine laughed out loud. I turned toward her. She was watching me, daring me to unlock the door.

"What's going on here?" I asked. "Katherine, why is Ellis here? Why do you have him locked up?"

"Let me out of here!" Ellis' voice was strained. "Heidi, are you still out there? Talk to me! Is anyone there?"

"*I'm* out here, Ellis." Katherine was in no mood for games. "Now shut up!"

But Ellis didn't shut up. "She wanted me to meet her kooky grand-mother! She told me she wanted company for the drive to Joplin! Heidi, I've been locked in here for three days, I think! What day is today? I haven't eaten for days! My clothes are dirty! It stinks in here! Katherine! Help me please!" Ellis sounded disoriented and weak. "I love you, Katherine," he cried. "Why are you doing this to me?" Ellis was crying as he pled for his life. "Please, I'm so hungry! The rats in here are biting my ass! Katherine, please, I love you!"

"Shut up!" she screamed at the door. You don't love me, you never did! You took advantage of me Ellis Majors! Dating other women behind my back, saying you were going home right after school. I saw you, I saw you with my own eyes! You've been cheating since the beginning of our relationship, if that's what you want to call it. I was in a relationship by myself. You were never interested in me. I bought you everything, that filthy watch on your arm, all that gold jewelry. I paid full price for it, too! You made me look like an idiot at school and at home! My parents are barely speaking to me! All those clothes I bought! You know what, Ellis? I followed you one night. Remember the night you said your aunt was sick and you had to take her to the emergency room? I stooped to your miserable level and followed you. I saw you out on a date! That lousy bitch was worse than this lousy bitch!" Katherine pointed at me. "She was ugly and poor! I checked up on her and her horrid family. Her brother is in jail for God's sake! And her mother works in a school cafeteria! They use food stamps! What was wrong with me, Ellis? I gave you everything! Every stinkin' thing you ever asked for. I used my own money that I shouldn't have touched. Now it's your turn to pay! It's your turn to feel bad and cry your eyes out! How does it feel, Ellis? How does it feel to be on the other side of the fence, huh?" Katherine was banging on the door. "Huh, Ellis? How does it feel not to be king anymore? I bet you don't feel so well now, and you look awful! The famous Ellis Earl Majors is now the little man he always was. I made you the person you are now! You are nothing without me!"

Ellis did not reply.

Katherine became even more enraged. "Did you hear me Ellis?" she roared. "How does it feel? How could you pick a nobody like Heidi? How could you pick that tramp I saw you with? Imagine, dating someone with two tone fingernails and streaked hair. Ellis—*are you listening to me?*" Katherine had snapped. She continued to cry and pound on the door. The water in both tanks began to churn. The furry creature hopped around as if the floor were also boiling hot.. The stone lion roared as it walked circles around the two tanks of boiling water. I stood watching and wondering how long I had to live.

"Katherine, it's time." The voice came from the doorway to the hall. It was Katherine's grandmother. "It's time, Katherine," she repeated. "Open the door." Obediently Katherine composed herself while her grandmother came into the room. The old woman was dressed in a flowered dress and sagging stockings. Her worn pink house shoes and limp yellow apron were caked with mud. "Come and get the key, Katherine. It is time." Katherine glided toward her grandmother and held out her hand. The old woman put her hand into her apron pocket and retrieved an old skeleton key, which Katherine took and turned like a robotic soldier. I watched in horror as she headed toward the door that stood between Ellis Majors and the light of day. She slowly turned the key in the lock and opened the door. The putrid smell of feces came pouring out, permeating the entire room where we were standing.

"You stinky boy!," Katherine laughed. "Ellis, just look at you. You're a mess!" Ellis was in the far corner of the little dark room, sitting with his chin resting on his knees. He looked like a scared newborn fawn. "It's time to get up!" Katherine lumbered over her victim demanding that he get to his feet. Ellis stirred a little and put his head down. He never uttered a sound.

"Can't you see he's in shock, Katherine?" I said. "He can't move."

"Katherine, get him out here!" The old woman barked loud and shrill. Katherine reached down and pulled Ellis to his knees. His pants were completely soiled, the shirt he wore was wrinkled and dirty, and his face was drawn and ashen. There were dark rings around his brown eyes. His lips had white puffy foam in both corners and his chin sprouted a three-day beard. Ellis looked like a dead man walking.

Katherine laughed again. "Oh, Ellis, I'm tired of this pitiful act. Get out there! You heard my grandmother. It's time. Now get out there." Ellis walked, taking tiny steps.

"What is going on here?" I couldn't help but ask.

"Silence. There will be no talking." Katherine's grandmother waited impatiently by the large tank, her arms folded. The stone lion sat quietly in the corner with the furry creature at its side. The water sputtered and exploded, sending blazing droplets to the floor. The old woman bent down near the side of the tank closer to her and turned a black knob. The fire beneath the tank burst into a raging inferno. She then moved the stepladder to the front of the tank. "I believe we are ready."

Ellis began to weep, shaking his head from side to side. I stood in horror, unable to move a muscle. As Katherine marched him past me and the animal kingdom in the corner, Ellis looked back at me with a grief-stricken stare. What could I do to help him? I was so weak I didn't know if I could overpower Katherine or her wicked grandmother.

"Stop this madness!" I shouted. "Katherine, what are you doing? Don't do this to him, please!"

"Silence!" The old lady was disturbed by my shouting. "We must remain silent during this solemn occasion." Katherine stopped Ellis in front of the tank with the boiling vegetables. I could smell them. The scent of the onions were so strong, that I didn't know if my eyes were watering from them or from the tears I was still shedding.

"Ellis Earl Majors," the old woman said, sounding like a judge, "you have led a shameful life of deceit and disgust. You have hurt my granddaughter for the last time. You have sinned before us and God. You now must cleanse your dark dirty soul in this holy water. With the grace of God, I sentence you to death by boiling. May God have mercy on your tormented soul." The old woman paused with a gleeful cackle. "Now, that's what I'm supposed to say according to the bible, but I hope the devil rips your wretched soul from your malicious body and stabs it with the poisonous sword of eternal purgatory. Now take your last steps up the ladder and thrust your body into this holy water! NOW!"

The stone lion began to roar and lunge on his hind feet. The furry creature was also very excited.

"Stop this Katherine," I shouted. "Please don't kill him. God help us—please don't do this! Ellis! Ellis! Katherine, please don't do this. My God, in the name of heaven, spare his life!" I suddenly remembered the promise I'd made to God in August, my promise to get all A's if God would save the life of the old janitor. Well, I had not gotten all A's. Three A's and two B's were the grades I'd received the semester before. Was God angry with me? I didn't even know if the old man was alive or dead. Did I dare pray again in an attempt to save the life of Ellis Majors?

Ellis had one foot on the first step of the ladder. I ran over to the tank and grabbed his arm. Katherine knocked me back and to the floor.

"Do not interrupt, Heidi!" she shouted. "The devil does not like to be kept waiting! He has an evil, sinister soul, and now he must pay with his life."

"Ellis—stop!" I was amazed at the energy I'd suddenly found. Ellis now had both feet on the step. His tattered, soiled clothes hung off a pathetic physique. He was headed toward the second step. Soon he would climb to the top of the ladder of death.

The water continued to churn while the fire crackled underneath the large steel tanks. Now Ellis was at the top of the ladder. Katherine and her grandmother stood patiently, looking up at him. Ellis turned toward the three of us and remained silent. The steam from the water captured his face, causing him to cringe and wince.

"Ellis, no!" I shouted again. "Please don't do it!"

Katherine walked over to me and slapped me with the back of her hand. "Didn't I tell you to be quiet? We're busy here! If you keep all this noise up, your turn will come sooner!"

My cheek instantly got hot and swollen. I could only watch the horror that was taking place before my eyes as Katherine and her grandmother both stood with their arms stretched up to the ceiling and began chanting in tongues.

Ellis found my eyes once more, swallowed hard ... and flung himself backwards into the boiling inferno among the vegetables. The splash and his scream were blood-curdling. I imagined the water filling his lungs as he tried to fight the piercing pain. He was probably trying to hold his breath inside a scorched throat and keep his burned head above water. The thumps against the side of the tank indicated that Ellis had not given up, but soon there was only the sound of the boiling water liquid. My thoughts raced to the flesh of Ellis Earl Majors being torn savagely from his muscle bound frame. His eyeballs floated among the broccoli flowerets and the grains of corn.

Katherine snapped out of the trance she was in and raced up the ladder to check her victim. She bent over the edge, looked in, and smiled. The beefy smell filled the room once more. "Ellis told me he knew how to swim; I guess that was another one of his filthy lies."

"Well, he does know how to float!" Katherine said. "Do you want to see, Heidi? Do you want to see what your precious little Ellis looks like now?" Katherine reached into the soup and retrieved Ellis's black onyx cufflinks. "I'm surprised I even noticed them among all of these bones!" Ellis's remains had drifted to the surface of the soup.

"Look Heidi," Katherine said. "I paid good money for these. I wonder how much I can get for them if I pawn them. I'm a little short." She held the items in her hands wondering exactly what she would do with them. "Maybe I'll keep them for the memories, the sweet memories of revenge." Her flippant behavior made me sick. "Dinner will be served promptly at six," she said, "and, Heidi, you're our guest of honor!"

Katherine's grandmother quietly left the room, obviously exhausted by the morning's activities.

"No, no, Katherine, please!" I begged, but Katherine only breathed a sigh of relief and said, "Now that this is over, let's get to you, Heidi!"

Chapter 24

"Eat up." Katherine was looking at me from across the dirty table in the dismal kitchen. I sat on a rusty folding chair that rocked from side to side. In front of me was a bowl of brown liquid with boiled vegetables floating on the surface. I could hardly keep my head up. After Ellis's grizzly murder, Katherine had escorted me back to the locked room I now called home. This time I had been in the room for two days without food, water, or bathroom privileges. My clothes were soiled and torn, my feet, swollen and blistered. I was so weak I could hardly speak. My body ached from lying on the cold cement floor.

"I said eat up, Heidi," she told me. "You always wanted to be close to Ellis. Here's your chance." Next to the bowl were a bent, crusty spoon and a dirty napkin. Katherine came around the table to my side and forced the spoon in my right hand. "It's all the food you're gonna get," she said threateningly, "so you'd better eat up." I looked up at Katherine wishing I could strike her or run or do anything to save myself. I lifted the spoon and placed it into the bowl and stirred. The soup was thick with jagged brown meat and lots of onions.

"She won't eat it?" Katherine's grandmother had entered the kitchen with the same clothes on I remembered from two days ago, except that now her apron was covered with fresh blood. "After all the time I put in skinnin' that boy, and she won't eat her soup? He wasn't exactly what you'd call tender. All those grade-A vegetables I cut up, too? The recommended daily amount for a Mama's girl." The old woman was clearly annoyed at the insult. "You will eat this or die," she said to me. "I can promise you that!" I could hear the roar of the stone lion coming from somewhere in the house. Katherine's grandmother padded over to my side of the table and placed her hand on top of mine.

"Look at all of this fine meat in here! We won't have to go to the market for a week! Why, even our lion enjoyed this feast." The old woman began to stir with my hand. She then scooped up a spoonful of the human soup and jammed it between my lips. I thought she'd broken my teeth, but when I felt around in my mouth, I found that my gums were gouged and bleeding.

"Swallow or you'll be sorry."

Cringing at the thought of swallowing, I held the soup in my mouth, but some of the broth slipped down my throat anyway. I could feel the death juice dripping onto my lips. Katherine and her wicked Grandmother both stood over me, waiting for that first gruesome gulp.

I couldn't do it. I spit the soup and the entire contents of my stomach onto the middle of the table. I couldn't stop heaving and spewing, my body expanding and contracting with every breath I took. Finally, all was quiet. I put my head down on the table and wept. I listened for the next command, afraid of what would happen to me. But I heard nothing, not a sound. Slowly I lifted my heavy head from the table and looked around. Katherine and her grandmother had disappeared. I sat for a while with the flesh of Ellis Earl Majors on my breath.

I finally worked up the nerve to turn around to see if anyone was watching me. I was alone. I grabbed the dirty napkin and began wiping my face and clothes. There was a roll of paper towels on a wooden cart next to the sink. I hobbled over to the familiar white roll with pink swirling lines, grabbed the paper towels off the roll, and turned on the faucet. The rusty warm water was quite a sight, but it was all I had to work with. I wiped my mouth and hands and made a feeble attempt at cleaning the front of my filthy, tattered suit. I ran the water over my hands enjoying the warm sensation as I wished for a nice warm bath and a dab of deodorant. I rinsed out my mouth several times, squirting the water out between my teeth.

"Having fun, Heidi?"

I turned around to see Katherine standing behind me with her arms folded. She wore a beige pantsuit with matching hose and shoes. Good old Katherine, always dressed up for a special occasion.

"The police found your rental car," she told me in a sneering voice. "They even came to the house and spoke to my grandmother. Apparently your parents are really worried about their precious baby. Your picture is all over the news. Unlike our Ellis, you're famous. No one really cared about him. He hasn't even been missed … yet. By the way, my grandmother told the police she never has any visitors. She told them if she should see you, she'd give them a call. She even invited the nice policemen in for tea." "Oh, yes," she continued. "I'm glad you got to witness our family ritual. I know you think it was a bit barbaric, but it's the way we do things around here. Our family has done it this way for centuries. Your good friend, Toni Steptoe, was quite a fighter. Even though she couldn't see a thing, she sensed she was about to be doused in boiling water. Blind people are very special. I was very impressed with her. Now the illustrious Professor Vital and the red head kid were both dead when they were dunked, so they were no fun. That was a twofer day. And you know what? I practically ran out of seasonings! We made do with the bare minimum. I believe I added celery to their soup. I try to make sure everyone gets treated fairly, you know."

"I must be frank with you Heidi," she went on. "You're next. I haven't quite figured out when because I'm having so much fun torturing you. My grandmother wanted to kill you right away for what you had done to me, but once again, I saved your stupid worthless life. You really make me sick, you stupid bitch!"

I stood watching Katherine as she spoke to me about taking my life. I wondered when it would be and if I would be able to step up the ladder with dignity. I agonized over my friend, Toni Steptoe. What was she thinking when she took her last steps? Did she scream, or violently flap her arms in an attempt to grab onto something … anything that would keep her head above water? I wondered if she died instantly. Or had hers been a long, excruciating death? What was I thinking? Katherine said she had been a fighter till the very end. Could I really believe that?

Katherine stood watching me, as if trying to make a decision. I tried to think of something that would persuade her to prolong my life. I needed a plan to get out of this house of horror. My feet were badly infected, but given the chance, I would run like the wind.

"Now what am I going to do with you?" Katherine stood tapping her feet as if I were her naughty child. "I could shoot you in the head, but your big cranium would explode and gush with blood, and I'd be stuck cleaning that nasty mess up. Although I could boil you afterwards."

I had to think of something fast. My mind was empty.

Katherine was still thinking of things to do to me. "Perhaps I could give you to Clarence. You've seen him. He's our pet lion. I'd certainly enjoy watching him tear your arms and legs out of the sockets. He's partial to fall-off-the-bone meat! Oh, shoot." Katherine pouted like a child. "There is one problem with that plan. Grandmother loves baked tongue, and I'd have to fight Clarence for yours. She'd be so heart-broken if she missed her favorite meal!"

"Could I just have a glass of water?" I managed to speak out. My weak attempt at buying time was almost comical.

"Why sure, Heidi," Katherine replied. "Sure you can have a glass of water. Allow me to get it for you!" She calmly walked over to the old cupboard and opened it, retrieving a glass with a gold stripe around the edge. She placed the glass under the encrusted faucet and turned on the water. When the glass was full, she held it out to me. As I lifted my hand to grasp the glass, she said, "Oh, I forgot, I want to give you something." She reached inside her pants pocket and pulled out a dark object and plopped it into the glass of water. Then she handed the glass to me. A large dead roach floated to the top.

I collapsed and my head banged on the floor. I couldn't hold on to the gold-rimmed glass. It tumbled to the floor and exploded into a mil-lion pieces. The dead roach lie near me with its feet stretched up toward the ceiling. I could hear the stone lion roar in the distance. I wondered if Katherine ever boiled animals.

It must have been getting late, for I could see that the sun no longer shone through the kitchen window. After Katherine made me pick up every sliver of glass, I was escorted to the dining room, where I was forced to sit at the table that had the candelabra with the invisible can-dles for a centerpiece. The flames danced against the haunted backdrop of the dreadful house. Katherine sat across from me, gazing at the stains on my clothes, repulsed at the stench that surrounded me.

"I want you to play a game with me." She spoke as if she were a first grader speaking of hopscotch.

Still weak from malnutrition and lack of sleep, I looked at her with strained eyes. I did realize that I was dying little by little.

The chair I sat in housed the skull of Toni Steptoe. I had awakened Toni when I pulled the chair out from the table. "What kind of game?" I managed to squeak out. I decided to humor Katherine and try to get on her good side … if there was such a thing.

"It's a game that you've played before, but not very well."

Suddenly I heard Toni's voice, whispering to me from underneath the chair. *Watch out, Heidi. Don't trust her. She's planning to kill you.* Katherine appeared not to have heard the skull's voice. *Don't play with her, Heidi,* Toni's skull said again. *Please don't play the game. I'm begging you--please don't!*

Katherine reached down beneath her chair and produced the Ouija board I had awakened just a few months ago. "You were so good at this before, Heidi," she said. "How about another go-round?"

"Where did you get that? That board belongs to my family!" I was unexpectedly cocky. "What have you done with them? Where in God's name did you get this?" I felt a renewed burst of energy. I jumped up from the table and leaned over toward Katherine. "I asked you where you got it! It's a simple question, Katherine. I expect an answer. It's been in my family for over one hundred years!" I pointed toward the board. "This Ouija board belongs on the third floor of my house! It was never to be disturbed—ever!!" My eyes stung with hot, salty tears.

Katherine sat chuckling at me, getting a charge out of my hysterics. "Well, we've really got our dander up, don't we? Hit a sore spot, have we? Heidi, I wanted to play a nice little game with you and now you're mad. Is it that you think I don't know how to use it? You must remember Heidi, I was there! I was in your bedroom that night. I saw your clothes. I saw your dumpy, tacky clothes come flying out of the closet, I heard the pigeons cooing from the fireplace, I saw the perfume bottle tumble off the dresser and crash to the floor. In fact, allow me to let you in on a secret. *I was the one causing all of those nasty little disturbances.* I think I blinded Toni quite nicely. Plucking her fingernails out was a nice touch wasn't it?

"Now," Katherine crooned, "am I a worthy partner? Will you play Ouija with me?" Her crooked smile sent chills over every inch of my body. I quietly sat down again and remained silent. "Well," Katherine said, "now that I have your undivided attention, let's have some fun before it's your turn to die."

I shifted in my seat, gently rocking the skull of my best friend beneath me.

Be careful, Heidi, Toni warned, *she's the devil times two.*

"Shut up, you stupid Indian! Mind your own stinking business. I wish I could blind and kill you all over again!" Katherine was bent down under the table screaming at the skull. "I'm gonna throw you back into the boiling water, Hiawatha—how about that! How about I take that stupid headband from you? Would that help to shut that big yap of yours?" Toni was quiet, and so were the skulls of Professor Vital and the red headed kid. The head skull was sleeping through the entire ordeal.

Katherine rose up, again peering at me with her piercing eyes. The flames flickered and crackled morbidly in the darkness. Katherine's face had an eerie red aura surrounding it.

"I'm going to ask you one more time," I said. "Where did you get that board?"

"Take it easy, missy. I was given this Ouija board with your family's blessings."

"No one in my family would have given you that board!" I was practically out of my chair.

Shhh, Heidi, she's gonna kill you. Toni was still trying to warn me. The stone lion roared.

All this talking now agitated the skulls. Professor Vital began rattling off the difference between a television rating and a share and the red-headed kid sang *"Itsey Bitsy Spider"*. The nurse delivered a baby. *Push! Push! Now take a deep breath!* The room was actually very loud. I watched Katherine watching me. She was elated by my eternal confusion. Professor Vital switched gears and was now mentally in his backyard dressed up like a woman serenading the moonlight. I remembered the nasty rumors that rattled the campus about his bizarre behavior. He continued to talk to the moon and stars. *Star light star bright, first star I see tonight. Hickory dickory dock, Old McDonald had a farm,* the redhead sang.

I looked at the board lying on the table. It was wrapped in the original red silk scarf the old gypsy had given my Grandmother.

"Believe me, Heidi," Katherine said. "The board was given to me by someone close to you. Now let's play. First, we must have complete silence."

Toni whispered up to me, *Don't let complete darkness fall in the presence of the wretched Katherine Sharpe. Don't do it, Heidi.*

"Red rover red rover send Heidi right over!" The redhead was humming to himself.

Doctor, she's flat-lined, the nurse warned. Heidi felt chills rise on her arms. The redhead was in concert with himself singing Prince's "Little Red Corvette."

"Shut up!" Katherine screamed. "Now, let's play."

I watched Katherine crack her knuckles. The smell of beef drifted throughout the room. Thinking about Ellis, I cringed.

"I'll go first." Katherine carefully unwrapped the Ouija board and gently put the scarf around her skinny neck. "How do I look?" she asked me. "Don't I look marvelous?" She was ready for the death game to begin. "Now let's both put our fingers together on the pointer." Katherine's fingers were long and very clammy. We sat across from each other with eyes locked in place, skin grotesquely touching.

"Let's see, who could we raise tonight?" she wondered aloud. "Heidi, do you have any suggestions? Do you want to see any mummified restless soul rise from the dead? Elvis?"

I sat in complete silence, and so did the skull of Toni Steptoe.

Katherine pointed her head up to the ceiling as if she were in deep thought. "I know!" She snapped her fingers. "I've got it. Let's bring back Ellis! Isn't this fun? It's just as much fun deciding as doing! Let's see if Ellis is truly resting in peace!" Katherine was elated with her idea. "You start, Heidi. Bring your king back from the dead." I shook my head no and dropped my eyes. "All of a sudden you're a weenie?" Katherine taunted me. "A scaredy cat! OK, I'll start, but you just feel free to jump right in."

Katherine took a deep breath and started. "O restless spirit in the dead of night," she intoned, "come to us in the form of Ellis Earl Majors." She bent toward me and said, "I can't believe I remembered that prick's middle name, but it makes for a more interesting séance, don't you agree?" She giggled and continued her invocation. "Release his tormented soul from your grasp. Ignite the evil flames of hell. Bring his wicked corpse from the grave."

I was too afraid to say anything. All was silent until the skull of Toni Steptoe sniffled. I prayed she wasn't crying. The nurse skull sighed, and baby skull cried for its bottle.

The stone lion roared again in the distance. The wind whipped the trees and the rain punished the earth, pounding it with black hail. Lightning streaks poisoned the skies. Suddenly, I heard chains rattling. The noise was so thunderous that Toni's skull began to cry and Professor Vital's skull wailed out in pain.

Elizabeth, I'm comin' to get you, honey! It's the big one! The door of the dining room was consumed by a dark shadow. The redhead screamed, *He played knick knack paddy whack give the dog a bone"*. I trembled, with my fingers still in contact with Katherine's. I wanted to close my eyes but couldn't. The dark figure proceeded toward us, taking slow, lumbering steps. The chains were tightly bound to its ankles and around its waist. The lightning illuminated the room with a fiery authority. The redhead hummed Prince's "When Dove's Cry."

"Show yourself, prisoner of the grave!" Katherine intoned. The smell of damp earth filled the room. The shadow was now up to the table. Ellis' corpse was draped in rotted black cloth with maggots slithering all over it. He rocked side to side with quick violent movements. *Why, Katherine, why did you trip like this? Why did you do this to me?* Ellis's voice was strained. He could barely speak. His grunts were morbid and unrecognizable. I managed to look at the scorched bone face of a zombie standing next to me.

"Speak to us," Katherine said, sounding like a psychopathic schoolgirl.

Why did you do this? I loved you! We had it going on, Katherine! What we had was special! Most folks would kill for what we had! We were soul mates!

"Soul mates?? We were not soul mates, Ellis! Are you crazy? We were as different as night and day! I am rich, you were poor. I have class and you, my dear sweet Ellis, had the manners of a pig. I am smart and you were an idiot! We had nothing in common, so please don't let me hear those filthy words again! Do I have to go over this again Ellis? You used me! I had to kill you. It was only right!" Katherine was visibly shaken. Even in death, she allowed Ellis to rattle her cage. It was now my turn. Ellis turned to me and said, *Why didn't you save me, Heidi? Jesus Christ, you watched her murder me! Look at me! Now I'm burning in everlasting hell!*

Underneath the robe, I could see Ellis's body had no flesh. His bones were covered with mud and dried blood. He could hardly stand. The trail behind him was wet and slimy. His eye sockets were filled with slimy maggots. I was afraid one of the nasty insects would jump onto me. I was terrified to even look in his direction. I couldn't believe I was communicating with a dead man.

"Ellis," I finally managed to protest, "I couldn't do a thing! She would have killed me, too! I'm so sorry! There wasn't a thing that I could do!" I put my head down on the table and cried.

"Enough of this crazy talk!" Katherine cried out. "I'm tired of talking to you, Ellis Earl Majors. Be gone and have a wonderful life in eternal hell! Heidi, let's get rid of this creep." Katherine began chanting and rocking in her seat, while pushing the pointer all around the Ouija board. Ellis grabbed his heart, or the spot where his heart should have been, and collapsed to the floor. His bones clanked on the hardwood. He then struggled to his feet and slowly padded over toward the door. "Ahhhh," he screamed as he disappeared into the darkness. There were still maggots poking around on the floor.

"Wasn't that fun, Heidi? Let's bring someone else back. Now do you have any suggestions?" Katherine's face glowed in the broken flames. The furry creature came out of nowhere and jumped on her shoulder. Startled, she jumped out of her seat and grabbed the animal by its throat, instantly breaking its neck and slamming it to the floor. The creature made a high-pitched hideous noise and died. "I've been wanting to do that for a long time," she snarled as she returned to the table. "Remind me to throw that miserable thing into the boiling water later." She sat down with the grace of a swan and smoothed out her clothing. Katherine looked at me and said, "Now, Heidi, who will be next? Who would you like to see?"

CHAPTER 25

We sat at the dining room table with the Ouija board from hell for what seemed like hours. Katherine suddenly flew into an uncontrollable rage, screaming about how life wasn't fair and how she always fell for the wrong man. Then, as quickly as the rampage started, it stopped and all was quiet. The furry creature lay broken and bleeding near her chair. Its sixth toe on the hairy left foot stood apart from the rest. The flames blinked and popped as Katherine the chameleon changed her colors again. I was totally exhausted and too afraid to disturb the she-devil. The board remained on the table, separating what I thought was good versus evil.

Outside, it was still raining, and I could actually hear the hum of cars driving by. The stone lion's roar was reduced to a cat's purr. Katherine was sitting with her back straight against the chair, staring into space when I heard it. The sound was very faint at first, but as time passed it became louder and louder. It appeared to be a signal, one bump, then two more. I knew Katherine heard it, too, but she pretended she didn't. I sat listening to the rhythm, *Bump ... bump, bump. Bump ... bump, bump.*

"He's going to pay for making so much noise," she said through gritted teeth.

"Who is that?" I asked without thinking.

Katherine was irritated by the interruption. She glared at the Ouija board, then slowly looked up at me. "It's one of your kind," she said. A do-gooder bleeding-heart pain in the ass." Her eyes remained locked on me as if contemplating leaping across the table to strangle me with both hands.

The sound became louder and louder. *Bump ... bump, bump.*

Katherine could no longer ignore the obvious. She began stomping on the floor and screaming into the hardwood. "Will you shut up down there?" She was looking under the table. I thought her anger was directed toward the skulls, but it wasn't. "I told him to stay quiet down there! Grandmother instructed him to never interrupt us!"

"Who is that, Katherine? Who is making that noise?"

"That is none of your business, young lady!" Katherine snapped, "Keep your mouth shut!"

"Who could that be?" I was beginning to feel the fatigue consuming my body. I was so hungry I would have eaten the mush I was fed three days ago, with or without the dead grasshopper at the bottom of the bowl.

The bumping got louder and louder. Katherine's face was crawling with rage. She stomped, kicked, and scratched the floor with the heels of her expensive shoes. "Be quiet, you old man!" she shouted again. "Shut up! Go away! You deserve exactly what you got! Shut up and leave me alone!" I thought she would have a heart attack right on the spot. Katherine Sharpe was so upset she forgot I was there.

Suddenly she jumped up and took off running and screaming for her grandmother. Her voice echoed throughout the house. I sat there, frozen, trying to figure out what to do. The house was unexpectedly quiet. I could hear labored breathing trying to form words. It seemed to be the voice of an elderly man in excruciating pain. I bent down to inspect the skulls. Toni Steptoe's skull was wide awake, looking right at me. Professor Vital was sleeping like a baby, the red-headed boy was humming quietly to himself, the nurse was staring off into space, and the chief skull was counting beers on the wall. It sounded like he was up to 996.

I saw that there was a new addition to the skull family. By the sound of his voice, I could tell it was the old man from the fire at the university pool. *I don't know how dem peoples expected me ta clean that whole buildin'*, this new skull was saying. *I declares, I was jus an ole man, tryin' to feeds my family.* I cringed, remembering that horrible night. The old man had been burned in the pool by black acid. Katherine Sharpe had been on her killing spree and I hadn't known it yet.

And then I heard a new voice that did not belong to any of the skulls. I could hear someone whispering my name. *Heidi*, it said, *Beware of Malmspada.* The word *Malmspada* sent chills down my spine. Whose voice was that? I quickly checked the skulls again. No dice.

This voice clearly did not come from any of them. Was it alive? *Heidi, listen to me*, it said again. *Beware of Malmspada*. The voice was tired, strained and shaky. *Bump ... bump, bump.*

"Heidi, please ... help me! Let me out. Unlatch the door!" The voice was coming from the floor! Someone was trapped beneath the hardwood panels. There was a silver latch with a circular rubber seal. I flashed back to the hump in the dining room floor under the dining room table at home. Although it was covered by the carpet, I always knew it was there and was always afraid of it. "Let me out, Heidi. Set me free." The voice was barely audible. I slowly got down to my knees and placed my index finger through the round latch and pulled. I tugged on it, trying not to make a sound.

The trap door lifted and flopped back down to the floor. I realized I was kneeling on the edge of the door blocking the way to open it completely. I backed off and tried the latch again. It popped open. I could see only a few feet down the stairs. The trap door was too big to lift completely because the large dining room table was on top of it. I saw an old man on the wooden steps squinting up at light that wasn't there. His skin was ashy and cloudy, his eyes watery. I could only see his face. I had seen that face before, but I couldn't remember where or when.

"Be careful, Heidi," the old man whispered up at me. "If they catch you speaking with me, they are sure to kill you. Check and see if they are coming."

I quietly closed the trap door and shimmied from beneath the table and stood up. I couldn't hear a sound. Neither Katherine nor her grandmother was anywhere to be seen or heard. I tiptoed to the doorway and looked left and right. No one. I looked up the stairs. I still didn't hear Katherine or her witchy grandmother. I returned to the table and sat down for a while just in case the gruesome twosome returned. I listened quietly to the death sounds of the house. I could hear low gurgling echoes of the twin killer tanks and the rough purring of the stone lion. I was afraid to move a muscle, or even exhale. The flames continued to crackle and the morbid shadows danced on the old walls.

The old man remained under the floor, waiting patiently for my return. I stayed at the table for what seemed like fifteen minutes and then made my move. I slowly scooted the chair back across the hardwood and stood up. I was so hungry and dizzy I was sure I would collapse. I took one last look toward the door to the dining room and crept back under the table and pulled the trap door up.

The old man had not moved. He was still sitting on the steps, waiting for my return. "Are they gone?" He began to squint up at me with his hand protecting his eyes. "Heidi, do you remember me?" The old man had no teeth and his lips were sunk in like a rotten snaggle-toothed jack-o'-lantern. "Don't you remember that day at the student center?" he asked me. "You saved my life, Heidi! I wouldn't be here if it weren't for you!" I looked deeply into the old gentleman's eyes … and then it clicked. The janitor in the student center on my first day of school! This was Oliver Vaden! "Heidi," he said, "please listen carefully. I've got something very important to tell you."

I squatted down as much as possible to put my head between the trap door and the floor. The old man began to spit out his troubling story from a mouth that sank deeply into his face. He saw my eyes lock in on his soft lips and quickly offered an explanation. "They took my dentures and stomped them to pieces right in front of me!" His eyes darted from side to side anticipating light, whether it be sun or artificial. Mr. Vaden's bones poked through his wrinkled flesh.

"First of all," he said, "I want to tell you that you are in great danger. The old woman with Katherine is my loving wife, Martha Vaden. Katherine Sharpe is my granddaughter."

I had to let the news sink in. The janitor is married to the old witch? I shook my head, *no, that's not possible*, as if it would change anything. I swallowed hard to keep from fainting and allowing the trap door to come crashing down and chopping my head clean off.

"I've been working at the university for many years," Oliver Vaden said. My wife has been mentally ill for most of that time. She talked me into moving her to Joplin while I continued to work in St. Louis at the university. I never was good enough for my wife. I never could make enough money to make her happy. She wanted this large house, and was simply unbearable until I finally gave in and bought it for her. I took on odd jobs after work just to pay the mortgage on this place and the rent on my small apartment in St. Louis. I sent money to her so she could live comfortably… with out me. We never had an unpaid bill. I worked day and night so she could have the finer things in life. Martha demanded all of this expensive furniture so Katherine helped her pick it all out. But heck, we always had a good sturdy car to drive, and decent clothes to wear. It was never enough for her. She always thought we didn't have what others had. When we argued, she called me a hick straight off the farm. Gosh, I met the woman at a pig callin' contest nearly fifty years ago. Her family was no better than mine. Her daddy worked on a cow farm slingin' cow shit!" He stopped for a moment as if he were reminiscing the past alone in his mind.

"My son, Espy Vaden, and I never got along," he continued after a minute. "He also thought I was no more than an old country bumpkin who liked to wear overalls and a plaid shirt. What was I supposed to wear a tuxedo everyday? I worked day and night so my son, the big shot, could go to law school. I mopped floors and cleaned toilets until I was dead tired." Mr. Vaden dropped his head and sighed deeply. "He is my only son, and Katherine is his only daughter."

"Then why is Katherine's last name Sharpe?" I was trying to put this all together in my mind.

"Katherine changed it when she learned I was working at the university. She didn't want any connection with me at all. My son allowed her to do it. It was like I was a total disgrace to her." He stopped again, thinking about his family and what they had become.

"Let's see, now—where was I?" Mr. Vaden touched his dirty brow. "What I neglected to tell you Heidi is when my wife got sick, it was my son who thought it best for her to move to Joplin. Espy hammered it home to Martha that this was the best thing to do. He also wanted me to move as well. My son convinced his Mom that she'd be happier in a small town. I believed Espy was embarrassed and ashamed of his parents. The next thing I knew she was harping on moving. As I said before, I needed to continue working to pay for the care she needed. Katherine was elated when she heard the news that her grandparents would be moving six hours away from St. Louis, but when she found out that I would still be working at the university, where she would be attending college, she hit the ceiling. Now, Katherine and her grandmother have formed this heinous kind of bond that I could never understand. My granddaughter had disowned us both, but now, I'm the one she hates." The old man was baffled. "I don't even try to comprehend this madness. I'm just trying to stay alive."

"Shhh, I hear something." Mr. Vaden began to tremble in anticipation, then, he lowered his voice and continued. "Katherine and her grandmother are evil, Heidi. My wife was the most wonderful woman I had ever met, but over the years, she changed. Her mind went south after she got sick. My son always catered to his mother. He always wanted to keep his parents separate from his friends. We were not allowed to go to his undergraduate or law school graduation. He told everyone that we were both too ill to attend. If it weren't for me, Heidi, Espy would have never been able to go to that private college.

"When Katherine was born, Espy could not have been more proud. His mother and I didn't find out, however, until days after the baby was born. Can you imagine? Grandparents not even knowing their only grandchild was here? Katherine's mother, Augusta—we always called her Gussie—was a beautiful educated woman from a decent family. She worked hard to keep my son happy."

The stone lion purred again in the distance. My neck began to cramp after bending down for so long. Katherine and her grandmother had still not returned. What would they do if they found me talking to Mr. Vaden?

"Gussie was the daughter of a deranged woman," Mr. Vaden continued. "Gussie's mother went mad shortly after Katherine was born. My son didn't find out until after then that Gussie had an inherited dark side. My daughter-in-law was adopted by a doctor and his wife with no ties to this psychological madness. No one knew her real background. She appeared to be stable for the first ten years of their marriage, with only minor problems. But a little after their tenth wedding anniversary, Gussie started to break to pieces. She was admitted into a mental institution and it was there that her medical history was exposed. With the double whammy of mental illness from her grandmother and her mother, Katherine was sure to turn out twisted."

"I knew something was wrong with that girl from the very beginning," he said after another pause during which we listened to the stone lion roaring again. "Even as a baby, she'd go out of her way to step on worms and smash them until there was only a wet spot left. She tortured all of her dogs by burning and kicking them. My son always insisted this demented behavior of hers would pass, that she was a sweet little girl. But she just wasn't normal! Everyone tried to ignore her temper tantrums at school. She terrorized her classmates and bit her teachers. She was a bad little cuss, but smart as a whip. Made straight A's all of her life. It was the darndest thing."

My heart broke for Mr. Vaden.

"Heidi, could you find me something to eat?" he whispered. "Make it something soft." He focused on me as best he could through the slits of his eyes. It was still quite dark.

⌐ I whispered, "I cannot get you anything, Mr. Vaden. They barely feed me. They tried to make me eat soup made of Ellis Majors! I am risking my life speaking these words!"

"Then you better run, my child," he said. "Get up and run!"

"I can't leave you down there to die! I've got to get us both out of here."

"I am a weak old man, Heidi. I would only slow you down. But if you do get away, I know you'll come back and get me!"

I heard footsteps behind me. Katherine was returning. I signaled to Mr. Vaden to get out of the way as I slowly closed the trap door. He didn't make a sound. I barely made it back to my assigned seat when Katherine appeared in the doorway behind me. She had regained her composure.

"Did you miss me Heidi? I've missed you. Since you were such a good girl to sit tight and not try to get away, I'm going to reward you." I closed my eyes and never turned around. Her frosty attitude was back.

CHAPTER 26

"I overheard you speaking with him, Heidi. I know you know he's down there. I was so touched by your sympathy towards my grandfather, but it will cost you your miserable life."

I stayed in my seat, barely breathing. I hoped and prayed that Mr. Vaden was listening to the conversation.

"I'm not as bad as he said," Katherine said. "I never stepped on worms until they were only a wet spot. I stopped way before that! I must admit the part about the dentures is true. I wanted him to die a slow agonizing death, so I thought if I took his yellow stained teeth and did not feed him much, he would lie down and die. It would be easier than chopping him up and baking him for Christmas dinner. The old goat is still hanging on, though, banging and pounding to get out. I can't believe he's still alive. The part about my mother is all true. She was in an institution. My real grandmother, let's face it, was crazzzee! Heidi, do you think I'm nuts? Do you think I'm off my rocker?"

Did she really expect an answer? Was I supposed to say she was as loony as her mother and grandmother?

"Why, no, Katherine, I don't believe you're crazy. I just think you wanted a little company, and that's the real reason you brought me here."

Katherine contemplated the response. "Well, what about Ellis?" she asked me. "Was I insane to boil him?"

My mind raced for the correct answer, one that would not upset this madwoman. I had to convince her I really didn't believe she was crazy.

"He treated you badly, Katherine. He deserved what he got. I would have done the same thing."

"Bravo, Heidi! That took a lot of thought. I almost forgot how smart you are. I almost fell for that crap. Now it's time for you to retire to your room for the evening." Her voice changed as she peered right through me. "Now get up."

Obediently, I padded up toward the room I now called home. I was allowed to go to the bathroom, but I wasn't given anything to eat. After Katherine pushed me into the small mausoleum and slammed the door behind me, I slowly slid down the wall. It was still dark and clammy. I could hear the rodents scurrying across the floor. I kept my legs and feet close to my body, hoping I wouldn't get bitten. I had no idea where the rats were. I listened to Katherine's footsteps travel up and down the hall. I was so tired. I tried to keep from nodding off, but finally the lack of sleep got the best of me.

I had no idea what time it was, or how long I'd been asleep, when I heard the scratching sound behind the wall I was leaning against. At first I thought one of my four legged roommates was clawing at the walls. I was dazed when I realized I could hear someone calling my name. Where was the voice coming from? "Heidi," the voice whispered, "let me in." *Let me in?* Who was that? Suddenly, I felt the wall behind me move. I was nearly pushed over by a hidden panel in the wall. I watched in horror to see who would appear.

My eyes strained to see the body emerge from the hidden door behind the wall. He smelled of sweat and raw sewage. It was Oliver Vaden! "Shhh, Heidi," he warned me. "Don't make a sound. They have no idea this hidden tunnel runs all through the house. I only discovered it about two days ago. When I heard Katherine throw you into the room above me, I realized I could get to you by crawling through this narrow passageway. It's our way out, Heidi. It's your way out!"

I couldn't believe what I was hearing. The words were music to my ears. I scooted closer toward Mr. Vaden and tried to process the thought of freedom. I began to tingle with joy. I could see Mr. Vaden much more clearly now. It was a miracle he wasn't dead. Although he was barely hanging on physically, his spirit was very much alive. The tunnel reeked of human waste, and the bricked path was smeared with feces. Mr. Vaden had been surviving in eternal hell.

"Listen to me Heidi," he said. "This tunnel leads to a door to the back porch. Like I said before, I am old and weak, I could hardly run fast enough to get away. Besides, I know there are two dogs guarding the back porch." I was elated to be hearing a getaway plan. "They feed the animals religiously at nine every morning. I know, because whatever the dogs don't eat, they give to me." I thought about the scraps they'd fed me. Was it dog food, too? My stomach churned with an acidic burn.

Mr. Vaden continued. "I have listened to the sounds and figured out that Katherine must feed the dogs on the patio on the west side of the house. I can always hear the heels of her shoes clicking on the bricks. I can't believe she dresses up to go nowhere! Anyway, the dogs usually gobble up their food quite fast, but on some days, Katherine treats them to raw steak. It takes a while for them to devour the meat." Mr. Vaden's breath was labored. "Katherine talks baby talk to the dogs like they're her children. If I remember correctly, there is a side gate on the east side of the house. I overheard Katherine and my wife talking about a broken lock on this gate. They wouldn't dare call a repairman for fear we would be discovered, or the skulls might decide to scream."

"You know about the skulls?"

"Yes, Heidi. I've been here a lot longer than you. Besides, one of the skulls is a former co-worker." I instantly remembered the janitor from the university's pool facility. "I heard them all boiling to death except for the good professor," Mr. Vaden continued. "When he got here, he was already dead. I couldn't bear to hear the agonizing screams. He yelped day and night. There was no way I could calm him down. Katherine taunted him more in death then she did before she killed him."

"But—" I didn't know what to say.

"But that Toni Steptoe," Mr. Vaden said, "she fought the hardest. I was silently praying for her when they forced her up the stepladder. She gave Katherine some real competition. Katherine made the stone lion stand guard, growling and snarling in an attempt to scare Toni. With her Indian heritage, Toni wasn't afraid of animals, so the lion didn't faze her. I never heard such a commotion! It sounded like a heavyweight fight! Toni was screaming in tongues practically bouncing off the walls. My lovely wife pressured Katherine to speed up the process because the battle bored her. Unfortunately, Katherine came up a winner, but she knew she'd been in the fight of her life."

I was mortified that my best friend had died such an atrocious death, but I was proud of her for not giving up. Katherine would be in for round two if she came for me. I would be fighting for my life and defending Toni's honor. I would not give up.

"They are both mad, Heidi. You must get away as soon as they feed the dogs the steak. When they feed you, try to eat as much as you possibly can. You must have the strength to run to the east gate. But you must remember that if the dogs catch you, or if Katherine and Malmspada catch you, they will surely kill you. Malmspada is an old woman, too, but in her mind she has the strength of two bears."

"Mr. Vaden," I whispered, "what does Malmspada mean?"

He took in a lot of air and blew it out. It took him a while to gather thoughts that appeared to make him sad. His lips vanished into his face. When the lips reappeared, there was another story tumbling out of them.

"Malmspada is the pet name I called my wife for nearly fifty years. It was a playful name that I created when we were in love. I had no idea it would ultimately represent something so diabolical." Mr. Vaden switched gears. "Remember the bone, Heidi? The one my sweet dear sister-in-law dug up for you in the tunnel beneath the school library?"

I didn't want to recall that horrible day in the library, but I certainly did remember. Estelle Adams was a loving old woman on the outside, but was really a repugnant grisly witch with a forked tongue.

"You remember, don't you? The tibia she dug up from the damp earth?" He was watching me as closely as he could. Through squinting eyes, he watched as I replayed the experience over and over in my head. He knew I remembered. "That bone was a human tibia."

I closed my eyes tightly, trying to push the horrid thoughts out of my mind, but it was impossible. I flashed back to the tunnel beneath the library and how frightened I had been while trapped in the underground graveyard. I remembered the old woman's serpent tongue and the long, thick, scaly snake that had almost squeezed the life out of me. How could I forget?

"Estelle belongs in a loony bin," Mr. Vaden said. "She has no business working with innocent students."

"I thought for years," he continued, "that her superiors would find out how crazy she really was, but so far no one has noticed! The kids seemed to like her as much as you did. She plays the gentle grandmother role so well, but I know the truth." Again, Mr. Vaden fell silent, reluctant to tell a story so terrible. He shook his head and rubbed his eyes until he could barely open them. I looked at the old man's filthy clothes and grimy hair. He was bone thin. His face was sunken and wrinkled. It was only then that I remembered the glasses he wore when he soared to the floor that day in the student center. I supposed Katherine and her Grandmother took them, along with his dentures. His hands trembled as he snorted and cleared his throat. How well I recalled that sound.

"Do you remember the ghost that appeared before you and Toni, late one night one your back porch?"

I did recall the ghost, but it had the face of Katherine Sharpe. "Wasn't that Katherine? It looked and sounded like her."

"Yes Heidi, it looked like Katherine, but it wasn't Katherine. She came to you in the form of Katherine, but it was really someone else. Someone you know, someone … close to you."

I was puzzled. The ghost had worn a white gown with a frazzled hemline. Her fingernails were blood red. That much I couldn't forget. It had been very dark that night. The ghost was holding the furry creature in her hands. Toni Steptoe thought the animal was her own grandmother, but I had no idea who it was. The dogs next door had barked up a storm. I remembered thinking that all the ruckus would wake up my parents and the entire neighborhood. This ghost definitely had the face and the heart of Katherine Sharpe.

"Heidi, brace yourself," Mr. Vaden said. "This isn't going to be easy."

Who was the ghost, really? I didn't know if I could stand to find out. I braced myself for a stab in the heart.

"The ghost was your mother."

What? My mother? What was he saying? I wanted to strike the old man. I wanted to hit him straight in his fleshy mouth. I could have killed him. "My Mother?" I was speechless. I felt my body go limp.

"Listen to me, Heidi. It's true. I know you don't want to believe this but it is true. The ghost took on the form of Katherine, which was believable to you at the time. Your mother is a part of this madness."

I listened in horror, not believing the words I was hearing. "Shut up! I don't want to hear another word! How dare you say that about my mother! You're old and feeble, you have no idea what you are saying! You crazy old man!" My blood turned to ice. The face of my mother consumed my mind. She had the face of an angel and the disposition of a saint.

"I hate that I had to be the one to tell you this, but your mother is as evil as my wife, Estelle, and Katherine."

Silence. Complete silence. I was floored by this information. My head was spinning and I was sick to my stomach. This could not be true! This wasn't true! I didn't care if Katherine or her sick, reptilian grandmother heard me.

"You are wrong, Mr. Vaden, dead wrong," I shouted. "My mother would never be a part of this terrible game. I would appreciate if you would not speak about my mother again. She is a kind, loving, gentle woman without a harsh bone in her body."

"Speaking of bones Heidi ... that bone that Estelle dug up. It belongs to your mother."

Mr. Vaden paused, waiting for all of this to sink in. After all, he had just told me that my mother, my wonderful saint of a mother was a monster, a killer.

I put my hands over my ears and shook my head violently. I didn't want to hear any more of this morbid tale. "My mother couldn't—" I finally managed to say. "She wouldn't. She is my mother, a mother would never ever be capable of such hideous acts." I thought back to the time when I accidentally threw away all of the Christmas gifts I had purchased with my allowance. I mistakenly thought the bag was full of trash. My mother had replaced all of the gifts the same day. I was touched by her generosity and never forgot how much love I felt for her that Christmas season. A woman with a heart as pure as hers could not possibly be a part of this killing game. And what about my father? Was he a part of this too? What was I saying? I was actually entertaining the thought! Mr. Vaden remained painfully quiet. Even through squinting eyes, he could see how devastated I was. I sat cross-legged against the wall with my head tilted back. I rocked my body in hopes this was all a bad dream, but when I heard Mr. Vaden speak again, I realized it was a nightmare and I was living it.

"Heidi, please listen to me and listen well. Your mother has a long scar on her right leg, doesn't she?"

I didn't want to nod my head. Instead, I sat in a confused stupor. My mother did have a scar smack dab in the middle of her leg. It was an awful scar, one that had scared me when I was little. I remembered asking my mother if she was going to die because of the horrible scar. She would reply, "Of course not, honey, Mommy's going to be around for a long, long time." I hated that scar.

"They took the bone as a sacrifice, Heidi. She underwent a very painful operation by someone who was not a doctor. It is usually performed by a madwoman who truly believes she has solid medical knowledge. She had to allow them to take the bone to prove her loyalty."

I sat in absolute amazement; watching and listening to a man dismantle a lifetime of happiness. My dad even teased her about the ugly scar. It was a raised, snake like splotch that could be seen a mile away. I recalled my father wanting her to have plastic surgery, but she wouldn't hear of it. My mother never tried to hide it. In fact, it seemed she was quite proud of her "war wound," as she often called it. She paraded around with that scar like a trophy.

"Heidi, there's more."

"I don't want to listen to another word! Stop it! Shut up! You are talking about my mother!"

Mr. Vaden was quiet for a beat, then he continued. "Have you ever heard a noticeable pop when your mother walks? Can you hear a ... a weird kind of crackle?"

She always popped when she walked. It was something I always heard, always. Even while walking down a busy street with horns honking and sirens screeching, the pop was there.

"Katherine has that pop, too, and so does my wife. It has something to do with the loss of the bone. The day I saw my granddaughter's scar, I quickly tried to push it out of my mind. It was the worse day of my life. The worst! I pretended it wasn't there for years. The old man inhaled deeply. My only grandchild was one of them. When I met my wife, she already had the scar. I never thought anything of it. For years, I just believed it to be an old childhood scrape, but it wasn't. Boy was I wrong." Mr. Vaden actually chuckled.

I didn't know if I could stand to hear any more. This bad news was enough to last me a lifetime. I braced myself for words that would feel like a hit by a Mack truck. I shook my head and shouted, "No, no, no!"

"Be quiet, Heidi. They'll hear you! I gotta tell you this for your own good! No one would have ever told you! You would have eventually found out the hard way. You would have awakened one day and your tongue would be forked. The inherited blood will mutilate you soon."

I inhaled so deeply, I thought my chest was going to explode. The smell of warm feces hauntingly floated around the tunnel. The walls began to move in closer and closer. My blurred vision and dry throat made concentrating difficult. I fully expected an alien to jump out of my puny little chest. I checked my hands for webbed fingers and felt behind my ears for scaly skin. Nothing had happened so far. I guessed I still looked fairly normal. When would this transformation occur? The neon green eyes of Estelle Adams permeated my thoughts.

The mice began to chase each other in bizarre circles, biting and tearing at their tails. Long sharp claws scraped across the floor with wicked enjoyment. I hoped this was not some type of mythical ceremony inducting me into the witch's hall of fame. The mice soon disappeared into the darkness. I waited for the inherited conversion to take place. We sat in complete silence with only breathing sounds between us. I had to depend on someone, and Oliver Vaden was my only hope. I secretly prayed for another favor from God. I hoped he still wasn't mad at me for not making straight A's. A faucet was dripping somewhere in the house of horrors. One drip, then two. One. Two. The wind blew dangerously outside. I felt a cool breeze enter my body. Was this the beginning of the inevitable transformation? I flashed to the ghost that haunted our street. Was she here with me? Had she ventured inside of my body? Was I her? Was it my mother's presence? Did I believe this madness? It was too much to absorb, too painful to digest.

I could hear the old lady laughing at something. I pictured her with her head back, hacking like an old crow.

"Heidi, you've got to get out of here. You must try to escape when Katherine feeds the dogs. I have no idea what they have planned for you. Or for me."

"But what about you, Mr. Vaden?"

He looked blankly off into the distance with a cold blind stare.

"If I am missing they will kill you for sure. They will assume that you helped me. I just can't leave you here. I've got to take you with me."

"Heidi, look at me." I slowly found his eyes, the eyes that were soft yet watery and bloodshot. "What makes you trust me? What makes you think I won't try to kill you if I am one of them too?" He was definitely a beaten man, a man at the mercy of a deranged psychotic murderer. "You have to save your own life." He was still attempting to salvage my poor pitiful soul. "You are still relatively pure until they take the bone from your leg. The initial change is more physical. Katherine wears layers of makeup to hide rough scaly skin. Her complexion is the result of plastic surgery and expensive cosmetics." I flashed to Katherine's flawless skin, and to Mrs. Adams's lizard-textured skin near her ears. "Your initiation," Mr. Vaden said, "could be webbed feet, fanged teeth, or bloody tears. But the removal of the bone—that's the icing on the cake. Whatever you do, do not allow them to take the bone from your body. Do everything you can to fight them. Use every ounce of your strength to get away, or … die before they rob you of your soul."

CHAPTER 27

It was a chilly, rainy, dark morning. The wind had howled all night, keeping me awake in the torture chamber I currently called home. My weak body, riddled from constant tremors, lay helpless on the hard cement floor covered with mice droppings. I listened as the morning arrived at a snail's pace. The birds sang death songs. They seemed to have knowledge of the great get-away. The dogs barked with nervous agitation.

Mr. Vaden had been up all night calculating my escape. It was the day, according to habit, that Katherine fed the dogs the special rare steak. She usually opened the door quite early, leaving click clacking sounds floating in the air from the heels of her shoes.

Mr. Vaden was in an anxious mood. "Today is the day," he said, determined the plan would be carried out successfully. I instantly became more nervous as I wiped sleep from my tired eyes. I stretched, yawned, and arched my weary back.

"I think I'm too weak, Mr. Vaden," I said. "I'll never make it. If only I could have one more day to rest. Maybe Katherine will feed us today."

"There is no time to rest. Today is the day. Tomorrow could mean death. We must escape today."

We both sat waiting with our backs against the wall, our legs against our chests. Mr. Vaden remained in his side if the penitentiary and I stayed in mine. We could not risk Katherine checking in on either one of us.

The plan was to stay put until the coast was clear. I tried to process the instructions when we heard Katherine open the back door. My heart raced and my breathing stopped. "Right on time," he whispered coarsely. The demonic popping sound pouring from her leg amplified the moment she arrived. My eyes darted from his face to my tingling, splintering feet. I was not ready for a life-threatening escape. If I failed, it would surely be fatal …. for both of us.

The sound of her heels on the wooden back porch was exactly the way Mr. Vaden described it. I hoped he was right about everything else. It was Katherine's habit to distribute the meat as evenly as possible to each dog. By Mr. Vaden's calculations, it would take about seven minutes from start to finish. From the second the door opened to the minute it closed was precisely timed. We both began crawling toward the end of the tunnel that led under the back porch. My raw knees picked up bits of debris that tormented my open sores.

"How are my babies this morning?" We heard Katherine say in a motherly tone. The dogs moaned lovingly for their wicked mistress, raising their heads in sleepy delight. The sounds of the dogs running toward her, pounding the barren land, indicated that every move was going according to plan. "She'll now begin her baby talk." Mr. Vaden was right. "Mama loves her babies, yes, and do you love your Mama?" Mr. Vaden had it down to the second. We finally reached the end of the passageway that led to the rest of our lives.

I could actually see daylight peering through. The rain had dwindled to a nasty drizzle, just enough to slow me down. My heart raced in anticipation of freedom. I could practically taste it. Mr. Vaden shook with anxious enthusiasm. I would never forget him for saving my life.

"Now, Heidi," he whispered, "There is not a second to spare. You must go exactly when I tell you to. Get ready. She should be on her way back to the porch. I have got to get back to my room because she'll throw me the slop that the dogs didn't eat. I must be there to get it." The beads of perspiration on Mr. Vaden's forehead danced the freedom jig. He listened carefully, not wanting to miss a sound. "You're gonna make it, Heidi." His words were broken and choppy. "Please make it for me." Every excited breath was an agonizing struggle.

The dogs were busy devouring their breakfast. *Now was the time…*

"Go now, Heidi, go right now!"

I pushed through the trapdoor leading to the backyard. I didn't hear it come crashing down behind me. Good ol' Mr. Vaden had caught it before it slammed shut. I looked toward the dogs. Wagging tails and bobbing heads greeted me a cheery hello. I took off like a jet. The canines were much too absorbed in breakfast to care about the thin, frail girl running for her life towards the gate with the broken lock. My legs

had the energy of ten men. I had no idea where my strength was coming from. My feet sank into the soil with every step. Luckily the earth
was damp, and since I had no shoes on, my movement was practically
silent. My toes squished through the mud, smushing dirt under each
toenail.

I never looked back to see if Mr. Vaden was watching. I just kept
running toward that beautiful gate. When I finally reached it, my body
exploded into the splintery wood, causing it to swing open without a
hitch. I was through the gates of heaven in record timing without the
dogs chasing me. My heart threatened to detonate at any second. I
tasted freedom for the first time in weeks.

I stood outside the fence, pausing for a second to catch my breath
and figure out my next move. I didn't want to come face to face with
any stone lions lurking about. I tasted freedom, breathing in the moist
air and swallowing it whole. I searched the house for roaming eyeballs
and large-barreled guns sticking through the curtains in the windows,
but the thick dusty curtains were still conveniently drawn. I saw or
heard no evidence of the sinister Katherine, her insane grandmother, or
the oversized stone kitty-cat. I glanced up to the cloudy sky feeling the
rain drops on my ashen face. It was warm for January, if it was still
January. The rain didn't freeze. It simply fell upon the grass, touching
each blade. I had to keep moving or risk getting caught.

I looked out toward the road. There was no traffic. What kind of
town was this? Where were the bank tellers, the receptionists, the garbage men, the truck drivers? Should I flag down a car, assuming one
came along very soon, for help, or should I try to call the police? What
would I say if I did call the authorities? *Hello, I've been held captive in
a house with talking skulls, people being boiled to death, and an old
man living underneath the dining room table.* They would think I was
insane!

I needed to gather my thoughts. I could not believe I was really
free. I had to decide which way to go. I decided to travel back the way I
came in, which would mean a quick right turn down the road.

I scrambled toward the road, trotting along the fence like a lame
horse. I had lost the graceful stride I'd once possessed, but I still had
just enough velocity to keep me on the path. My problem now was getting past the lions perched on their high pedestals. Please, God, let the
second kitty-cat be real stone. I bowed my head and said a few extra

prayers, wishing I had gone to church more than I had. I hoped Mr. Vaden wasn't boiling to death in one of the large acid filled tanks. Making another deal with God was out of the question because I had certainly used up all of my favors.

I dropped to my knees and crawled along beside the fence like a thief in the night, checking behind me every other second. For the second time today, both shins were bleeding, but this time it was from chips of dirty glass. I glanced up at the second lion perched atop its mighty throne. The grisly stone mammoth's mouth was permanently open, displaying a mighty roar. Fortunately, the lion was stone and not flesh and fur.

I had cleared one hurdle. Now it was time for another. Taking a deep but silent breath, I stood erect, smoothed out my vomit-covered blouse, and bolted toward the main road. The open space made me vulnerable to hurled bricks and flying bottles. Katherine and her diabolical grandmother were capable of anything. I finally felt my mouth actually smiling for the first time in weeks. I ignored the fierce pain in my chest as I pushed past a large field with a menacing oil pump. The black contraption resembled the praying mantis hop-along bug in my basement. For a fleeting moment, I thought the metal monster was following me. I looked back to find the pump had stopped moving and turned at a sinister angle. It was glaring sheepishly at me, awaiting authorization to kill.

CHAPTER 28

T he fiendish pump was suddenly back in its original position. It resumed pumping its oil. I could hear a faint growl drifting across the cornfield. The contraption was grinding with the disappointed thought of a lost kill. It salivated and slurped up the oily film on its metal frame.

I continued to run along the side of the road until I heard the sound of a large truck. I stopped to listen to what direction the brawny engine was coming from and waved my arms frantically. The puzzled young truck driver cocked his head to the side, trying to decide if I was a raging lunatic. The truck had black writing on the side. I couldn't clearly make it out. It looked like TV … something. It was a satellite truck from the television station I'd applied to! What a break! If he would only stop, I could tell him who I was, and he could call and confirm my story. I knew the name of the station's general manager and his drippy assistant. The truck zoomed closer to me, its tires kicking up gravel and debris.

The driver's face conveyed to me that he was remembering strict company rules: no rides to hitchhikers, not even if they looked like they'd been trapped in a tunnel for weeks. The truck rattled past me, leaving puffs of dark smoke and rocky calling cards. His eyes met mine in his rear view window, apologizing for the inhumane act.

I looked back toward the house. It sat high, lurking on its dark foundation, challenging me to return. But no one appeared to be following me. I slumped over, limping along the gravel road, kicking glass bottles and French fry boxes. The rain intensified again, battering the wind-bent trees and the eerie stalks of corn. I buttoned my dirty suit coat and kept moving.

I heard another engine in the distance. This time it was a small car with a mean front grill. The car's husky grind burned up the road, kicking up trails of dust. Again I saw the face of a young man behind the wheel. My arms shot up as I waved vigorously in the moist air. I dared not scream for fear I was still too close to the house of horror. My waves caught the driver's eye, forcing him to reduce his speed and zero in on me. His perplexed expression desperately tried to sort out the situation. He was alone in the car, with no one to persuade him one way or the other.

The driver slowed to get a better look at the monster begging for help. My eyes pled for assistance in rain that was now a torrential down pour. The driver sped past me with a hostile mean streak, but, then, about ten yards up the road, he pulled over. He had stopped! I quickly picked up my step and trotted toward my waiting chariot. I had almost reached the rear bumper when the driver screeched off, burning rubber like a bank robber driving a get-away jalopy. The driver's window rolled down and a thin arm snaked out. He flipped me off in grand style.

My heart sank to an all-time low. I kept walking. Cars were now zinging past me at high rates of speed. People were gawking at me and shouting nice little nasty words. I kept hoping someone would do the decent thing and call the police from a cell phone. Now I knew why the homeless felt like the scum of the earth. Men honked and waved, one guy even blew me a kiss. Females cruised by in complete disgust with the word *prostitute* forming on their lips. I trudged along, hoping for an angel to descend upon my pitiful soul.

Eventually, I noticed a farm house about fifty yards up the road. Katherine was probably in that house too. Hesitant to make the same mistake twice, I decided to keep the faith that a decent human being would pick me up. I had walked another mile when a beat up car coughing up a mechanical lung glided to the side of the road. Watching warily to see if the driver would take off, I made my way toward the car. As I got closer, I could see the rust stains and holes in the body of the car. There was a faded AAA decal on the bumper, no license plate, and an old MIZZOU TIGERS sticker on the rear panel. I looked through to the front windshield and saw spider web cracks covering the glass. Who was my guardian angel, a black widow spider?

The passenger side window rolled down completely, allowing the static filled music from the radio to pour out. The head I saw was small and round with very short hair. The body barely reached the top of the dash. The person never turned around until I was near the door. She had to be at least eighty years old.

Her skin was wrinkly and saggy, yet her voice was sweet. "Do you need some help, honey? I was on my way to the market, but I can drop you somewhere." Her glasses were half-moon cat eyeglasses like my grandmother wore. They bobbed from a frayed string that rested on a faded flowery dress. The car reeked of mothballs and stale gin. There was more red lipstick on her chin than on her lips. She smiled crookedly with a set of false teeth two sizes too big. The choppers jumped out of her mouth, resting on her lips. She quickly grabbed the dentures, adjusted them and continued talking. "You look like you're freezing. Get in!"

Reluctantly, I grabbed the door handle and opened the squeaky door. The rusty sound could have awakened the dead. The door finally opened completely with a loud crack, and I slid slowly into the front passenger seat and slammed the door shut.

"Thank you so much," I mumbled, still afraid of what might happen. "Is the police station this way?" The woman coughed and burped air that smelled of week-old salami. I fully expected her to turn into a serpent with a forked tongue and one eye.

"Are you in some kind of trouble, dear? What on earth happened to you? Yes, the police station is right up the road a little ways."

"I just need a little help." I searched for the correct words, hoping that I sounded normal. Stale air tumbled out of the vents, assaulting my face. At least I was not walking. The rain had let up, but the road was very slick. Dark clouds had given way to patchy sunshine. The old woman poked down the road at a snail's pace. Cars zoomed past her honking and staring.

"Have you had anything to eat?" she asked. "Would you like a bite of something?"

I was ravenous, but anxious to get to the police station, and even more eager to get out of this car.

"No, thank you," I replied. "You've done enough for me already."

"What's your name, dear?"

"Heidi Morgan," I replied. Annoyed at volunteering my real name, I realized I had made a critical mistake.

The old woman was thunderstruck. "The Heidi Morgan from the TV? They've been looking for you! I can't believe I didn't recognize you! You're that college student who's been missing for weeks! Well, I'll be." She was so excited she could hardly drive. "I've gotta get you to the police mighty fast. Your parents are pert near heart sick with worry. Wait'll Mabel hears about this! Heidi, where have you been? Your picture has been all over the television and in the newspapers."

CHAPTER 29

The old lady pushed on the rickety accelerator, forcing the car to lunge forward and pick up speed. I reached for a seat belt that wasn't there. I turned around to look out the back window … and there it was. The bone. Bouncing around full of life on the cracked leather seat. I turned to watch my deadly sweet driver. Her eyes were ablaze with snakes spiraling out of each socket. I squeezed my eyes as hard as I could and held on for dear life. How could I make the same stupid mistake twice? The car bucked over the yellow line, and swerved out of control into oncoming traffic. I closed my eyes and braced for the inevitable.

The sound of screeching tires, grinding brakes, and the blood-curdling yelp of the old woman was all I remembered.

I woke to the smell of wet gauze, antiseptic, and the sound of a static-filled public address system. The bandage was wrapped so tightly around my head that I could not lift either eyelid. I was totally helpless and completely in the dark. My entire body ached. I couldn't move a muscle. I was scared and alone. "Dr. Thomas to the ER. Stat!" Was I in a hospital?

I visualized beeping computerized machines next to my bed with IVs dripping clear fluid into my veins. The contraptions always frightened me. No wonder Mr. Vaden had been so terrified that awful day in the student center.

I imagined busy nurses marking charts and taking temperatures. I was lying under rough sheets, still feeling cold and miserable. My head was awkwardly propped up with uncomfortable pillows. I guessed I was in a small room with a glass sliding door, a paper towel dispenser on the wall, and a corner sink with a square mirror above. I guessed I was in intensive care. Pain shot down my leg like hot coals. The medicinal smell mixed with Pine Sol turned my already upset stomach. I tried to lift my battered body off the bed, but found it impossible. Someone on the PA was now paging a Dr. Booker to the ER. I hoped Dr. Booker was high-tailing it down the hall to the emergency room. I tried to reach for a side table. Hopefully there was a phone on it. All I grabbed was air. I heard a moan close by. Someone was really sick.

I could hear voices floating very near.

"Will she be OK, doctor?" It sounded like my mother's voice. I had to be hallucinating.

"My name is Dr. Anthony," he replied. "I treated Heidi when she arrived in the emergency room last night."

"Will my daughter be OK?" It was my mother! How did she get here? How did she find me?

"First of all, she's in a coma, Mrs. Morgan. She sustained severe trauma to her head, spinal cord, and legs. There is a lot of glass embedded in her face. We can remove the fragments in her cheeks and forehead, however, I will have to operate on her right leg. I want to be honest with you. I don't know if she'll ever walk again."

Who were they talking about? Who would never walk again? Me? I'll never walk again?

"Joplin Memorial hospital is an excellent facility. She'll be in the best of care."

The male voice sounded like a young dark haired doctor with grey eyes. I imagined a stethoscope around his neck bouncing happily on a broad chest. I guessed that the white coat he wore was open from the front with his name printed in swirly black letters. "I'll have to remove the tibia in the right leg," he said, "and replace it with a plastic tube to support her body weight. I have consulted with another surgeon and he concurs with this diagnosis."

Then I heard the voice of the devil.

"Heidi will never walk again? Are you sure, doctor?" It was Katherine Sharpe, the evil, despicable Katherine Sharpe, the same monster who had kidnapped and starved me to death!

"Exactly what happened?" my mother asked the doctor. "What did the police say?"

I couldn't believe they were in the same room together asking questions about me. Didn't they know I was awake? Couldn't they see me moving?

"She was in a head-on collision. All we know is she was in the car with Mrs. Brewster, who, according to the police, picked her up along the side of the road. Mrs. Brewster was eighty years old, and was legally blind. She shouldn't have been driving in the first place. Luckily, Heidi didn't go through the windshield like Mrs. Brewster did. No one should have to die like that." The doctor's voice became low as if he were fighting back tears. "She baby-sat me as a kid. I'm really gonna miss her. She was like a grandmother to me."

The old woman who had picked me up was dead. Everything was eerily quiet, perhaps a moment of silence for the old woman. The doctor continued. "Heidi's legs were mangled from the impact. I had to operate immediately because there was a great deal of damage. I believe I repaired most of the damage, but there will be more operations, and hours of physical therapy. She's young and strong, and with injuries such as these, sheer dedication and the will to walk again will be vitally important. Firefighters used the jaws of life to remove her from the car. She wasn't wearing a seat belt. She's a very lucky young lady. Hopefully she will wake from the coma very soon."

Coma? I wasn't in a coma!

The woman on the staticky PA system barked out more commands. I heard wheels turning on slick tiles. The sound reminded me of Mr. Vaden's cart that dreadful day in the student center. I smelled roast beef and garlic. Maybe it was dinnertime. I hoped the meat wasn't that of Ellis Majors. The clatter and banging of stainless steel dinner trays filled the air.

The old lady was dead, and it was my fault.

"Will her leg look normal? Will it sound normal?" my mother asked.

Sound normal?

Dr. Anthony waited a beat before answering the question. I envisioned him crossing his arms and tilting his head the way doctors do when searching for the correct response. "Sound normal?" Dr. Anthony was confused. "What do you mean *sound normal?*"

I heard my Mother squirm. "What I meant was, will she have a pop in her ankle, knee, or foot when she walks?"

"She was in very bad shape when she arrived at the ER. Like I said before, there was severe trauma to her right leg. I can't promise that there won't be a limp if and when she walks again. As for a popping sound, I just don't know. It's possible that, as she grows older, as we all do, she will have a certain amount of strain on her legs. My grandfather swore that when it rained he could feel it in his bones. Right now there is no way to tell.

Dr. Anthony, will there be a scar?" Katherine asked innocently.

I could tell that Dr. Anthony was beginning to get exasperated, and a little annoyed at these odd questions. "I will have the assistance of Dr. Forest, a plastic surgeon who works miracles on scars." He replied. "I'll show you exactly where I will make the incision." I heard the snap of what sounded like an x-ray on the square viewing contraption attached to the wall. "Here's where the most damage is." I listened to what sounded like a pen scraping against the x-ray.

I heard the click of Katherine's heels as she moved closer to the doctor. I recognized the click-clack from the torment at the haunted house. "I will go in right here." I heard the pen draw a circle. "I will remove the bone, and replace it with a plastic tube that will keep her leg straight."

Katherine and my mother remained quiet. What was going on?

Then it hit me like a ton of bricks. The most horrible thought. I suddenly remembered Mr. Vaden's repeated warnings. I could not let them remove my tibia! The bone had to remain intact so I would not become *one of them*. I needed it to remain pure!

"Katherine, since you are Heidi's best friend, you will need to get her through all of this. She really needs you now more then ever."

"I will do the very best I can, Dr. Anthony. I will never leave her side, ever." Katherine spoke in an innocent tone.

Katherine would finally succeed in killing me! I was unable to tell the doctor that I wanted no part of the operation.

"How soon will she need the operation?" My mother sounded concerned.

"As soon as possible."

I had to stop this madness! I had to get away from Katherine. Again.

The room fell silent. The heater hummed gently in the dead air. I finally heard whispering and movement. What was going on now? I heard my mother's voice again. "Katherine, we've finally done it! I've been waiting for this all of my life! Heidi will finally be one of us. This is the best day of my life."

One of them? What was she saying?

"Finally my little girl's soul will be free."

Then it all clicked. My mother's leg. Mr. Vaden was right! She was part of that wicked, bizarre group. I had to get away somehow. I had to fight with every ounce of my strength. If I didn't, my heart would turn to stone, and my soul would be lost. I felt helpless. I had to do something—anything—to get the doctor's attention. Wait a minute! Could he be a player in this game, too? Did I have a voice? Was I capable of speaking? I was just about to shout when I heard someone else walk into the room. Everyone got quiet once again. Was it another physician? I smelled men's cologne.

"Is this our only solution, doctor?" a man's voice asked. "Are there any other alternatives? I don't want my little girl to be mutilated like this!" It was my father! He didn't have a scar. He was not one of them! *"Dad,"* I thought as hard as I could, *"please help me! We really need to get out of here! Dad, they are going to kill me. Please!"*

"This is really the way to go, Mr. Morgan, and unfortunately I need to operate as soon as possible. We need to get the papers signed to secure the OR. Heidi has experienced a very traumatic ordeal, and she needs to begin healing mentally and physically. She will need all of your help when she wakes up to find that there is a possibility that she may not walk again."

I closed my eyes and tried to scream. Nothing came out. All I could do was allow warm tears to tumble from bandaged eyes. Suddenly the woman on the crackly loud speaker belted out an urgent page. "Dr. Anthony, code blue. Dr. Anthony code blue! Room one three six two. Stat!" Dr. Anthony tore out of the room knocking over what sounded like a small stool or chair.

"Hon," my father said, "did Dr. Anthony tell you if he spoke with Heidi at all? Has anyone spoken to her?"

"I don't know," my mother answered flatly.

I tried again to speak, and again, nothing came out.

"I suppose she was already in the coma when she arrived at the emergency room," Dad said.

"We'll have to wait until Dr. Anthony returns." My mother sounded disappointed.

"Well, I'm calling the police to find out exactly what happened.

Heidi was far away from her hotel and the television station." My father was relentless. I heard him pick up the phone and ask the operator for an outside line.

"Oh, my God! I almost forgot!" My father slammed down the phone. "I'm parked in a no parking zone! We were so worried about Heidi, I left the car in the first place I saw! A ticket in this hick town has got to be an arm and two legs! I'll be right back. It's probably towed away by now!" I listened to my father zip his jacket and slam the door behind him. My heart sank.

The room was instantly quiet. I felt my mother and Katherine watching me. The awkward silence was deadly. I heard them walk toward my bed.

"Heidi, we know you are awake." Katherine had plopped down on the side of the bed. I could smell her perfume. "You can stop faking it now." She was back to her heinous ways. Someone had taken my hand and was squeezing it.

"Now that your father is gone for a minute," my mother said in a sweet voice, "you and I can have a nice sweet mother-and-daughter talk. Katherine has informed me that you know our little family secret." I felt my mother's breath cover my face. She kissed my forehead with rough lips and a wet forked tongue. I shook my head away from her face.

"Now, you will have this operation, and this bone is coming out! If you utter a word of this to your Father, I'll kill you myself." Her breath was hot and moist. "Katherine has done you a favor by preparing you for this life you are destined to live. You will do as I say."

I shook my head and squirmed away from her side of the bed.

"You should be proud of your heritage, Heidi. Look at all the power you will have. Your enemies will be helpless against you!"

"Let me tell you exactly what you'll be able to do..." My mother squeezed my hand so hard it felt like a vise grip. "You'll be able to torture, disfigure, kill ... the list is endless!"

All I could do was cry, and try to hang on to my soul for as long as I could.

Shelly McDuffie lives in St. Louis, Missouri with her husband, Tony, and dog, Max. She is currently working on her next novel.